T0274507

THE UNFINISHED

CHERYL ISAACS

THE UNFINISHED

Heartdrum
An Imprint of HarperCollinsPublishers

Heartdrum is an imprint of HarperCollins Publishers.
The Unfinished
Copyright © 2024 by Cheryl Isaacs
All rights reserved. Printed in the United States of America.
No part of this book may be used or reproduced in any manner whatsoever without
written permission except in the case of brief quotations embodied in critical
articles and reviews. For information, address HarperCollins Children's Books, a
division of HarperCollins Publishers, 195 Broadway, New York, NY 10007.
Library of Congress Control Number: 2023948461
ISBN 978-0-06-328738-9
Typography by David Curtis
24 25 26 27 28 LBC 5 4 3 2 1
First Edition

FOR PETER AND DIANNE,
KONORÓNKHWA

ONE

NO MATTER HOW FAST I RAN, IT FOLLOWED. Something buzzed around my ear, persistent like a bad memory— too tiny to see but driving me mad and forcing me to swat blindly with every other step. But it wasn't the only cause of my bad mood. I slowed and came to an unsatisfied stop at the end of the main loop, exactly where I'd started; a finger drawn along my forearm came away practically dry. I'd barely broken a sweat. Not even worth checking my watch. The fact was, these trails weren't going to get me any faster. And I did need to get faster for a scholarship to university, something that I'd recently realized was a necessity for me. This was supposed to be a celebratory run. I'd given my last exam a good-luck kiss and was looking forward to a summer of running, working in the bookstore, and hanging with my friends at FallsFest, eating funnel cake until one of us puked. But I was stuck on the tame main loop through the forest, getting more pissed off by the second.

It wasn't that I didn't like the forest—I did, I always had. It was a constant in my life, running the trails that my mom was eternally warning me not to leave, like a single step off the path would be the end of me. Besides, she had nothing to worry about. The trails were maintained, but the bushes were wild—as if I would go into the brush looking for things to stick and bite me.

The forest was immense, surrounding my little town on three sides, like a defense against the rest of the world, or like it wanted to keep us all to itself. No matter the time of day, the light coming through the trees was soft and dappled, creating shifting patterns on the ground.

I drew in a deep breath. The air here was warm and a little sweet. For me, this was what green smelled like. Different kinds of trees—maple, aspen, birch, and fir—all lived together here, with massive outcroppings of limestone and the underground streams that popped up intermittently. There were tons of birds—blue ones, red ones, little white ones that looked like they were wearing tiny black caps. I enjoyed the forest. It was beautiful and quiet in every season. But what it offered was no longer what I needed. During the year, the cross-country team ran meticulously planned routes along the back roads and finished with a long stretch along a two-lane highway, only considered safe because our coach was looking out for traffic. But the season was over, the team dispersed, and if I tried to run those routes alone, half the town would see me and snitch, and then I'd have to deal with the wrath of my mom, which could be considerable.

But sticking to the forest trails was getting old fast. What I needed was technical terrain, not wide, groomed paths. All the good trails were much farther away from home, but since I hardly ever got the car, here I was—like an Olympic-class skier stuck on the bunny slope.

"Excuse us!"

I set my jaw and managed to keep the eye roll internal as I stepped aside to allow a couple with a stroller to go by.

For God's sake.

I returned the wave the toddler gave as they passed even though I was seething inside. I scuffed my shoes in the dirt, considering my options. This day had been going so well, and now frustration sat coiled in my chest, set to open up, expand, and swallow the whole day.

Just settle down. I released a slow breath and shook out my hands.

I could run the loop again, knowing that there was at least one stroller out there to dodge. Unless . . .

I tracked back from the trailhead a bit to what was barely enough room to pass through the bushes lining the path. An opening onto a deer trail. Sometimes . . . I stood on the balls of my feet and peered over and through the brush, and sure enough, the trail seemed to open up a little. Enough for me to run, anyway. Definitely not enough for a stroller. It was barely enough to wriggle through, yet as I continued to look, the bushes seemed to open. They were pulling back on either side, ready to accommodate me, ready to welcome me if I'd like to enter. If I wanted to take just a few steps in, surely I could find my way. I wasn't supposed to leave the main trail any more than I was to run on the highway alone. But the difference was that no one would see me here, a thought that drifted through my mind, which had suddenly gone honey-soft and warm.

It was quiet under the canopy of trees, just my footsteps, the twittering of unseen birds. Even the buzzing stalker was gone. The light cast a soft rose-gold glow over every leaf on every tree, the filter that colored my best memories. It was hot, but the wind had picked up, making the heat enjoyable rather than hellish. This was already better than the main loop. The sun beat down and I closed my eyes for a moment, letting my head drop back, soaking up the heat warming my muscles, the sound of insects buzzing, and the delicious knowledge that school was almost behind me and summer stretched out as far as I could see. No pressure, no stress—just me and the forest trails.

The little voice in my head was soft and soothing.

The tree canopy is so pretty.

It was.

Quiet and dark and soft. Perfect for a run.

Just a little one.

Noise from the trail made me look back. Back? How had I gotten here? I turned in a slow circle, feeling fuzzy like I'd just woken. I hadn't stepped through the bushes. I'd never left the main trail. Yet I looked back through the brush and saw the colorful flash of three cyclists heading along the trail to the main loop.

I should definitely go back.

I got only two steps back when I felt it. A tickle in my brain. Not a thought, but an actual itch. A scratch from the inside. And even though I knew I shouldn't, I turned my back to the main trail.

Keep going.

I did.

Three steps into the brush, and the dark waxy leaves leisurely brushing against my legs made me pause to consider ticks. Spiders. Things that bite. But bravery, faith in modern medicine, and my body begging to run sent me gingerly hop-shimmying through the bushes with their deep red berries until I saw it. The trail showed itself, clear and welcoming, after thirty feet. No stroller or cyclists here.

Perfect.

It was the best feeling, to need to pay so much attention to the footing that my head emptied and went quiet. There was no school, no job, no parents, no worries. My eyes tracked the ground coming up in front, relayed the information to my body, and together, we just went. Mindless bliss.

My first run had been for cancer research when I was seven, and that was all it took. Ever since then, I ran. For fun, in races, on teams. It had been and still was the closest thing I could imagine to flying.

The buzz of my watch startled me out of my zen. A little satellite-shaped thingy with an *x* through it blinked up at me. Signal lost. I slowed to a walk, checked my heart rate, and looked around to find the brush and bushes were gone, replaced by a grove of pine trees, so close together I couldn't tell how tall they really were. I continued in farther until the trail was gone; a uniform carpet of pine needles spread out in front of me that swallowed my footfalls whole. Without a trail to follow, I came to a stop.

The air here was still and cool. Dense. It gently enveloped me with a hint of sweetness. A snug and comforting embrace. I could sit down and lean against one of the corrugated tree trunks. I could sit down and stay here, content to not take another step, ever. The thought of running vanished from my mind. A bead of sweat slipped down the center of my back.

I looked up into the branches and spun slowly. Shades of green everywhere. The tips of the branches were covered in needles that were still soft to the touch, fresh and bright. Closer to the trunk, the needles were older and thicker, a green so dark, it bordered on black. Above my head, the branches wove together to form a vaulted ceiling. A forest cathedral, that's where I was. No wonder the GPS had crapped out. Not even a sliver of sunlight could make it through to the ground.

Which, I now realized, made it hard to know the direction I'd come from. A slow 360 was no help. The forest looked the same in every direction. Pines. I bit down on my lip, but it wasn't an emergency yet. I hadn't walked that far inside the grove, just a few steps. Right? Another circle gave me the same information as the first. Pine trees, all I could see. And the sun was—where? Trail runner's code—keep track of the sun.

Shit.

Okay, okay. I closed my eyes and took a breath to soothe the fluttering tightness in my chest, a calming technique perfected in the hours and hours I'd waited at school for Dad to remember to pick me up, watching everyone else leave, half-convinced that I'd be waiting forever.

In through the nose for four, out through the mouth for four more.

Okay. You're in the forest. Somewhere. You've spun around so many times now that there's no hope of determining which way you came in. But! It's not anywhere near dark yet, and your watch battery is at a healthy 65 percent. Conclusion: walk until you find a signal.

Okay, but which way? I just had to go far enough to get out of the cathedral and back into the sun. A sunny sky meant a happy watch.

Crack.

A single branch snapped. I spun, because bears. A wave of adrenaline swept over me, my skin tingling in its wake, my hands curling into fists. I searched the darkness of the pines and saw nothing. I looked up, scanning overhead. But that didn't feel right, either. The noise had definitely come from down here, on my level. A single crack like a gunshot, and now silence. If it was a bear, it wasn't coming any closer. Not yet.

Time to go.

Once I picked a direction, it was really hard to walk. Didn't running from bears make things worse? Maybe that was dogs. My mind hummed as I went along at a pretty good pace, periodically checking my watch for signs of GPS life.

The instant I spied it out of the corner of my eye, relief flooded my body. The glint of sun on parked cars. I had no idea how I could be so close to the parking lot, but thank God. I'd gotten myself all worked up for nothing. Walking again, I changed direction slightly to aim for the lot. If there was a fence, I'd hop it, climb it, barrel right through. Whatever it took to get out of the forest that no longer felt like a friend.

The pine branches closed in a little here, suddenly stubborn and unaccommodating. I had to push to get through, one arm extended out to protect my face.

You'd think that the opposite of relief *flooding* your body is relief *receding*, but it isn't. It's your heart *sinking*. When you realize that what you glimpsed through the trees isn't a parking lot—it's water, and you're farther out in the middle of nowhere than you feared you were.

I emerged from the trees and stepped into the edge of a huge circular meadow. The comforting sweetness of the pines had dissipated. The view here was different but still pretty. Mounds of long, soft grass sloped down to a perfect circle of a pond in the middle.

But even as I thought it, the word *pond* seemed wrong. It was water, sure. It had to be. This was what I'd mistaken for the parking lot, the sun glimmering on this pond. But I'd never seen water like this. The longer I looked, the more I got the impression that it was the sunlight itself that was moving, shimmering. The water was so still, it looked fake.

I stood for a long time, for no reason. Just looking. The air stirred against my skin, breath on the back of my neck, raising fine hairs and sending a shiver down the length of my spine. The longer I looked, the more seeing felt like . . . remembering.

I shook my head. Fake water or not, it didn't matter. What mattered was that I had no idea where I was. Every year, I marked up little side trails and shortcuts that I favored on the forest maps handed out at the park gate. This pond wasn't on any map I'd ever seen, but I was definitely nowhere near the parking lot where I'd walked in. I let out a long, slow breath, envisioning the building panic leaving me in a plume. *Calm down.*

I should just turn back into the trees and try again. Choose a different direction.

And I would. That's exactly what I'd do, as soon as I finished looking at the pond. The . . . water?

It was water. What else could it be? It was weird, this clearing in the middle of the forest, like the pond had just been dropped here. No stream seemed to be feeding it; it was just . . . there. It wasn't big, no farther across than the swimming pool at the community center.

A breeze picked up and brushed the side of my face, but nothing else around me moved. No insects buzzed, no birds sang. The panic I'd felt a moment ago was gone, suddenly absent like the natural noises that should be there. I stood, aware of the stillness watching me, waiting to see what I'd do. The pond remained unrippled, the grassy moat unruffled. It was pretty here. Or it should be. I stared at the pond. The water.

I blinked slowly, my mind warm and fuzzy. An unknown pond in the forest. It sounded familiar, but the more I tried to grasp the thought, the further it floated away and out of my reach.

Chirrrp!

I jumped a little. My watch, reconnecting with its people. Thank God.

Chirrrp!

Actually, a glance confirmed it was telling me that my heart rate was climbing. While standing still. Which was unlikely. I frowned and held my wrist up to the sky, as if that bit of elevation could help it connect with the satellite. Still nothing. But back into the trees was the way out; it simply had to be. Okay. Time to go. I scanned the tree line and chose my point of entry, back and to the left of where I stood. Let's go.

Okay.

This was me, going.

No reason to wait.

Except, what was that? Something down there, right at the water's edge. It was hard to see from this angle. I squinted upward. The sun was still high in the sky, no worries there. I had plenty of time. Why not take a look? I just wanted to see what was out there. There was no harm in getting a little closer.

One step into the meadow and I discovered that the mounds of grass were solid. Hundreds of tiny mountains of earth covered with long silky grass. An illusion of fluidity where there was none. I picked my way carefully between the mounds, slowly approaching the water.

Wouldn't want to break an ankle here.

The thought—mine?—almost stopped me, but I was so close, and I really wanted to see the water, if that's what it was. I scrunched up my nose and tried not to breathe too deeply. It definitely didn't smell great. There could be some contaminated sludge that the county was hiding out here where they thought no one would find it. A few more carefully placed steps forward and I stopped.

Nope. Not sludge.

Just water. Staying out of the mud to protect my fairly new and expensive shoes, I gazed down into the pond. Just water, but perfectly still. And perfectly black—a fluid, inky well. The only thing visible was my own hazy reflection and a muted version of the sky behind me. It was just water, but it was . . . There was something not right. The longer I looked, the more I was sure of it. Like something standing off to the side, just far enough that I couldn't make it out. I knew what it was, I knew it. It was on the tip of my tongue; I just couldn't quite get hold of it. I leaned over a little farther, closer to my reflection in the water. I hated this feeling—knowing something but not being able to name it. I frowned.

My reflection smiled.

I staggered backward like I'd been shoved. The grass was longer now, denser and deeper. It seemed to twine around my ankles, but that couldn't be possible. I pulled one foot free, overbalanced, and landed hard on my back. The slippery green blades curled around my fingers and cinched tight. I scuttled backward like a crab, grass still clinging to me, the heart rate alarm chirping cheerily.

Chirrrp!

I wanted to get up, wanted to run, but I also didn't want to take my eyes off that water.

Nothing will crawl out. Nothing at all.

It's just water.

It's just grass.

I lurched to my feet and ran. My ankle jammed on one of the hard grassy mounds, but I kept going, eyes on the pines that had somehow gotten so far away. Afraid to take my eyes off the water before, now I absolutely could not look back, could not see what was there.

Nothing at all.

Diving onto the pine carpet like I was sliding home, I spun around on my back and finally looked.

Nothing at all.

Just a pond in the middle of a meadow. Under a sun that was not black and a sky that was not gray.

From which nothing was crawling out.

Get out.

The scraped heel of my hand burned. I gripped a fistful of needles, unmoving. Afraid to.

Get home.

Still not taking my eyes off the meadow, I carefully rose to my feet.

Get away.

This time, it was easy to decide which way to go, but now the brush was dense and unyielding. Thorns scratched at my legs as I pushed through, back toward the main trail. The bushes that had parted so easily before now refused to budge.

Chirrrp!

Was there someone behind me?

Someone else in the brush, a heavy presence at my back. I couldn't turn to look, regardless of the little voice. A vine with waxy green leaves curled across my right wrist as something unseen brushed tenderly against my ankle. My heart pounded, but my skin was cold. I had to move. I had to calm down and go, because I could hear the thing behind me moving.

Run.

I shoved away the whispers, clenched my fists to regain control of my body, and did what I do best.

I ran.

Without stopping to take a breath, I plunged back into the brush, leaves and branches slapping, snagging, scratching against my legs. Ripping free of thorns stuck in my skin, I started moving forward again, no longer able to run against the green gripping me, but lurching forward like I was wading thigh-deep through rising water. I kept my eyes locked on the small opening ahead in the brush because it was my way out, and it was closing fast with the darkness right behind me.

I had to stay focused on where I wanted to be. Back on the useless, manicured trail, back among strollers and cyclists. Panic propelled me forward until I popped through and stumbled out into the path of cyclists, eliciting shouts and a flurry of bells, my watch singing its resurrection song. Reconnected to the satellites and to reality. Off-balance, I spun around to see where I'd been.

And saw nothing but brush. No one there. No trail.

What.

What had just happened?

I started walking in the direction of home and then sped up a little. I needed to get home. But it was more than that. Somewhere small, where I couldn't fully admit it, I knew I was really in trouble.

The hypnotic little voice that had lured me off the trail had not been mine.

TWO

OUR HOUSE WAS NOTHING SPECIAL: A SMALL, gray-sided, one-level deal with the obligatory patch of grass out front and a pot of geraniums on the porch. But I'd never been so relieved to see it. I stood on the mat inside the front door, just wanting to be still for a moment, to give my heart a chance to settle down. The same rack I'd put my shoes in since kindergarten was now over-flowing, one of the few things in the house that my mom hadn't changed. I took two deep breaths, focusing on the wall, smooth and cool under my palm.

As I untied my shoes, my hands shook a little just from running home so hard. It wasn't anything else. Leftover adrenaline, yes. But just from the run. Not anything else. Not from finding a big nothing in the forest. That wasn't it at all.

A long exhale with my hands on my knees. Classic recovery position for a run that I shouldn't need to recover from.

"What"—Mom stepped out into the foyer brandishing my phone and blocking any escape—"happened to you?" She crossed her arms across her chest and waited. She was all muscle and sinew like me, lean and angled; she could have been a good runner—she was built for it. But Mom wasn't the running type. Not on the trails or in life in general. She was more likely to turn and fight than flee.

Her name was Violet, which was a terrible name for her, evoking a shrinking, timid person. But her family had a thing for flower names, right up until Mom broke the cycle with me. Mom went by "Vi," which was much more appropriate, basically another word for *compete*. Perfect for someone who'd never back down. Which wasn't great for me at the moment.

Mom raised her eyebrows at me, still waiting for an answer. "Well?"

Got lost in the forest. Had a panic attack. Ran home like a demon was on my tail.

"I went for a run."

Her eyes narrowed. "You're all scratched up."

I rubbed lightly at the welts that were starting to sting on my legs. "I was looking for blackberries." I surprised myself with the lie, but Mom had already moved on to the next item on her list of grievances.

"You can't just go out." Her voice got tight, like she'd told me this a million times. Which she had. "You need to communicate—I'm not a mind reader!"

"Okay." Which was my part of this conversation we'd had a million times. It was bound to get her wound up, but it was better than the only other thing I had to say at the moment, which involved me almost breaking an ankle and freaking out over nothing. Which is all we seemed to do lately—freak out on each other. Since my dad had left, Mom had gone into next-level mom mode, more in my business than ever, but I didn't want her to worry about me any more than she was obligated to—she had enough going on. So, the more she poked, the more I hid.

And honestly, I really didn't want to tell her about the pine cathedral or the creepy pond. It was just stupid, anyway. It was all in my head, and if I told Mom about it, there would be a cautionary tale about rapists or being eaten by wild dogs. She had a million of them.

"When I was your age, there was a girl . . ." Seriously. If only half of the stories I'd heard over the years were even halfway true, Mom must have been the only survivor in her graduating class. *Overprotective* should be her middle name.

"You know better than to go out without a phone, Avery." It was too late. A full-blown lecture was incoming. The hands were on the hips now; nothing for me to do but sit down on the floor and get comfortable, slowly pulling the laces of my shoes. "I'm willing to give you a certain amount of freedom, but you're not an adult. I'm still on the clock." Mom tapped her chest.

"I'll be away at school in a year. Then you're off the hook." I shrugged but watched my mother closely. This was my new hobby—looking for tells, digging for information. It seemed wrong that school was not something everyone had the money for, but it was true, and I was one of those people.

Mom had never flat-out told me that I was on my own, but I knew she worried about paying for school almost as much as I did. I apparently came from a long line of withholding, denying, squish-your-feelings-down-into-a-little-ball kind of people. I wasn't stupid. I heard the rattle of my dad's car when he did actually come to pick me up on his Friday nights. I knew my mom waited as long as she possibly could before she paid the bills. Buying my new running shoes was a big deal, and yes, shoes were expensive, but how could we afford university if shoes were a problem? And by "we," I mean me and Mom. The eye-roll emoji was the only suitable response to Dad and any promises he made these days.

Mom's pursing of the lips, the slow and deliberate blink of her large, dark eyes—this is what someone withholding information looked like. I should know; I did it every day.

"Yes. Well." Just as I'd suspected, mention of school had derailed the lecture. "Just—" Mom waved my phone in her hand vaguely and turned toward the kitchen. "Go have a shower before dinner. Ihstá Lily's here. You smell like—" She wrinkled her nose. "You smell worse than usual."

I wiped my hands off on my shorts and slid up the wall and onto my feet, hoping to quiet whatever was beating its wings high up in my chest, threatening to progress into my throat. In the kitchen, I could hear Mom's aunt Lily having what sounded like a very serious conversation with the cat.

I blinked, and Mom won. As always.

"Take your shower. Dinner will be ready soon." Mom turned and went into the kitchen, where something was bubbling on the stove, trying to escape from a pot.

Out in the hall, I hesitated. Going left would take me into the living room with its gray marshmallowy-soft sofa and nothing but photos of me on the walls. Beyond that was the immaculate dining area with a table used only for meals with Lily and holding cast-off junk the rest of the time. And at the very back of the house was the very uninspired standard white kitchen, which was fine because neither Mom nor I were cooks—the microwave and dishwasher got the most action. But today the kitchen would also hold more questions. Aunt Lily was there, yes. But so was Mom, and in her current mood, maybe doing what I'd been told for once was the way to go.

So I padded down the hall to my right, the same dove gray as everything else in the house, hopping on one foot to pull off my socks as I went. The door to Mom's bedroom was closed as usual but not shut. The socks got tossed into my room as I passed, and I continued to the bathroom at the end of the hall that was essentially mine.

In the bathroom, I waited for the water to heat up to scalding and tugged the elastic out of my hair, hissing when it took a few strands with it. I always kept my hair long even though I never did anything but pull it back, which was kind of pointless, but for the few minutes a day it was down, it was pretty—long and shiny and dark like Mom's. Above the counter, my reflection in the mirror stared back at me—skin with a hint of copper like my mom's and big hazel eyes that were the only gift from my dad that I got to keep.

A shower had been all that I wanted, but now that the water was actually on, there was something I didn't like about the way the drops rolled down the glass door. One particular drop slid, stopped, slid faster, and then disappeared when it got close to the bottom, mingling with all the other drops along the base of the door. Like they were massing, looking for a way out.

I bit down on my bottom lip and held it, my old go-to before a race. The sensation focused my mind, helped me dive in and do what I had to, even when I wasn't sure I could. Even if I was afraid. Which was before every single race, really.

I peeled off my stinking running clothes, leaving them in a heap on the floor just like Mom hated. I was more careful taking off the silver chain around my neck, a small silver turtle dangling from the end. I let it lie on my palm for a long moment, watching the light bounce off the beveled shell before setting it carefully on a towel on the counter. The turtle necklace was my souvenir of Lily as she used to be, her gift for me at one of the last powwows we'd gone to together. That was our thing—every July she'd invite my mom to come with us, but Mom had always found a reason not to go. I hadn't minded then, having Lily all to myself. That last time, before Lily started to change and couldn't drive anymore, while we were waiting for the grand entry, we'd made our way around the vendors' tables circling the arbor; I'd been drawn to the long colorful beaded earrings, but Lily had leaned far over to the back of the table and plucked the silver chain with the tiny turtle—mostly shell, with only the suggestion of four feet and a head. She'd held it up to the light and smiled before nodding to the woman behind the table. I'd worn it ever since, keeping it safe every time I showered, just so Lily could see me wear it. She was different now, frail and insubstantial; I tried to make her smile whenever I could, and wearing the necklace was an easy way to do that. I wore it so often now, it was like a part of me—my security turtle. Thinking of Before Lily made my throat go tight, so with the necklace safe in its towel nest, I ran my hands through my loose hair and turned back to the shower.

Drops of water pattered against the glass shower door, quiet but insistent. Waiting for me. Something had changed; taking a shower shouldn't be this scary. There was something wrong with me, but I couldn't put my finger on it. Maybe the pond actually had been toxic sludge. Maybe I'd inhaled fumes.

Mom had always told me to stay on the trails, but there were so many of them and not all were well marked. They twisted so far and wide through the forest, looping back on themselves and intersecting, that it was more like a labyrinth—even locals could get lost. Then there was an old story about a pond—finding it would wake some kind of monster, but surely an urban legend couldn't be what had her so riled up and me so . . . off? I wasn't sure, but I didn't want to ask for clarification.

I didn't like to use my words. Ask questions. Words could do things.

I had discovered this a couple of years ago, when my dad still lived with us. I hadn't been oblivious; no kid is. I'd known my parents were in trouble, even if the variety of trouble was—to me—ill-defined. I was sure even the cat had known. But I hadn't ever truly believed that he would leave—or get kicked out, depending on who was telling the story. No kid does.

So there I'd been, this knowledge drifting like a fog through the house, making it hard to see, hard to know what was safe to say and what wasn't. Night after night of sitting at the table between my parents, neither of them saying anything of value. People called it an elephant in the room, but I knew it was a fog. A dense white fog that you moved through as if you could see just fine, when in fact, you were walking blind.

And then one night, I'd cracked, because a person could only take so much. In the middle of dinner—roast chicken, spinach salad, and sweet potatoes—I had asked if they were going to get a divorce. My parents had frozen, staring at their plates. The silence felt like it had always been there. When it became clear that Dad was going to sit this one out, Mom had put down her fork carefully, like the placement of cutlery on china had consequences that history would turn on. She'd faced me, put her hand on my shoulder, and looked me in the eyes.

"Avery, none of this is your fault."

But I instantly knew it was. I'd spoken the words, given the idea power. I'd made it real.

After that, things had happened fast. After months of creeping around the edges of the idea, of terse, whispered arguments, my parents sprang into action. Three days later, Dad had a new address and there wasn't a trace of him left in the house. It was like I'd given them permission. I'd spoken it into existence.

Which is why I needed to keep my mouth shut now, even if there was something dancing in a very unpleasant way up and down my spine like the remnant of a nightmare, a gauzy sliver that I couldn't quite grasp. The water, and what I'd seen in it—why give voice to something like that, why open a door when you didn't know who was knocking? Nothing bad had actually happened; no reason to add another worry onto my mom's pile. Like everything else, I could deal with this myself.

I gripped the shower door and released my lip. The whole room was starting to fog up, and that's the last thing I wanted—to be immersed in water when I couldn't see clearly.

I pulled the door open and stepped in.

Dinner was excruciating.

As soon as I sat down at the table, the bubbling contents of the pot were staring up at me from my plate. Pasta. Again. Mom working day shifts at the hospital meant she was home to make dinner—which was nice. But she'd never really been an inspired cook, and pasta was easy and quick to throw together after picking up her ihstá from the retirement home.

Mom brought her over for dinner regularly, and I'd certainly never objected. Ihstá Lily was precious: if a bird were transformed into a human, that would be my great-aunt. A sparrow, maybe, something cheerful but fragile. Coiffed hair and too-big cardigans made her look more substantial than she actually was. She was seated at the circular oak table, smoothing out the paper napkin onto her lap. Even now, with a failing memory and faulty knees, my ihstá was elegant.

"Hi, Ihstá." I sat down and repelled Buttons's attempt to jump onto my lap.

Lily's fork clattered onto her plate mid-twirl. I looked up to find her watery brown eyes on me, huge and unblinking behind her glasses, eyebrows pinched together in obvious concern.

"Are you okay, dear?" Hushed, like someone might be eavesdropping.

"Avery's fine, Ihstá." Mom placed a half-filled glass of water in front of her aunt, like you'd give an unsteady toddler. "She just had a hard run today."

"Karhá:kon," Lily said to Mom, like she was looking for clarification.

Trees? I was having trouble following this, but I'd clearly upset Lily just by walking in and sitting down. I'd never been fluent in Kanyen'kéha, and now I only occasionally heard it when Lily lost track of what language she was speaking. It wasn't the kind of thing you could study in high school, which Lily had said was a crime years ago, but honestly, I think Mom was afraid it might do me more harm than good, marking me as different in a world that only claimed to value diversity. As a result, I was stuck there, listening to my great-aunt question me in a language someone else had decided I didn't need—Mom, for one. But deep down, I knew she had her reasons.

The summer I was six, we'd gone out to visit Mom's sister, where I'd been happy to play with my cousins, but I'd still stayed close to Mom and Dad while the grown-ups talked about work and stuff, so I'd seen Mom's face when her sister leaned forward in her lawn chair, playfully slapped Mom's knee, and laughingly said Mom had an "apple life."

On the ride home, Dad had been buoyant, smiling and tapping his fingers on the wheel, already planning another visit to "the country." Beside him, Mom had been stone-faced and silent. I didn't understand until much later why being called an apple made my mom so angry. We never visited those cousins again. Now Mom spoke Kanyen'kéha only to Lily. I guessed my mom knew how dangerous words could be, too.

"Mom." I prompted her to remind Lily of my ignorance and speak English to me.

"Ihstá." Mom patted Lily's hand.

"Oh, yes. You were in the trees?" Lily turned her intense gaze on me and put her weightless hand on mine. If I reached across the table and took Mom's left hand, I'd complete the circle. But things between us were the way they were, so I didn't. I curled the edge of the gray woven placemat under my fingers and gave Lily my most reassuring smile.

"I'm fine. I just got a little lost," I said. I shrugged uber-casually. "Well, not lost. I found a new trail."

"A new trail?" Mom's fork stopped midair, her voice sharp. "What new trail? Where?"

Lily's watery eyes were on me again, brows pinched even more. "You found it." Her words were barely a whisper.

Mom stared at me like she'd never seen me before, eyes searching my face for information. If ever there had been an opportunity for a lecture, here it was. I'd walked face first into this one.

I played with my fork a little, still casual as ever. "Um . . . I found a pond."

"Stay away from the water." Mom's voice was low and soft, the one she'd used to either lull me to sleep or scare me into good behavior in public. "I've told you before—don't ever leave the trail."

Oh my God. "Mom. Seriously."

So I'd run off course on a deer trail and freaked out a little—why was I getting the lecture face? It was just an old story. She was supposed to make me feel better, to laugh and tell me not to be so dramatic. But I didn't feel better, not at all.

And she didn't laugh.

"Don't mess around out there, Avery. I don't want to hear about training." Her voice remained low but firm and serious. "Stay on the trail or you won't be running out there at all." Mom glanced at Lily and patted her hand again.

Why was she acting like she'd found weed in my backpack? There was a pond out there that I'd found by accident. This was not a Level-Four Emergency, but the most rebellious I could get without inviting total lockdown was to stare back at her.

"People have disappeared in there." Lily's fingers curled around mine, papery-soft, more like the memory of fingers than the real thing.

Partly true. The forest was massive, and out-of-towners got lost practically every summer. Sometimes they came out on a stretcher, or in a neck brace, but they came out. They didn't *disappear*. Things like that don't happen in real life.

Plaintive meows, and suddenly I had a cat in my lap. Mom got up and headed to the kitchen with a sigh, my misadventure in the forest suddenly gone from her mind. "Didn't you feed him?"

"I forgot." One of my few duties—keeping the cat alive—that I wasn't excelling at today. Buttons nudged my hand with his head, basically forcing me to pet him. Cats, at least, didn't have issues with being clear about their needs, a skill I admired. His fur was creamy white and silky soft because although I'd forgotten to feed him today, a quick brush when I got home from school was part of our ritual and a chance for me to decompress. Lily loved Buttons almost as much as I did, so I was surprised when she ignored him and leaned toward me.

"I'm worried," Lily whispered.

"Don't be worried—I'm fine. Wakata . . . karí." I stumbled to string the words together.

"Wakata'karí:te," Lily corrected softly, removing her hand from mine and shaking her head gently. She reached out to me and brushed the silver turtle with trembling fingers. "People disappear forever in that place. . . ."

That place again, stuck in her head on a loop. It was hard to talk to Lily these days—this ghost of my great-aunt. I preferred to remember her as the woman I'd planted a Three Sisters garden with every spring, who'd taken me to powwows. But all that was left now was a frail old lady who drifted in and out of reality, so I did what I could to make her feel better.

"It's fine, Ihstá. I won't go again. I just found it by accident."

"You only find it if it wants you," Lily murmured to her plate.

I shivered. Lily had always been full of stories; she'd passed them down to my mom, where most of them had stopped. That's all this was. An old, barely remembered story about an even older place.

Lily poked at her pasta, murmuring something like a song. I didn't understand a word. I shoveled in a forkful and chewed slowly, making it impossible for me to say anything to upset anyone else tonight. I'd just keep my mouth shut until Mom took Lily home and I could go to sleep and not be conscious for a while.

In bed that night, with Buttons curled up in his spot behind my knees, the image of the unnaturally still black water I'd found kept pushing its way into my mind. I'd been on those trails, in that forest, since I was the one in a stroller, yet I'd never come upon that pond, and it wasn't on any map I'd ever seen. Which shouldn't bother me. It was a big forest, after all. I pushed away the image of the water, and once again, it returned, like an unwanted guest shouldering their way through a half-closed door.

I took slow, deep breaths, my tried-and-true method of winding down enough to sleep. I focused on my body, trying to relax my feet, my legs, my hands and shoulders, but as soon as my focus moved on, each muscle snapped back tight.

Mom padded down the hall to my door, stopping me mid-breath.

I couldn't take any more confrontation today; I was still so weirdly wound up that sleep wasn't going to come easy, and I didn't need more conflict. So when the doorknob turned, I closed my eyes and evened out my breathing, as if that could fool my mom. The door opened too softly to hear, but the fragrance of her rosemary shampoo wafted across the room to me.

The edge of the bed dipped, but I'd committed to feigning sleep and was too stubborn to give up now. If she wanted to continue her lecture, I wasn't going to provide a willing audience. But when she finally spoke, her voice was low and soft, as if she'd fallen for my act and was speaking to herself.

"When you were born, your dad and I were pretty young," she said, one finger barely grazing my hair. "Even before we left the hospital, I was afraid that they would take you away from us. They do that, you know. Still."

I'd never heard any of this from Mom before, but it made me feel bad for her. Most parents got a moment when there was nothing to do but bask in the joy and relief of a baby arriving, but Mom hadn't, because the government had a history of snatching Indigenous kids. Worse, I hadn't ever really thought about what that must have been like for her. It was so tempting to give in and open my eyes, but Mom and I were enough alike that I sensed it was easier for her to say these things if we both pretended I was asleep.

I felt the barest pressure of her hand on the blanket over my leg. "I know you're too big for anyone to take now, but I guess that fear never left me."

Buttons shifted, as if he were listening, too.

"Just . . ." Mom sighed and gave my leg a little pat. "Just promise me you'll be careful. And smart. I worry about you, you know."

That was as close to an apology as I'd ever heard from my mom, which sent a little shot of warmth through my body. But as she rose and slipped out the door, the chill, the image of the black water and the tension it brought, chased every bit of warmth down and stamped it out. Mom did worry about me—I knew that, and I didn't want to add to it.

"I'll deal with it myself." I whispered to Buttons as the door clicked shut. "It's nothing, anyway."

That night, I dreamed I was back in the forest, at the edge of the pine cathedral.

The air there was cool and fresh. I was safe.

But my legs were traitors, taking me into the meadow against my will.

The long grass smoothed out, paving my way. I didn't want to go but couldn't stop.

The water that was placid and smooth rippled just once, a single raindrop hitting the surface from the other side.

It stilled again, and for a moment, I thought it was okay.

But then another drop.

Another raindrop from the other side, where the sky is always gray.

My heart was pounding. I knew then that I wouldn't get away.

Something was coming for me.

Something was coming through.

THREE

WHEN I WOKE, GASPING FOR AIR AND SCARING the crap out of the cat, I did anything I could to stay awake, afraid of being sucked back into the dream. Getting up would set off Mom's internal mom-alarm no matter how quiet I was, so I lay there, eyes wide open, trying to do the opposite of what I'd done last night. Mustn't fall asleep. But my bed was warm and comfy. The light outside was still soft, and at heart, I was a lazy person. Only one thing to do.

I picked up my phone, the sudden brightness searing my eyes. Six a.m. I waited a few seconds, then typed and hit send before I chickened out.

You awake?

When Key called, I picked up right away. I always did. I picked up for my friend Stella, too, but Key was different. *BFFs* didn't cover it. We were two puzzle pieces that fit together.

"Where've you been?" he said. His voice was a little gravelly with sleep. I'd woken him, clearly, but it was worth it to me. With exam madness happening, I hadn't seen him much recently.

I closed my eyes and snuggled back into my bed. With his voice in my ear, the dark became warm and comforting. Sometimes I liked to pretend that he was right there, in the dark beside me. It was a secret fantasy of mine, but every once in a while, I would catch him looking at me, his eyes gone soft and warm, and get the feeling that maybe it wasn't the secret I thought it was. Key's voice wasn't deep, exactly, but it was smooth and rich. Like, if his voice were an object, it would be something buttery-soft and caramel-colored. Something expensive and indulgent. Like a luxury car or . . .

I was really tired, like I really had been running all night and not just in the dream.

"Where've I been?" I smiled at my phone. "Where've *you* been?"

"Killing my exams." Matter-of-fact statement that was most likely true. Key killed everything. "I think a celebratory cinnamon roll is in order. But no Stella. Just you and me."

Key was always celebrating something and dragging me along with him. Last spring he'd gotten one of his photos published in the paper. He got good grades without even trying, and his family was whole and happy, but he was fundamentally different from me. He saw reason for celebration everywhere, where I saw the problems first. The world loved Key and he loved it right back while I held it at arm's length, forever skeptical. Technically, Key should be the kind of person I couldn't stand, but the truth was quite the opposite. Unlike me, with a select circle of friends I'd cultivated over the years, Key practically trailed friends, acquaintances, and well-wishers everywhere he went. But where he went was usually to me, a fact that never crossed my mind without a little tingle of . . . something, deep in the center of my chest.

"Sounds good." A surge of something bright and sparkling swept through me at the thought. Cinnamon rolls meant the café, which actually sounded like the perfect place to be right then.

"Cinnamon roll for *me*," Key clarified.

"Right."

"Not to share."

This was an old game, and I loved it.

"Not at all." Shaking my head solemnly.

"You buy your own for once."

"That's very harsh."

"So you want to skip it?" he teased.

"Meet you there."

The café opened ridiculously early to accommodate the swarms of cyclists that showed up this time of year, zipping in packs along back roads and forest trails. It was quiet at this hour, but Key and I were never the only ones there.

I'd scooped up some clothes from the floor and stepped into the first pair of shoes I'd seen, made sure the front door closed with a barely audible click, and taken off. Key had probably showered and selected something from a real hanger in his meticulously organized closet.

The coffee shop was not much more than a nook, a coffee niche, really. Ten round tables and chairs scraped loudly on the tile floor when pulled out; abstract art on canvases were the only decorations except for the fairy lights around the counter. It was a bare-bones kind of place that didn't need to be flashy—all the food was homemade and the coffee was exquisite. Everything was warm and cozy and the whole place somehow always felt like a refuge on a rainy day.

At this hour, the only other customers were a young white woman with a baby sleeping in a stroller and an older man sitting in the corner working on a newspaper puzzle. I was settling in at our usual table, against the wall under a four-foot-tall painting of what looked like a tree preparing to take flight, and enjoying the sensation of my hands warm around a hot mug of coffee when Key pushed through the door, nodding to the waitress politely but only truly brightening when he saw me. He was lanky in an athletic way, even though the closest he'd ever been to an athlete was when he was sitting next to me. Big brown eyes and a mop of dark unruly curls he claimed to never bother with but also never cut and that managed to always look good—to me, anyway. It reminded me of my favorite photo of Key. On the wall of his living room, one of the first tripod shots he'd done when he was ten, on a blindingly sunny beach in Jamaica in the middle of his whole extended family, laughing as they crowded into the shot, their backs to the ocean where a wave was forever about to break. The only part of his face not obscured by his windswept curls was his smile.

"Hey," he said, those same curls bobbing as he dumped his backpack on the floor and dropped into a chair.

"Hey." I sipped my coffee, scalding hot and a little bitter, which was perfect.

And just like that, with the coffee hot and Key's smile warm, things started to get better. My shoulders dropped and my jaw softened. I closed my eyes and smiled, letting my mind drift while listening to one of my favorite sounds—Key talking about anything. A sip, a sigh, and I got a little floaty.

"So then Simu Liu comes into the coffee shop and tells me that he needs my help to save the universe. Not Shang-Chi—Simu Liu. I tell him yeah, sure, because who says no to Simu Liu, right? So he'll be by to pick me up at eight. What do you think? Cool, right?"

I nodded, downed the rest of my coffee, and licked my lips.

Key shook his head like he wanted nothing more to do with me. He raked his fingers through his curls and gripped two fistfuls, one step from yanking them out.

"Oh my *God*."

"What?"

He leaned forward and pointed his finger at me. "You're not even listening."

"I am."

"What was I talking about?"

"You're . . . working tonight. At eight." I struggled. Key didn't work on weekdays.

Key shared a disgusted look with the tabletop, folding his napkin into ever-smaller triangles.

"Not even a little bit."

"Sorry. I'm really tired." I tried puppy-dog eyes, but Key was the king of that.

It was true. I'd rolled through the initial burst of energy just getting here. Now I was dragging again, feeling like I hadn't slept at all. I sagged back in my chair.

Key reached over and tapped the back of my hand twice. Our secret code. *You there?*

"You do look like crap," he observed.

I managed a saccharine smile. "Thanks, Key. You always know just what to say."

"Seriously." He caught my eyes and lowered his voice. "Is everything okay?"

"Oh my God." I leaned back, making my shoulders relax and drop away from my ears to show how okay everything was. "The concerned eyebrows. I didn't think I looked that bad."

Pursed lips and a shrug. "I wasn't going to mention it, but . . ."

I lightly slapped the side of his head and simultaneously tried to scoop his cinnamon roll. Key took the hit and protected the pastry.

"I need sustenance," I whined.

"Okay. But you're not supposed to eat crap like this." Ever mindful of my training, Key broke off a teeny tiny piece of the roll and dropped it into my outstretched hand. "There you go, baby bird." He quickly licked his finger, unwilling to let any form of sugar escape him. But he had that look on his face now, the look I had first seen in the schoolyard years ago. I'd been the victim of a mean-girl squad dump, sitting alone, and Key had come over with this look on his face, ready to save my world.

"So, are you going to tell me what's going on, or do I have to guess as usual?" Key tilted his head at me. "Honestly, Ave. It's like you're two different people—the person you pretend to be and the you I know you are. It's all or nothing with you. That must be exhausting."

He had no idea.

I might as well surrender.

I shrugged. "I just didn't sleep well."

No follow-up questions, because he didn't need any. He had the Look.

"Weird dreams," I said, my eyes flicking away from his unwavering brown ones.

His concerned eyebrows turned to possibly scandalized eyebrows. Key docked his chin on his fist, awaiting further details.

"Not like that. Like . . . weird. Scary."

Still nothing.

"You should be a psychiatrist. You have this whole"—I waved my hand in front of his face—"thing going on."

"And how does that make you feel?" Key smiled.

I could do this all day. This was real. Joking with Key, snug in our coffee shop. This place always smelled like cinnamon, the light was soft but not dim, and in the background a woman always sang about being in love or being out of love at just the right volume. The dreams felt far away and stupid suddenly. I sighed, and my chest loosened, letting my lungs fill completely in a way they hadn't for the past few days. I put my hand up for a refill.

We both fell silent as the waitress came to our table, stood beside us, and poured, all three of us pretending that she wasn't interrupting anything. The sound of coffee gurgling happily into a cup is reassuring, especially when the coffee is needed. But the *smell* of fresh coffee, that heady aroma—number five on my list of Top Ten Things I Love but Will Never Tell.

I watched it flow into the gleaming white cup, just the sight of it making me feel safe and snug and warm. The coffee neared the top, but the happy gurgling had changed. I frowned down at it, because this wasn't right. It sounded now like a much larger quantity of liquid.

It was trickling, streaming, rushing. Rapids when it should be a brook. My pulse boomed in my throat as I watched the color change—it was no longer a deep brown but an inky black. My beloved aroma turned fetid and foul. The black liquid reached the top of my cup and spilled over, sending thin sentient fingers slithering toward Key's hands resting on the table, seeking him out. I gasped and startled so hard my knees hit the table.

"Ave?" At the sound of his voice, my head snapped up. There was the hint of a frown and genuine confusion in Key's face, and I didn't blame him. A glance down at the table confirmed that my coffee was a normal dark amber and safely in my cup. The table was clean and dry, and the waitress gave the ceiling a long-suffering sigh before she walked away. What was happening to me?

"Ave. Scary how?" He lowered his voice but didn't look away. He wasn't going to let this go, and honestly, I wanted to tell him. Then I wanted him to tell me it was nothing, that it would stop, that I had no reason to be afraid.

"I got lost in the forest." It came out of me like a secret.

The concerned eyebrows were back.

"In your dream."

"No. No. In real life. On my run."

"Okay."

"I got lost and found something. This pond that was . . . weird. I got scared because I was lost, I guess, but I had this dream that I was back there and I don't want to be. I'm afraid something's going to suck me in or . . ."

Or something is going to crawl out.

I rubbed my hands over my face and sighed. I was doing a crap job of explaining. It sounded like nothing, and I sounded unstable.

"You've gotten lost in the forest before," Key tactfully pointed out, talking around the last of the roll. "Remember that time your mom and dad had to go out with flashlights because you—"

"Yes, yes. I didn't keep track of the sun and got lost. Yes. Thank you. We all remember the flashlights."

Key put up his "don't hurt me" hands. "You were seriously lost then."

"Yeah."

"In the dark, even."

"I do remember."

"You were super lost."

"Thank you."

Key smiled and gave up the ribbing. He always quit just before I got truly mad. It was a gift he had.

"Being lost is scary," he said, opening his hands like his opinion was an offering. "Maybe this is about the future, you know? Like, you're at a crossroads in life. School, decisions, maybe it's about that." He sat back, looking really pleased with himself. And it was a sweet bit of analysis, honestly.

But no.

"I'm not lost in the dream. It's . . . it's not really even the dream." I looked down at my hands on the cream-and-beige-flecked table. As much as I didn't want to think about it, I wanted to get this right. If I could explain it, make him understand, maybe it would leave me. Maybe I could speak it *out* of existence.

"When I got lost in the forest, I found this pond, this water, but it wasn't normal and it shouldn't have been there. It freaked me out. It was still and black." My reflection. "And I thought that maybe I saw something." If Key laughed now, if he thought I was crazy, I would never mention it again to anyone. I'd just quietly go insane. Like a good girl.

But Key's face had gone expressionless. "You should stay on the trails."

I stared. "What did you say?"

Key lowered his chin and raised his eyebrows, getting as close to my mom's lecture face as humanly possible. "In Crook's Falls, you should stay away from the water."

The music and voices around us faded until it felt like Key and I were the only two people in existence. I'd been running the trails for years and had never heard any of this from him.

"Key." I leaned forward and kept my voice low. If he was messing with me, I wasn't amused. "What?"

"A mysterious place in the forest? That doesn't ring a bell?"

I sat back so hard and fast my chair squeaked on the floor. "Come on."

Just like my mom. He was talking about stories so old and ridiculous, they may as well be written in calligraphy in a dusty leather-bound book kept on a shelf in a haunted library. The black water in the forest that hid until it was hungry. Nobody knew where it was because no one who found it ever came back. Everybody in town had heard that urban legend. It was a Crook's Falls thing. And I wanted reassurance that it was not real, that what had happened then—and just now—was a result of my stressed, burned-out self.

Key shrugged, slowly spinning his phone between us on the table. "Yeah, but a legend is not a myth. There's a kernel of truth somewhere, and who knows where it comes from? You should ask." He tapped the table. "You know, in your community."

I flicked his phone with my finger so hard it went skittering across the table, forcing Key to snatch it before it sailed off the edge. He wasn't making me feel better about the legend, and now he had to bring this up.

"Why don't you call up your cousin Asha and see what she's up to?" I countered, a fight brewing in my voice.

He looked at me like I'd lost my mind. "Because the last time I saw her we were five, before she left Jamaica for London."

"Exactly." I folded my arms. Other than Lily and Mom, I didn't know anyone in "my community," and Key was aware of that. Mom and Lily were the only Kanyen'kehá:ka I really knew, which honestly had always bothered me. It was like I belonged to a club but had never been invited to a meeting. And the story—legend—had nothing to do with "my community"; it was just small-town boredom. Now I was in an even worse mood than before I got here, and it was all his fault.

I started carefully tearing my napkin into even strips and sighed. Key set his phone face down on the table and did the slow blink to let me know he was being patient even though I was being unreasonably bitchy. Which—maybe I was.

Another sigh, the closest I could currently get to anything resembling an apology. Fortunately, Key spoke my language.

"Should we go?" he asked softly, already pushing back his chair.

We left some money on the table and pushed through the door into the air that had gone still and hot, our argument already fading.

FOUR

"WE STILL HAVE TO MAKE OUR PLAN OF ATTACK for FallsFest, right?" Key gave me our customary one-armed hug as we parted, taking things back to normal so I didn't have to. "Stella's getting pretty hyped."

"Stella's always hyped."

"True." Key conceded. "But FallsFest is worthy."

The two-week countdown to the highlight of our small-town summer, a tradition for us and plenty of junk-food opportunities for Key. Fiddling with my backpack for a moment gave me time to send a surreptitious glance back at him, check out his body language to make sure we really were okay. Key's easy stride and swinging arms reassured me, so I turned left onto Spruce Street, and right onto Forest Avenue, all the way into town to my job at the bookshop. There were pretty little cottage-style houses on my right, the edge of the forest on my left. Proximity to the forest meant that though the houses here were small and old, the people who lived in them had the money to keep them perfectly maintained—immaculate lawns, precisely edged flower beds, not a dandelion in sight. Everyone was willing to pay big bucks to be close to the forest.

But not me. Not after finding that weird pond. The sidewalks in this part of town were perfect—no uneven, crumbling concrete here to trip me up—but I kept my eyes down out of habit, putting one foot in front of the other, trying to get on autopilot and failing. My body was wired and humming from the caffeine, but I still felt like a zombie—a very unpleasant combination.

I took in some nice deep breaths as I walked, hoping the oxygen would either wake me up or calm me down, because the black water was still on my mind—part of me dismissing it as pure drama, the rest fixated on figuring it out. Key bringing it up hadn't made me feel better at all. Across the street, a sprinkler rose out of the lawn and sprayed a mist fine enough to be carried over to me on the breeze while a lawn mower grumbled to life somewhere nearby.

I turned down Meadows Way, leaving the forest behind. Nothing here but houses on both sides of the street. Nothing to creep me out, nothing to think about except how I could calm the fuck down. Yoga? Meditation? Ocean sounds might be good. Yeah, listening to some waves would be nice and soothing right about now.

I came to the fanciest lot on the street, which spanned almost the whole block—same little house as everyone else, but a huge yard enclosed by a living fence of lilac bushes taller than me. I raised my left hand and let it brush against the green leaves, releasing the scent of the flowers as I passed. The leaves were soft, whispering against my palm and slipping up toward my wrist. Cool, green, and smelling like summer. The movement rippled out and up, my hand sending the bushes shivering all the way to the top. I let my hand drag a little harder into the hedge, pressing into the dense green.

And felt something press back.

I stopped, but the hedge continued to shiver half a step ahead of me.

And then stopped.

"Hello?"

The hedge was too dense to see through, but I sensed something solid on the other side. I listened for movement, but there was only the chirping of birds and the *sst-sst-sst* of the sprinklers. I wiped my hand on my shorts, suddenly wanting any remnant of the lilacs gone.

"This is why I need to calm down."

This was exactly why. There was nothing there except my imagination. It was just like the coffee, so I needed to suck it up. I gripped my backpack straps with both hands and kept walking, eyes on the sidewalk, desperately trying to ignore the lilacs rippling and swaying beside me with every step. I bit my lip and tried to think of anything else, but my brain stayed stuck on the rustling of the leaves right next to my arm and the quiet whisper underneath that would turn into actual words if I let it. Swallowing around the lump in my throat, I sped up, but the rustling of the bushes kept pace.

Nothing there. There was nothing there on the other side of the hedge, and I was going to feel so stupid when I passed the gate and could see that. But the sight of the little white wooden gate set in the hedge didn't make me feel better. The closer I got to it, the more I dreaded passing. I didn't want to see whatever was keeping up with me. My head told me there would be nothing on the other side, but another, smarter part of me told me that a pale, wrinkled hand would appear through the leaves, grab my wrist, and drag me to the other side, a dark place where I couldn't breathe and didn't know which way was up.

The cute little gate six steps away may as well have been the gaping jaws of hell. I broke into a run and the rustling followed suit, both of us racing to get to the gate first. I shut my eyes as I passed and then broke for the end of the block and darted across the street. Screw Meadows Way. I turned onto the bike path that would mean an extra five minutes to downtown but that had nothing but open lawns on either side.

I finally slowed, eyes straight ahead, sweat pooling on my skin under my backpack. Aunt Lily's words echoed in my mind. *"You only find it if it wants you."*

I tried to push the idea down, squish it into a little ball and ignore it, but I couldn't. Whatever I'd found in the forest, whatever lurked in that black water . . . had it followed me home?

I hurried the rest of the way as fast as I could without actually running. Now that it was summer, I was doomed to walk to work every morning—there would be no rides from Stella in her Mini. Hopefully not every walk would be like this one. I breathed a sigh of relief when I reached Frank's Books, the center of the north block bordering the town square. The storefront was all glass and dark wood, a designated heritage building Frank had fallen in love with and bought after he retired. "Born to be a bookstore," he always said of it. I slipped my key in the lock and turned, watching my reflection in the glass set in the big oak door.

"Hey!"

If I hadn't been holding on to the brass door handle, I would have shot straight up into the stratosphere. As it was, I startled hard enough to get a weird look from Jackie, owner of the most glorious long red hair I'd ever seen and frequent co-author of my biology homework. She stood on the sidewalk in shorts and a T-shirt with neon-pink bikini string peeking out from the collar, a white apron draped over her arm, looking at me curiously. She was all curves and sociability, both qualities I lacked and sometimes envied her for.

"Hey, Jackie." I tried to rearrange my face into something more casual but didn't let go of the door handle. "You opening?"

Mehmet's Kebabs was another Crook's Falls staple, a tiny to-go shop wedged between a florist and a bakery. It had only opened last year, but every lunch hour there was a line down the block. The fast success in a town as monochromatic as Crook's Falls had taken some by surprise, but Mehmet really knew what he was doing behind the grill.

"Yeah." Jackie lifted the apron as proof. "Mehmet's kid is sick, so he's actually trusting me to open and prep. I bombed my last exam of the year, so I had no excuse. You done?"

"Yeah." Exams were done and I was free for the summer, but it wasn't starting out great.

"I'd planned to spend today getting some sun." Jackie pouted. "Me and my bikini in the backyard, just enough to make my new dress pop so I'll be radiant for FallsFest. A white minidress." She mimed the dress on her body. "My sister thinks she's going to borrow it, but she is so wrong."

I nodded, fascinated by her ability to talk to anyone about anything. Once she started talking, you were just along for the ride, but I had never minded her chattiness; in biology class it was a nice distraction from drawing cells and cutting up dead frogs, and I admired talents that I didn't have.

"You okay?" Jackie stepped closer to peer at me.

I was getting really tired of people asking that, but she meant well and I did look like crap, so I nodded. "Just tired."

"Same." She blew her bangs out of her face. "You should come out with us sometime. Let loose."

"Us" could mean anything—Jackie was kind of like Key in that she didn't have a circle, she moved in all of them, at home no matter where she went. "Stella always comes without you."

"Thanks." More nodding, even though I didn't have the stomach for the kind of outings Jackie was talking about. Key and my other BFF, Stella, were in their element in social situations. But I was, if not shy, definitely reserved. Parties were things to be endured, not enjoyed—my nightmares.

Except for this new one I had.

"Anyway, I gotta go." Jackie glanced down the block and sighed. "If that grill isn't sizzling by the time Mehmet gets in, you'll never see me again." She headed down the sidewalk at her customary trot, always in a hurry to get wherever she was going.

"See you around," I called.

She waved her hand over her shoulder in reply, leaving me alone with my reflection.

I stayed a moment, watching and waiting to make sure that the world reflected behind me was as it should be. Cars passed, birds flitted. Nothing lunged out to grab me. But I was distrustful of what I saw now, glancing over my shoulder just in case before hauling the door open like it was resisting me.

Inside the store was mercifully cool and quiet, the sounds of the town muffled by the old doors heavy enough to repel invaders and a massive window that would invite them in. To the right of the door, the counter ran parallel to the window, which seemed like wasted space to me, but my boss, Frank, insisted that we had the whole window on the other side of the door for displays. Secretly, I think he liked sitting sandwiched between the counter and the window, perfect for his people-watching hobby. I flipped the sign on the door to Open; it was hand-lettered and vintage like everything else. The store itself was an antique, with original wood everywhere, including the tall shelves that stretched from the front of the store all the way to the little office by the back door. Even the two wooden stools Frank and I occupied up front were reclaimed from somewhere. The only new things in there were the books themselves and the air conditioner Frank had replaced last summer. Frank's Books was a town staple, a place everyone passed through at some point, whether they liked books or not. It was my job but it was also one of my favorite places to be.

Backpack safely stashed in my little cubby underneath the front counter, I found the list Frank had left me in his precise handwriting. *Sweep, price, shelve.* Definitely not rocket science, but one of the reasons I liked this job. I wasn't the kind of person to meditate in a yoga class. That was more Stella's thing. I always felt like someone was cheating and opening their eyes, watching me and judging. But even I knew—and Key agreed—that meditation, stillness, was exactly what I needed. Some part of me was always running, and I didn't really know how to stop. Even watching a movie with Key, my mind would be going like a hamster wheel, my body thrumming until he looked over. "Ave, seriously." So *sweep, price, shelve*—a mind full of nothing and my body in gentle motion—yeah, I was fine with that. I flicked the switch on the wall and the five milk-glass lights came to life, casting a warm glow over everything. Spending time here was good for me: repetitive mindlessness or grabbing a book off the shelf and getting lost in a different way.

But I never quite got to my zen. All day I felt sluggish, heavy, like I was wrapped in a wet blanket. Sleep deprivation is what it was, making pretty much any place look like a good spot for a nap. The bench at the back of the bookstore, behind the back two bookcases, curled up on the floor. The front counter.

A peek at the old train station clock on the wall gave me the bad news that I still had thirty minutes until Frank arrived to take over, and thirty minutes felt like more than I could manage standing up. I climbed onto my stool, staring out at the store with dry, gritty eyes. My sweeping had sent dust motes drifting through a shaft of light coming in the window. I picked one and followed its path— falling, rising, spiraling down and then back up. Side to side. Back and forth. My eyelids grew heavy, wanting to close.

And why not? I could just put my head down. Five minutes, tops. I couldn't see the office from here, but I would hear Frank come in the back door before he saw me. I slipped off the high stool behind the counter and peered down the length of all five rows of bookcases. No customers. Unless somebody was standing right at the end of a row, hidden from this angle. The only way to know for sure if the store was empty was to actually walk all five rows. Which sounded exhausting.

The coast was clear enough. What was Frank going to do—fire me? I hopped back up on my perch and settled my head onto my folded arms on the counter, surprisingly comfortable. It wasn't even a nap. I'd pop right back up if someone came in.

I sighed deeply into the cozy darkness of my elbow. My eyes closed, and I let the heaviness in my body tug at me, let it pull me down, under the layer of clear consciousness and into that in-between—the glorious level of awareness that beautiful, sweet sleep is almost in your grasp.

My breathing deepened, and sunlight dappled the backs of my eyelids. The comforting scent of paper and wood gave way to a slight aroma of earth and green. I sank a little deeper. The muscles in my shoulders went slack. I breathed in the scent of pine, unaware of the barest smile that crossed my face.

The clock ticked quietly, but I no longer heard it. My right foot slipped off the rung of the stool and hung free. Late afternoon sun streamed in the window, but I didn't see. The scent of pines stirred and disappeared, chased by something else. Far off in the distance, I heard something. A bell? Not enough to pull me out of this delicious comfort, not enough to rouse me, because I'd gone far beyond resting my eyes.

Desperate for sleep, I let it envelop me, felt myself sink further. Felt its hand around my ankle, a grip that tightened and pulled, tightened and *yanked*.

The feet of the stool screeched on the floor as I jumped back and off. I hopped up on the counter and scanned the floor. Nothing but the overturned stool.

But I'd felt it. A hand.

Someone had grabbed my leg and pulled.

The *chirrrp!* of my watch politely informed me that I was approaching heart-attack territory. Unnecessary, since I could feel my heart pounding quite clearly. Feet back on the floor, I slowly slid my hand between the cash register and the wall, coming up with the latest in self-defense technology to ever grace Frank's

Books—a five iron with comfort grip. I'd lobbied for a baseball bat—wood, not aluminum—but Frank's late wife had been a golfer, not a ball player. So, there I stood with the five, gripping it so tight, my knuckles creaked.

Exquisitely awake now, I strained my ears but heard nothing. There was no one in the store with me. Except there was. I closed my eyes and listened again. There was someone in the store with me.

I had never really been a "run and get help" kind of person. I wanted to *know*. I liked to find things out for myself. So I didn't pick up the phone in the drawer, and I didn't bolt out the front door. I adjusted my grip, raised the five iron to head height, and slowly made my way out from behind the counter.

Down the first aisle—Coffee Table / Art / Atlases. I hated this aisle. Books were amazing, but why people bought giant books of art or scenery, I couldn't understand. Go and see it for yourself. The atlases—don't even get me started. Trees were dying to produce these things.

Halfway down the aisle, there was a creak. Not loud, hardly audible unless you were straining to hear. Which I was. It was the sound of someone shifting their weight on the old hardwood. The store was in good shape, but there were some spots in the floor that had voices.

Chirrrp!

Bottom lip between my teeth, I crept to the end of the aisle, wiggling the five iron behind my shoulder. The door to the back office clicked shut, and I came within inches of driving the five iron into the side of my boss's head.

Frank fell back against a table of featured local authors, and my follow-through hit the floor with a thud.

"What the hell!" Frank bellowed and swatted my hands away. "What the hell?"

"Sorry!" I clapped my hand over my eyes. Holy shit. "So sorry. Oh my God. Are you okay?"

Frank tore the five iron from my hand and held it up in front of me, brandishing the evidence.

"My God, Avery! You almost killed me!" Frank righted himself and tugged his cardigan into place. He huffed out an exasperated breath and ran his hand through his thick silver hair, staring at me the whole time.

"I'm so sorry. I thought there was someone back here."

Frank goggled at me and swept his arms out, identifying himself as "someone."

"I'm so sorry," I said again from behind my hand. What else can you say when you've almost taken someone's head off? "I was scared."

Magic words.

Frank left the club leaning against the local authors' books, opened the office door, and ushered me inside and into one of the two chairs facing the solid wooden desk that took up most of the office. Specks of dust drifted in the light filtering in the small window beside the desk.

"You thought you heard someone?" he prompted gently, eyes soft with concern.

"There weren't any customers, but then I heard . . . I'm not sure. I thought there was someone who shouldn't be here."

I left out the part about falling asleep and feeling someone pull on my leg. Because okay, maybe that part didn't really happen.

Frank was now all sympathy, his near-decapitation ancient history. He patted my arm and swiveled around in his old banker's desk chair to turn on his prized espresso maker that sat gleaming on a table behind his desk.

"You know, I have thought about you being on your own in here," he said over his shoulder. "That's why I never leave you to work on your own at night."

It was true. In the evenings, Frank always joined me. He was of a generation whose worldview included the fact that nothing bad could happen in the daylight and ladies needed to be escorted after sundown. Frank liked to think things through and be prepared for any eventuality. Hence the espresso maker. You never knew when there would be an emergency that required caffeinated comfort.

"It was just me you heard." The machine hissed, and Frank stood to organize the cups. "I came in earlier to look through these boxes."

"Yeah." I nodded. New arrivals, looked like. Frank loved the old books, but new releases were what paid the bills these days.

I accepted the tiny cup and biscotti he offered, only the slightest tremor in my hands. Frank settled into the chair beside me.

"It's an old building," he pointed out. "The pipes, the furnace, these floors—there are all kinds of sources for scary noises."

"I'm sorry."

Frank waved away my latest apology with his biscotti. "Enough."

The caffeine flooded through my body in a very pleasant way, washing away my fear and lingering uneasiness. It was lack of sleep is all it was. That stupid dream had kept me up at night, and now my system was all out of whack. I'd go for a hard run after work, tire myself out, and get a good night's sleep. Everything would be fine.

It would be fine.

"At least you know how to handle the five iron," Frank mused, downing his coffee.

"Yeah." I licked my lips and handed over my cup. "Still rather have a Slugger."

FIVE

I COULD STILL SMELL IT.

That's what bothered me the most.

There was a brackish, coppery smell that enveloped me at all times, almost overpowering. At first, I'd thought it was on my clothes. So all my running clothes had gone into the laundry. Everything. Even the winter gear I hadn't worn in months. Then everything hanging in my closet. On the floor of my closet. The pile on the floor at the foot of my bed. My mother was going to have a cardiac event when she saw the water bill.

I knew I wasn't the source of the odor because I'd asked Key. He'd leaned right in and taken a sniff, long and loud enough to get us plenty of looks at the coffee shop. He swore he smelled nothing.

"Just your usual shampoo and belligerence," he'd teased. I don't know if he thought I was making it up, but clearly no one was aware of it but me.

But it was there. It would sneak up on me, drift in like an invisible cloud—faint at first, then intensify until it was a stifling stench I could taste. I'd smelled it in the bookstore the other day, when I'd almost killed Frank. And the dream—I woke choking on the smell. Last night, I'd woken up thrashing *in the water*. In my bed, but in that depthless pond. I could feel it, and I could still smell it when I got up on Friday. And this time, it wasn't going away. It wasn't fading.

I was glad I'd told Key. Most situations could be improved that way, and he kept all sorts of information crammed in his juicy chess club brain. Most of the time it was useless, like the superiority of the metric system, or that you need to braid the dead leaves of daffodils at the end of the season, not cut them, or how often they clean out the Iced Capp machine at Tim Hortons. Okay, the last one was actually useful and had changed my beverage choices forever.

But I hadn't told him everything. I'd been pondering that fact the whole walk to school, the whole time waiting in line to return my books, and now, in the near-empty hallway. I bit my lip and pushed through the big double doors of the cafeteria to wait for Key to finish his exam. The room was subdued, since most people were finished and free for the year and just a few of us were tying up loose ends. I headed toward our table, passing by the bulletin board that was now naked except for exam schedules and one bright yellow poster. From a distance, it looked like the lost dog posters on the street—fresh off a printer that was almost out of ink, a name and a phone number and the heart-wrenchingly desperate "reward."

But this wasn't a dog.

Missing, not lost.

"Jackie." My cross-country teammate Sian came up and read over my shoulder. Tuesday afternoon, when I'd been at work, according to the text below a picture of Jackie posing, hips turned just so for the camera, working the angles. "You hear about her?"

I'd heard *from* her—what must have been hours before she disappeared. A shiver ran down my back.

Sian munched her way through an apple. "One minute she was

out tanning in the backyard after work . . ." Sian shook her head. "Her sister's in my chem class."

People disappear forever in that place.

Sian seemed like she would say something more, but maybe she was as much at a loss as I was. She made her customary free throw shot with the apple core, patted me on the back in farewell, and shouldered the door open, passing through and letting it swish shut behind her.

I sat down in silence, hanging my empty backpack on my chair and staring at the tabletop. This kind of thing happened all the time, I supposed, all over the world; people leave and never come home. But I'd just talked to her. It was a little too close for comfort. Too close to the bone, Key would say.

Had Jackie met someone on the other side of the lilacs? Had she fallen asleep when she shouldn't have? I ran my hands over the table, trying to ground myself here, in this world rather than the one in my nightmares. The table might be crawling with germs, but it was real. It was solid. Jackie was missing, and something was following me. I didn't want there to be a connection, but I couldn't help thinking about it. The image of that pond popped into my head, unbidden.

"Killed it." Key slammed his backpack down triumphantly on the cafeteria table and folded his long legs to sit on a blue plastic chair.

"What?" I looked up, startled by the noise, but also by those words.

"Exam. Remember those?" He smiled and raised a skeptical eyebrow.

"Right, right." I nodded a little too quickly and saw him catch it. "So, you're done?" I couldn't remember. School, exams—it all seemed like stuff that belonged to someone else, parts of a life I'd left behind.

"Done. Just want to pack up some photo club stuff." He stretched until his back cracked, his shirt riding up to reveal a narrow strip of brown belly. "You have anything left to do?"

I looked away from the unintentional display of skin and put my phone down. "Just returned my books." Thank. God. There was no way I could pass any kind of test in any subject right then.

Key folded his arms on the table and leaned forward. "Are you good?"

What could I say?

"Because you seem . . . not good." Key's dark eyes bored into me. I could never hide from him for long.

"I'm fine." But it came out as a whisper.

Key didn't say a word, just carefully placed his hands on the table, tapped his long fingers twice, and was still. He was really going to stare me down, right here in the middle of the caf.

"It's just . . . you know, that thing," I said with a sigh. If there was anyone I could tell, it was him. "I feel like there's someone watching me." My voice so low, I could barely hear myself.

He waited.

"It's like there's someone there." I shrugged. "But there isn't. I know that."

"You had a scare—"

"What's up, lunch bitches?" Stella bounced up to the table and dumped her backpack like she owned the place. She plopped down beside me, instantly at home wherever she went. The little silver ring she wore on her thumb glinted as she ran her hands over her dark golden curls in a constant unconscious attempt to control them. She was impossibly beautiful and had no idea. Stella was basically Opposite Me. "Happy last Friday of the school year!" Framed with jazz hands.

"Hey, Starla," Key drawled and slumped back in his chair. "Hey, man." He raised his arm so one of his photography club friends could bump his hand in greeting as he passed our table.

I pressed my fingertips to my eyes. There was nobody I loved more than Key and Stella, two people who probably wouldn't have been as close as they were without me. Bickering was their friending language, and usually it was entertaining. But not today, not when I was stressed and sleep-deprived.

"Guys." I flattened my palms to the table. It was smooth and solid. It didn't feel like every atom was about to go spiraling in a million different directions. That was just me.

Stella unzipped her backpack and pulled out her traditional lunch of orange slices and cheese cubes. Traditional as in every day for as long as I'd known her.

Stella's backpack was pink and purple and covered with the kind of sequins you could draw on. It was meant for little girls, but Stella saw it, liked it, got it. The first day she showed up to school with it, there had been snickers and raised eyebrows. By the end of the month, the backpacks were in every other locker. Stella barely noticed. "What's up?" she asked.

"You don't even know what we're talking about," Key scoffed.

"Don't be so pissy. Once you say it, I will."

"Eat your oranges, Starla."

Sometimes I found this cute. But not today. I shouldered my bag and headed for the door without a word. Behind me, there were indistinct accusations being lobbed back and forth and the squeak of sneakers on the floor. And then they were both there, an arm around each of my shoulders, a temporary truce allowing them to steer me toward the quiet of the library, a place where they'd have to behave. Mr. Abbas, the librarian who'd been mistaken for a student more than once, nodded to us with an indulgent smile as we passed, then went back to scanning in books. We'd all found refuge in the library at one time or another, partly because of him. We wound toward the back, filing past the tables piled high with returned books.

My hands felt kind of tingly, so I flexed them and wiggled my fingers under the table.

"What's going on, Ave?" Stella asked gently, because as obnoxious as she could sometimes be, Stella was just as perceptive as Key. I took a breath. Should I even say? Had telling Key made it real?

Ever in tune, Key filled her in for me, saying the things he knew I didn't want to. "She got lost on a run. Thinks she maybe found the black water and now it's . . . haunting her."

"I didn't get lost!"

Key shrugged and leaned toward me, lowering his voice. "Personally, I think you've got the story, the legend, all tangled up with getting lost. You do have a fear of losing your way."

"Yeah," Stella offered. "I heard the black water is really a sinkhole. You're just walking along and then—oops!—gone forever. They made scary stories to keep kids away from it." She patted my arm like that was it, but they were both missing the point. Yeah, it was a real place. I'd been there. That made things worse, not better.

"That doesn't—it's not . . ." I sputtered.

"Ave, you're under a lot of stress." As if Key were delivering shocking news. "You're trying to get a scholarship for school, and you're worried—I know you are."

"Maybe all your worry came out when you saw this place, and now it's taken on this, this—" Stella looked to Key for help.

"Yeah, yeah. Like now it represents all that pressure, right?" They nodded at each other.

"Maybe you should go to the doctor. My brother takes beta blockers before piano competitions, and they calm him right down. It's okay to need a little help." Stella patted my shoulder like I was a particularly nervous dog at the vet.

They didn't get it. How could they? Being under pressure didn't cause most people to hallucinate things stalking them. What was happening to me wasn't normal, and it was getting worse.

"Yeah, maybe." I nodded and pretended to accept what they were telling me. Because they couldn't understand, and I was too tired to try to explain anymore. They were trying to help, and they were giving me good advice. But they weren't haunted by the black water. I was. I knew this wasn't only stress, and I knew about the stories. But what if they weren't? Just stories. That's the thought that wouldn't stop rattling around in my head.

Stella gave me a two-armed hug that made something in my shoulder crack. "See? That's what we're here for. Don't you feel better?"

"Yeah. I do." I rubbed my shoulder more for something to do than from pain and slapped on a fake smile like the one I'd seen on my dad a million times, but I couldn't stop thinking about the poster. That wasn't just a story; that was real.

Stella dug in her bag for her orange slices, a clear violation of the No Food rule in the library. I rolled my eyes at that like I usually would, trying to be normal. I didn't want to talk about shadows in hedges or whatever had been in the store, but I wasn't sure Key was buying it. If anyone could read me, it was him.

"Moi, je mange une orange." Stella began narrating her snack, still in French mode from her exam. "Pas delicieuse, mais—"

"You're going to get us kicked out of here, Starla." As if Mr. Abbas would do that. Key kicked Stella under the table and grinned at me, faking it right back at me. He would let me put on a show for Stella, but he wasn't buying my "everything's fine" act. He knew.

"Did you hear about Jackie?" Stella talked around her orange, eyes wide. "I heard she ditched exams for the Indie Edge Festival."

"You believe that?" Key helped himself to one of Stella's cheese cubes.

"Je ne sais pas." Stella gave an elaborate shrug. "Jackie doesn't seem the type. But you never know. Some people are mysteries." Popping another orange slice into her mouth.

Key smiled at me and tapped his fingers on the table. "Yup."

I knew he meant me, and he wasn't wrong. But I had bigger problems. Someone had been in the lilacs, I was sure of it now, and someone had been in the store. I hadn't even mentioned the *thing* that had chased me back onto the trail.

I took a deep, slow breath.

"Do you really think Jackie just ditched?" Maybe I wasn't the only one who'd met something in the forest. "Like you said, it doesn't seem like her."

Stella shrugged, meticulously cleaning the white pith off her orange. "You never really know someone, I guess."

"Yeah." Under the table, I clasped my hands together tightly. "But what if something happened to her?"

"You mean like something dark and creepy in the forest?" Key knew where I was going with this.

"It's just a story," Stella soothed, offering me an orange slice. As if that would help.

"But what if it's not?" I pressed, my hands clenched under the table.

In a silence that went on a beat too long, I saw the look that passed between Stella and Key. They were worried about me, and so was I. But now I was worried about Jackie, too.

"You know what?" Stella swallowed the last of her orange and snapped the empty container shut. "We should look into it. The story."

"Stella . . ." Key sighed and let his head fall back like he'd just heard the worst idea ever.

I straightened up, because finally, we were taking action. "Look into it—how?"

Stella shoved her lunch containers into her backpack and zipped it up. "You know me, I'm the research queen." She turned a dazzling Stella-smile on Key and me. "We can look into the origin of the story. You'll feel better about it."

"Okay." Research. That sounded good. And Stella's confidence had a way of seeping into me. I turned to Key. "Okay?"

"Ave." Giving me his faux-serious look. "As if I could stop you."

"Let's meet up at Key's house tonight." Stella stood. "Jeremy's going to be practicing his competition pieces, so my house is out." She rolled her eyes.

"I don't know what you're complaining about." Key pushed his chair in. "The kid's pretty good."

"Yeah, it's fine." Stella linked her arm through mine as we headed to the door, waving to Mr. Abbas. "The first hundred times."

With both of them beside me, the panic lessened a tiny bit for the first time in days. I had disturbed something in the black water and it had come looking for me, I was sure of that. Maybe it had met Jackie first. But deep down, I knew I was the one it wanted.

SIX

WE PARTED WAYS AT THE FRONT DOORS OF THE school—Key off to catalog the photography club supplies before closing shop for the year, and Stella buzzing off in her Mini to her babysitting job. Thank God I wasn't working tonight. I was so tired, I'd struggled to zip my backpack closed before realizing it already was. There were no more books to lug home from school, no homework to do. Which was good because it wasn't like I had the energy to do anything, not even get home on my own two feet, not in this heat, so I cut behind the school to the nearest bus stop.

There were three other people waiting at the bus stop. On the other side of the square, I could just make out the marquee announcing a one-night-only showing of the Evil Dead movies. No thanks. When you sat down in the seats, they sagged so close to the floor, your knees ended up almost level with your shoulders. The floors were sticky in a way that newly built surround sound cinemas tried but could not quite replicate.

Next door to the cinema was The Bean, a coffee and dessert place funded almost exclusively by tweens. Stella and I sometimes got a cup there. The coffee was good, but the young, noisy crowd made it strictly a to-go situation.

From the bus stop, my view of the bookstore was bisected by the ornate water fountain in the center of the square. A relic from the town's glorious past, it was shaped like a three-tiered flower, each tier wide and deep enough for an adult to bathe in, except it was dry as a bone, and had been my whole life. The base was a pretty good place to sit and drink coffee, though.

I leaned against the bus shelter, not wanting to sit and get too comfortable. Everyone else at the stop was on their phones, earbuds in, staring at screens. Tired as I was, I needed to keep busy, stay awake, and not think about the dreams, the water, the darkness that was taking up so much space in my head.

The heat of the day was starting to lift, and a breeze was picking up. It was a reflex to close my eyes and let the breeze brush over my skin and stir my hair. It was barely there, but nice. Letting the wind caress my face was one of my Top Ten Things I Love but Will Never Tell. It reminded me of when I was little, long after I was tucked in for the night and on the edge of sleep. One of my parents would tiptoe into my room, gently touch my cheek and brush my hair back before leaving like a thief. I wished I knew which of my parents it had been. I'd never asked, and now it was too late. That part of my family's life was over.

The bus rumbled down the street, spewing exhaust that couldn't be good for any living thing. I wrinkled my nose and tried not to breathe too deeply. I had long-distance, scholarship-winning lungs to protect.

Gross.

The other passengers-to-be started falling in to form a loose line, because that's how we did things in this town. No jostling or jockeying for position, just polite lining up and waiting. All resentment reined in to be released at a more appropriate moment, in a more appropriate situation, like snapping at a partner or tugging on the dog's leash somewhat harder than was absolutely necessary.

I took my place like a good transit soldier and stepped forward.

"Afternoon, folks." Chatty Driver. He was better than Surly Drivers One through Three, but I wasn't in the mood for any of them. I made sure my earbuds were in place, the universal Do Not Disturb sign.

Two people boarded, but the third was having trouble swiping his pass.

"I just loaded it."

"Try swiping slower."

Unhappy beep.

"Okay," Chatty Driver leaned over. "Try swiping faster."

Unhappy beep.

"I swear, I just put twenty dollars on the card this morning."

"The whole system is fundamentally lacking," the old man in the front seat offered. "That's what happens when the town gives the contract to the lowest bidder."

My patience was wearing thin, both for what was going on in front of me and behind. I turned to give a civil but pointed look to the guy looming just over my shoulder but found only the empty bus shelter.

I could've sworn there was someone crowding me.

"Okay. May I?" Chatty Driver was now taking matters into his own hands, swiping the card with all of his expertise.

Unhappy beep.

I still felt like I was being crowded. I looked behind and again found no one.

Someone was there. Someone was watching me.

I knew this feeling from a hundred track-and-field events. I'd never had to look for my parents in the stands—I could feel their eyes on me or not. My dad could never fool me, arriving right at the end but faking, like he'd been there for the whole thing. I knew he hadn't. I would've felt his eyes.

Chirrrp!

A scan of the block showed three pedestrians, two deep in conversation, and one walking, on his phone, about to get hit by a van.

Yet still I felt it.

Chirrrp!

I just wanted to get out of there. Away from whatever it was that I felt but could not see.

"Maybe . . ." Chatty Driver rubbed the card with his green tie and swiped it again.

Happy beep.

Scattered applause from within the bus. Finally, the line could move.

The presence pressed in behind me again. I didn't want to turn and see no one there, so I shuffled forward too far and caught the heel of the woman in front of me.

"Sorry, sorry," I muttered, but didn't back off. I wanted on this bus. I wanted out of here now.

Chirrrp!

It was my turn to mount the steps and swipe my card. I took a seat near the back doors and hugged my backpack on my lap.

The presence at my back was gone, so I twisted around in my seat to look. As the bus slowly pulled away, something fluttered behind the shelter. It was partially obscured by a poster promoting eye exams—*No Eye-scuses!*—but I saw it. He was there. The man who'd been crowding me in line was moving away. Through the dirty plexiglass of the shelter, I saw him. Tall, long hair, long coat, all of him hazy around the edges. An impression rather than a picture.

I tried to get a good look, to focus on him, and found that I couldn't. My eyes wanted to look *around* him but not *at* him, my brain trying to tell me that there wasn't truly anything there to see. It could have been a trick of the light on the dirty plexiglass, or the reflection of the bus itself. It probably was. It was probably one or all of those things.

Except I knew it wasn't.

As the bus carried me toward home, I settled in my seat and hugged my backpack for comfort. It was all fine. I was safe. There was no reason for the skin on the back of my neck to be tingling. I tried to focus on the conversation Chatty Driver was having with the old man in the front seat.

"Rain, I hear," the driver said.

"No, I don't think so," the old man responded.

"I only know what the Weather Channel tells me."

"The Weather Channel would do well to look out the window. Those are cirrus clouds. They're not rain-bearers."

"Really?"

"Yup. My great-uncle was a lighthouse keeper on the Great Lakes. Taught me all about bad weather." He peered out the window and thumped his cane. "And I don't see it."

The sound of dripping water seemed about to prove the Weather

Channel right. I leaned my forehead against the coolness of the window. Four stops and I could get off.

"Well, you never know what might blow in," Chatty Driver said in defense of the maligned meteorologists.

The dripping was now trickling. A sharp, coppery smell wafted into the bus, slipping inside through the smallest gap and spreading.

Chirrrp!

I casually looked around for the source of the dripping sound. Hearing trickling water, but seeing no rain.

"Some people can smell it coming." The old man nodded. "Ozone in the air."

The smell was so stifling that I pressed my hand over my nose. Around me, the other passengers seemed unbothered by the noxious stink. At the first stop, the doors opened and closed, but the odor remained. I shifted in my seat, uneasy.

"Ozone," Chatty Driver confirmed. "A big hole in it. That's why we have to wear sunscreen, even in winter."

The trickling was louder now. I snuck a glance at the woman across from me, entranced by whatever was on her phone. The man opposite her stared ahead, lost in his thoughts, brown leather briefcase at his feet. The smell was invading me, I could feel it. It was wrapping itself around every strand of my hair, creeping into every fold of my clothes and settling in.

Chirrrp!

I bounced my knees a little on the hard plastic seat, trying to focus, and felt it. I took a quick glance down to confirm and then looked back up, fast.

Water.

Dark and brackish, covering the floor of the bus, inching its way up toward my feet.

I hugged my backpack closer and tried to make myself small.

"Sunscreen!" the old man scoffed. "Just a moneymaker. A cash cow."

I swallowed hard and felt the cold water rising over my feet. It wasn't real. It couldn't be.

"Well, you've got to be careful about skin cancer."

The old man shrugged. "We're all going to die."

The woman next to me tapped her screen and crossed her legs, oblivious to the water dripping from her dangling foot. The man's briefcase floated unsteadily, tipping back and forth like a buoy at sea. I closed my eyes and tried to breathe through my mouth around the choking stink.

Two more stops. With every turn, the water slapped against the sides of the bus.

Chirrrp!

I clapped my hand over my watch, knees bouncing constantly. My socks were wet, clinging to my skin. I could feel it. What was happening?

Even though I didn't want to, I looked down.

Water. Cold and black. It ringed both ankles, obscuring my feet.

"True," Chatty Driver conceded. "No reason to hurry it along, though."

"This is me." The old man rose and sloshed through the water to the front door, sending ripples off to the side, like the wake of a boat. "Nice talking to you." He nodded to the driver.

In the aisle, the staring man's briefcase bobbed on the surface of the water. No one else saw the water. No one else felt it climbing higher. Which meant it wasn't real. But I felt it.

I *felt* it.

I bit my lip and tried very hard not to cry. The bus engine hummed under the sound of the water lapping against the seats. It was well over my ankles now, dark and opaque.

The briefcase floating in the aisle shuddered, sending ripples out. It bobbed once more, then was yanked under the surface. I leaned forward, eyes locked on the spot it had been, desperate for someone else to acknowledge this, waiting for the man to notice his briefcase was gone.

Gone where?

Like a spider steadily climbing a wall, the water was still rising around my legs. I felt it, but it wasn't the only thing I was worried about. My attention was riveted on the irregular ripples in the aisle. The water wasn't just moving with the motion of the bus; something was moving in the water. Something long and sinuous, undulating unseen, just under the surface. I stared, breathing like I'd just run a sprint.

In the aisle, the briefcase suddenly resurfaced, and I jerked back. It burst up like it was trying to escape before falling onto its side to float downstream, toward the back of the bus. I watched it drift by, then looked around at the other passengers, on their phones or staring out the window. No one else was aware of the water approaching their knees or the quiet sound of the water sloshing from one side to the other as the bus turned a corner.

My feet were freezing in the icy water, but it didn't matter because it wasn't real. None of this was happening. I shook my head quickly, agreeing with myself. There was no water. I would talk to Key, and it would be fine. There was nothing swimming up the aisle, leaving a wake like a boat. There was nothing—

Something brushed against my leg.

I gasped and pulled my feet up, resting my heels on the edge of my seat. I wrapped both arms around my knees and scanned the water rising toward seat-level, chewing on my lip. Almost at my stop. I blinked my eyes rapidly to clear the tears gathering and pressed my lips together hard to stop the sounds that wanted to escape. I needed to get off this bus and away from whatever was happening.

But to do that, I'd have to put my feet down.

I'd have to let my feet disappear into the cold, murky water with whatever had grabbed the briefcase.

One block away. I had to do it. I reached up to ring the bell, gripped my backpack, and took a deep breath, the foul smell permeating me from the inside out. I let one foot slip down and under the surface. A heartbeat, then the other.

I stood and waded carefully to the door, the water strangely dense, pushing back against my legs with more strength than it should have had. I pushed aside a gym bag floating in front of me like it had teeth and reached up to ring the bell again.

Behind me, a splash—like a fish jumping. Or the flick of a large fin. I clutched my backpack and rang the bell once more, standing as close to the door as I could get.

Chirrrp!

"Let me off." Pressing my palm against the door.

There was movement behind me that I heard but did not want to see. If I stepped down into the stairwell, the water would be over my hips. I sighted the sidewalk through the window like a lifeline. The bus approached the stop excruciatingly slowly. I swallowed a sob, my pulse jumping in my throat.

"Please let me off." My voice cracked. I didn't even know who I was speaking to.

"Okay, okay," Chatty Driver muttered.

A wave built up behind me and broke against the back of my legs. The door hissed opened, and I spilled out.

Alone.

No water.

I watched the door close and the bus pull away from the curb.

I stood frozen, breathing hitching and pulse still racing. After a moment, I came back to myself and swiped at the stray tear I hadn't been able to contain. No one else had seen the water.

It was getting worse.

I went down the sidewalk, leaving wet footprints in my wake, desperate to get home but half-afraid of what would be waiting there.

Left, right.

Left, right.

It's not real, so it can't hurt me.

By the time I got to my house, I'd almost calmed myself down. I left the sidewalk to cross the lawn and took the porch steps in one leap. Inside the house, I shut the door behind me, peered out the window, and saw nothing but the street and neighborhood as it should be. I sagged back against the door with relief. I was going to have to tell someone what was happening, maybe even my mom. But what to say? Where to start? Before I even had my shoes off, she was on me. "Are you packed?"

Crap. All my plans, instantly derailed.

Father Friday. My dad would allegedly be there any minute to pick me up. A pang of guilt? Hunger?

No, definitely guilt. I'd forgotten.

Just like he often did.

"Um—I made plans," I started, but my mom's arms crossed quickly. He could forget. I couldn't.

Frustration built inside of me as I sent a quick text to Key and Stella—**Father Friday. Forgot. Meet later?**

I saw Key's text bubbles typing for a bit. Stop. Then start again.

Yeah. Call if there's anything weird.

I pulled my dedicated go bag for Father Friday from the floor of my closet. Fully packed and ready to go, but even before I unzipped it, I could smell that it was full of dirty laundry from the last time I'd needed it. Which had been a while.

Crap.

"Avery! Are you ready? He'll be here soon."

Maybe. Maybe not. Maybe I wouldn't be the only one with a faulty memory today. It would almost be a relief when the unraveling tether between me and my dad finally snapped. I dumped the contents of the bag on the floor and called over my shoulder.

"Yes! Relax!"

A few T-shirts from my closet. Jeans, shorts, pj's. Twice as much underwear as I really needed. Phone, charger, a book, running clothes, and shoes. In it all went at lightning speed.

Mom appeared in the doorway, leaning on one hip and arms crossed against her chest.

"Don't tell me to relax. You know I hate that."

By then I was casually reclined on my bed, squinting at my phone.

"Sorry, but like I said"—I gestured to the zipped bag next to me—"I'm totally ready."

Mom scanned my messy room, looking like she wanted to say something more, but I suspected my mother had been born with that look on her face. Thinly veiled impatience.

Her face softened, and I noticed dark circles under her eyes. She clasped her hands in front of her, which meant she was about to say something uncomfortable for one or both of us. "Are you okay?"

I wanted to tell her—I came so close. But the way she'd reacted when I first mentioned the pond stopped the words in my mouth. Mom had two basic reactions to anything I said. Suck it up, or total lockdown. I was already trying to do the first, and I couldn't afford the second. Not after the bus—I didn't want to be trapped anywhere. And if she was worried enough to ask me if I was okay, I didn't want to add to that burden by actually not being okay.

A shrug was all I could offer, not an answer but not a lie.

Mom shook her head, unsurprised. "Why don't you wait out front? It's nice outside."

Because I'm afraid to leave the house. Because the last time I was outside I saw a man who wasn't there. Because I'm a little concerned that I'm losing my mind but also terrified that maybe I'm not.

What I actually said, of course, was "okay." Mainly because it was better when my parents didn't actually see each other, when they didn't have to perform for me, because neither one of them was really good at it.

Hello, how are you? Nice weather we're having.

Like they were strangers; like they hadn't *made* me. It was excruciating for them and their audience of one, so much so that I was willing to sit outside and watch the sky go pink.

"See you tomorrow night." Mom kissed my forehead, and I gave a heartfelt air-kiss in return. Tomorrow night. Maybe. If he showed up. She turned in the doorway, and my opportunity to tell her anything was gone.

My dad was my dad, and I loved him, of course. But since no parent was perfect, it was complicated, and for us, our relationship was mostly a memory. Was it even possible to both like and love someone all the time? Like, *all* the time?

I sat on the bottom porch step, bag at my feet and checked my watch. Officially late. I hated that I did this, kept score on everything he did. I hated that it gave me a strange pleasure to tally up his every little failing. I *loved* him. But sometimes I hated him, too.

The leaves of the red maple whispered overhead, reminding me of the sound the lapping water had made on the bus. I took a quick glance around, but didn't see anything alarming in the vicinity. More importantly, I didn't feel anything. I pulled out my phone.

Hey.

It took all of three seconds for Key to reply.

What's up?

I stared at the screen and bit my bottom lip. How did I answer that?

Saw smthg on the bus. Kinda freaked.

Public transpo. Disgusting.

Ever since he'd gotten his license, Key had developed strong opinions about buses.

No. The thing.

What could I say? How could I explain? I didn't have to—I could just leave it. Make a joke and leave it alone.

A man.

I typed it quickly and hit send before I could change my mind. Telling anyone about the water—even Key—was out of the question. It had been too intense, too real. If I didn't say it, I could still believe it hadn't really happened.

I waited.

Waited some more, staring at the screen.

When the phone rang, I jerked back so hard, I almost dropped it. "Yeah?"

Key's tone was brisk and serious. "Explain. What do you mean?"

"I don't know," I said quietly. "There was no one there, so I didn't see him."

"But you did."

"Yeah."

I knew he was running his hand over his face, could see it in my mind. It didn't happen often. It meant he was truly worried.

"What man? Like, someone you know?" His voice was softer now, probing for information from someone he knew hated to give anything up.

"No," I hesitated, because this was just going to make me sound even more unstable than I already did. "He wasn't, fully *there*. You know?"

"No." Immediate response. He was done trying to soothe me. He wanted to know, to understand, so he could step in and fix it. I called him that sometimes—Mr. Fixit. It was just Key's nature. But some things couldn't be fixed.

I drew breath into my lungs as deep as I could and then let it escape through my mouth. I needed to explain at least some of this. He needed to get it. I didn't think he could fix it for me this time, but at least he could be there with me. I wouldn't be alone.

"It was like the impression of a man. Like a drawing that's just been sketched out but not filled in. He wasn't solid. He was . . . filmy. Unfinished."

Absolute silence at the other end.

"Key?"

A deep sigh.

"Ave, listen to me." His voice was low and rich, music that I felt in my bones.

"Okay." Tiny and soft, because I was afraid of what he was going to say.

"This can't wait. We need to figure this out. Now."

"I—"

"This is not normal, Ave." More than a hint of frustration that quickly bled out into concern. "There might actually be something . . . you know."

"Wrong with me."

"I don't mean—"

"I know." Silence on both ends. He was this worried and didn't even know how bad it really was. I hadn't even mentioned the thing swimming on the bus. "Okay."

"Come over when you can. After dinner?" he said. "Promise."

"Pinkie swear." Holding up a hand he couldn't see.

"You can't pinkie swear over the phone, cheater."

I hung up with Key and my phone immediately dinged.

Something's come up. So sorry. Make it up to you next time?

Staring at the screen, biting hard on my lip, I couldn't even be angry. I wished Dad had given me more notice—I was sitting on the freaking porch with my bag at my feet—but the only thing I felt was a whisper of relief, my shoulders sagging, knowing neither of us would have to suffer through a weekend of awkward silence broken by the occasional stilted conversation.

Maybe it was just as painful for him to be together as it was for me. It might be for the best—we could both stop trying to keep this dying thing between us alive. Maybe once it was gone, it wouldn't hurt anymore. I was glad, really. It was better this way.

But my mom was going to be pissed.

I gave a long, drawn-out sigh, my face tilted skyward, which was pretty much my usual response to parental stuff these days, before I got to my feet, shouldered my bag, and stood with my hand on the doorknob for a moment, preparing.

As soon as I stepped inside, Mom's head popped around the kitchen door. "Forget something?" she asked, but there was tension in her voice.

"Nope." Three strides down the hall and I launched my bag into my room from the doorway.

"Want to make banana bread?" She didn't even have to ask, and it was better if we didn't get into it, enraged on my behalf as I knew she was. Not making me say the hard stuff, that's how people showed they loved me.

I stepped into the kitchen and shook my head. "It's fine. Stella's going to be at Key's."

Mom pulled the skin back on the first brown-spotted banana over a bowl, breathing deep and slow, eyes on what her fingers were doing although she was probably imagining herself disemboweling my dad. "Did he even give a reason?" She didn't look up. Anyone watching would think that she didn't care, that neither of us did, but they'd be wrong. This was just how we were built, Mom and me, maybe out of necessity, maybe just because.

"It's fine." All I had to say on the matter, now or ever.

At the door, I slipped my shoes back on, trying to be grateful for the freedom I'd suddenly been granted.

"It's not," I heard my mom mutter as I stepped back out onto the porch and bounded down the steps.

Maybe not. But it had freed me to go to Key's and try to work out at least one of the problems in my life, so whatever hurt my dad had caused me, I'd pack it away and deal with it later. I was a pro at that.

My neighborhood was the kind of place where everyone had their own tiny but carefully tended patch of green. The houses all looked alike but not identical, and the trees were big enough to cast shade but not big enough to climb. It was an average middle-class kind of place; friendly enough, but Mom and I were the only ones on the block who weren't white, and I couldn't remember a time I hadn't been aware of that. Six more blocks would put me on Key's street, which was pretty much the same as mine except the Rogerses were one of four Black families in the neighborhood. The fact that I knew there were exactly four meant something, but Crook's Falls wasn't the kind of place that had those conversations out loud.

Movement in my peripheral vision made me turn, and I looked down to find a small white dog snuffling my shoe.

"Hi, buddy." I loved dogs, but both my mom and Buttons would hit the roof if I got one.

"Come on, Wilkie." The woman at the other end of the red leash tugged gently, smiling at me as if attention from a dog was something to apologize for. "Let's go." Key's neighbor—Cora?—took a step, but Wilkie seemed fascinated by me, not only not moving, but plonking his furry little butt down on the sidewalk and staring up at me. Wilkie had found a mystery, and that mystery was me. "Westies are stubborn." Cora—no, Cara—tugged on the leash and sighed.

"But so cute." I smiled and reached down, extending my hand, shocked when Wilkie sprang to his feet and backed away, barking furiously.

"Oh! Wilkie, no! Sorry." Cara's apology was no longer just implied, for her little dog suddenly seemed intent on shredding me with his tiny teeth. "Let's go." She tugged the leash a little harder, and Wilkie now wanted nothing to do with me. They continued along, Cara strolling, Wilkie trotting. I glanced back once more to make sure there was no tiny fluff of terror rushing up behind, to see Wilkie's head turn over his shoulder, apparently with the same thought.

Weird, but I was getting a lot of that lately.

SEVEN

I HAD SEVERAL BLOCKS TO GET OVER BEING rejected by a dog, which, honestly, stung more than my dad's text. Dogs were supposed to be the ultimate judges of character, and if that were true, I sucked. Dogs had always loved me. What had changed? I was still internally pouting about it when I turned up Key's driveway, a route I'd taken so many times, my body made the turns without me. Key's house looked a lot like mine from the outside, but once the red front door opened—

"Avery! Come in!" Key's dad beamed like he hadn't seen me just last week. Key's dad and mine were two different species—one hyper-involved and the other a ghost.

Key's house was a haven for me—all of the family warmth with none of the complications. My house was quiet and decorated in shades of gray, while Key's house was bright and lively, even when he was the only one home, like the energy of his family lingered. Everything was blues and greens, the scent of vanilla just discernible in the air. The walls were covered with wall hangings Key's mom made and tons of photos taken by Key—of family, the abandoned barn outside town, and some of the older buildings in town. I was always happy to walk through the door and slip off my shoes.

"What do you think, Avery?" Key's dad was the biggest man I

knew, in every way—well over six feet and the life of the party the second he walked in. Key was tall but not solid like his dad. They did share a certain quality that allowed them to move through life like the water was always calm, a serenity or maybe optimism that I could only dream of. His dad smoothed out his bright green golf shirt, turning this way and that in the hall mirror.

"I didn't know you golfed" was all I could think of to say in the face of all that green.

"So corporate. So cliché," Key said from the sofa, cueing up a movie.

"It is corporate." Key's dad worked in the brim of an obviously brand-new cap. "Golf is part of fitting in in that world and a price I'm willing to pay. I might even learn to love it! And a little respect, please?" He jabbed his finger in Key's direction, but there was no heat in this exchange, there never was. "This cliché bought you that photo paper last week." He tapped his chest. "Ridiculously expensive paper." He turned to inform me in case I didn't already know.

"Thanks, Dad," Key dutifully intoned, definitely not for the first time, and continued clicking through his queue.

"Don't forget the laundry. Don't leave that for your mother," Key's dad called over his shoulder. He set the cap on his head and bent to pick up a pair of startlingly shiny golf shoes. "Have fun, Avery." He straightened up. "But not too much." He pointed at both Key and me in turn. As if. Although sometimes I wondered if Key's parents' warmth with me was their tacit permission, their way of saying it would be fine with them if Key and I wanted to be something more than friends.

With his dad gone, Key and I sat in his living room, drapes closed for maximum viewing darkness, one of the Ant-Man movies playing as he worked his way through a box of cereal while we waited for Stella.

The crunching was deafening. Fortunately, Key had the dialogue in this movie pretty much memorized, and I didn't care. After what had happened on the trail, I was distracted but making an effort to be present.

"I'm not allowed to eat cereal on the sofa," I announced to no one in particular, patting the bright blue fabric.

"Correct." Key bobbed his head and popped another granola cluster. "*You* aren't."

I narrowed my eyes at him. "You—"

"You eat like a lumberjack." Key said, giving me the "sorry!" face.

"A lumberjack."

"Yeah."

"How does a lumberjack eat?" Because this was a new one.

"Like you. Like you eating cereal on the sofa and getting it everywhere."

More crunching.

I studied his profile, lit by the screen. A strong chin, nose with a hint of an arch to it, and plumper lips than mine could ever be. I could draw it from memory. If I knew how to draw. All I knew how to do was run, which was a gift with an expiration date. But people who could make things—like Key with his photos—that was lifelong. That was forever. He kept his eyes on the movie, but I knew he was really paying attention to me, waiting for my next move in the Granola Skirmish. Which was how this worked—Key gave me attention which I consumed like a black hole. What he got out of the deal—I'd never been sure.

"Okay." Key sighed, removing his hand once and for all from inside the cereal box. "That's enough."

"I haven't had any." I made a half-hearted grab at the box.

"Because you're not allowed." He turned a sweet smile on me as he meticulously rolled down the bag and closed the box flaps.

"You're very weird." Meaning *wonderful*. Meaning, *what would I ever do without you?*

"I'm preserving the survivors for maximum freshness."

"Yeah, for you," I pointed out. "You're the only one who eats that stuff."

"Riiight." He nodded. "You don't eat cereal. Or fries. Or ice cream. Or pilfered cinnamon rolls when their rightful owners step away for half a second."

He was never going to let that go. "You were in the bathroom for a long time." My best "c'est la vie" shrug. "What was I supposed to do?"

"Um, buy your own?"

I screwed up my face and waved away such an unlikely scenario. "I'm saving my money for school."

Key nodded, eyes back on the screen. "Those were the last words my fries heard, too."

I couldn't help the smile. It just happened when he was around. This was good. I had no idea what was going on in the movie, but the movie was just a backdrop. Me and Key, on the sofa arguing about granola—that was the star of the show. I knew it wouldn't last forever, that once the movie stopped and I'd gone home, the dark things skittering around in my head would return. But for a moment, it was more than okay.

He was right there beside me, close enough to reach out and touch. What if I did? He knew how I felt—he had to. I was the emotionally dense one, and even I knew he'd do pretty much anything for me. I knew how he felt.

Mostly.

But what if I was wrong? What if he pulled his hand away and it was all *Ave, listen* . . . What then? Was I willing to risk ruining what we had for the possibility of something more? Look at what had happened to my family the last time I asked a question. I'd never been a risk-taker.

I sat up, waiting for my stupid watch to announce my thundering pulse to the world. His hand was right there, long fingers idly rubbing the seam of the cushion. His hands were warm and strong and gentle. I knew this. His hand was right there.

Key slapped his knees and stood. "I'm going to make popcorn."

He tapped my head with the cereal box as he walked by, and I batted it away like he expected me to, when all I wanted was to pull him in. I sank back onto the sofa, my heart shrinking. Someone who wasn't a coward would have grabbed his hand as he passed. I'd had a chance and now it was gone. Would there be another?

I'm pretty good at lying to myself, so I just sat back and listened to the microwave beeping. We'd gone this long not talking about us; what was a little more?

A long series of complicated knocks at the door made me jump. Stella. Now it was time to shift from the best thing in my life to the worst—the black water. My heart sped up at the thought. I stood to get the door, clenching suddenly damp hands.

"Chill, Ave." Key came out of the kitchen, reading my mind.

I was trying. But I still had questions and no answers. That place was haunting me and not just in my sleep. There had to be some way to find out more, to learn what to do. I just needed to find it before this got any worse.

EIGHT

"HEY, KIDS!" WHEN I OPENED THE DOOR, STELLA bounced in like she hadn't seen us in years, toed off eternally spotless white sneakers, and curled up in her favorite spot, an impossibly cushy daffodil-green tub chair. "Oh my God, you have to see the painting Luci did this afternoon." She pulled her phone out of her back pocket and turned it toward us, displaying a shot of a dark haired, chubby-armed kindergartener proudly holding up an un-interpretable swirl of color, smiling so big her eyes had disappeared into her cheeks. "It's me and her. Isn't that cute?" Stella pressed her hand over her heart, doing her "aww!" face.

I nodded. "Very." I really liked my job at Frank's, but Stella genuinely loved that little kid.

"Sit, sit!" Stella waved at the sofa on the other side of the coffee table like we were at her house rather than Key's.

I sat down, and Key slotted in next to me, the vibe suddenly tense. I glanced at both of them but couldn't figure it out. Stella could be bouncy for any number of reasons, most likely that she'd spent the afternoon eating the endless snacks Luci's mom left them, mostly of the sugary and packaged variety. Key could be annoyed by her for any number of reasons. Sometimes he couldn't handle her and truthfully, sometimes Stella was a lot. But there was more.

Maybe it was just sleep deprivation making me paranoid, but I had the distinct impression that a conversation had taken place since we'd been in the library—one that I hadn't been a part of.

Stella was in hummingbird mode—definitely either hopped up on sugar or genuinely excited about something. "Big news." Stella stared into my eyes in a way that was a little intense. I looked to Key for help.

"Popcorn needs more butter," he murmured, rising.

"While Luci watched *Bluey*, I got to work," Stella continued, lowering her chin.

"Stell." I looked her in the eye to show her just how focused I was. "What?"

Stella shifted forward and took both of my hands in hers over the coffee table with its *National Geographic*s neatly fanned out.

"I've been digging a little, trying to find something that would help with your . . . dilemma." A covert glance around, as if Key's house was crawling with spics.

"Okay."

"Information is out there. About everything. You just have to know where to look." Stella's grip intensified, grinding my knuckles together.

"Stell, my hands."

"Sorry!" She released me with a grimace. "I'm a little wound up."

"No shit." I rubbed at the red marks on my fingers. "Continue."

"Okay." Stella leaned in so far and so fast, I anticipated a head-butt. "I looked—oh my God, that smells amazing!" Stella suddenly leaned dangerously far back to get a whiff of the popcorn Key placed in front of us.

"It's superhot," he cautioned, nudging the bowl into the middle of the coffee table. Almost, I thought, encouraging Stella. Almost like he wanted to interrupt. I shook my head when the bowl came my way. Key shrugged, abandoned the popcorn, folded his arms across his chest, and cleared his throat.

"Stell." It came out a little sharper than I'd meant it to. "You were saying?"

Stella nodded, swallowed, and treated us to jazz hands. "Microform."

I stared at Stella, sure there must be more coming.

There wasn't.

"Well, that's great." I'd had just about enough of being strung along by the two people I trusted most. "Thanks so much for this."

Key did the "move it along" hands.

"Right." Stella paused. "So you mentioned bad dreams about the black water, right?"

She was practically bouncing again. "Since I have some computer skills—"

"Coding camp," Key said to the table.

"It was a coding leadership *program*."

My hands clenched into fists on my knees. This was the caf all over again.

"Anyway"—Stella shot me a glance and continued quickly—"I went digging for information on the black water. Like I said, information is out there. It never disappears—not if you know where to look."

"And?" I prodded, my voice tight. Information was what I needed. Not dreams, not vague warnings from my family or small-town nonsense. I needed to know what was haunting me so I could stop it, end it, and get back to normal.

"Microform." Stella pressed all ten fingertips to the table like a final chord, smiling and waiting for applause. "The local newspapers are digitized now, but the old stuff isn't. Like the really old stuff. But!" She raised one finger. "You can search online for the *contents* of the old stuff. And then find it on microform. Which I did." She took another piece of popcorn, popped it in her mouth, and sat back proudly, her crossed arms mirroring Key's.

"What did you find?" I was finally interested. "The black water?"

"Kind of." Stella chewed, trying to keep her curls out of her mouth. "Not by name, but reports of disappearances. Like, a lot of them."

Was she saying the stories were true? I laced my fingers together to keep them still. Every time Mom or Lily had warned me about leaving the trail, there really *was* something out there, more than steep ravines? My mind raced, flipping through every version of the story I'd heard about the forest like cards in a deck. Which ones were based on fact—one? A few? All?

I licked my lips, my mouth gone suddenly dry. I knew Stella had skills and I knew both she and Key wanted to help me, but I guess I wasn't so sure now that having things confirmed was what I wanted. Key proffered his water bottle, but I brushed it away and shifted to the edge of the sofa. "So what happened? To the people who went missing?"

Stella shrugged. "Every time, they chalked it up to kids running away or getting abducted—like who gets abducted in Crook's Falls? Running away, though, I can see that. . . ."

I could see her attention drifting. "Stell."

"Right. I mean, just way too many people have gone missing to not be suspicious. Except no one was." She licked her buttery fingers, pulled out her phone, and found her notes. Stella never did anything halfway. "They go in clumps. There would be nothing for years, and then all of a sudden people just went missing."

"Like Jackie." Key was leaning forward over the table with me now, meaning this must be new information to him, too. I turned to him, but his dark eyes were steady, giving away nothing. "How could that many people go missing without it being national news?"

The thing was, it wasn't news, not to us. Now that I thought about it, there had always been someone going off and just . . . not coming back, but it was like a fuzzy blip. There was always some kind of explanation for it, and we all just accepted it, a normal part of life in Crook's Falls. But maybe there was nothing normal about this town.

"There was a big one about forty years ago." Stella squinted at the ceiling, doing the math. "But twenty years before *that*, there was a huge one. Just like the story—people went into the forest and set off these waves of disappearances. But for each one, there was some worn-out explanation and that was the end of it. Ran away, bad marriage, running from debt." She ticked them off on her fingers. "That is très weird, no?" Eyes wide, Stella hugged herself and leaned closer. We must look like we were plotting, heads inches apart over the coffee table.

Very weird. Maybe some of those things were true, but what if most of them weren't? What if the town was unable or unwilling to see the truth? The black water could take people and no one would blink. It could just keep happening, over and over, forever.

A shiver slithered down my spine like the thing I'd seen on the bus.

"Almost a whole family just went—poof!" Stella snapped her fingers. "The Millers. And I looked in the phone book—the library has phone books still!—and, voilà!" She turned her phone to Key and me.

F. Miller, 1300 Miller Road

Next to me, Key exhaled slowly.

"Road trip!" Stella loud-whispered, clapping her hands delicately.

NINE

IN THE FRONT SEAT OF KEY'S CAR THE NEXT day, I was about to vibrate out of my skin. In biology class, I'd once seen a video of a tarantula molting—that's what it did—vibrated right out of its skin, becoming a whole new, fresh spider. It seemed like a great idea at the moment. Shed your old life and become someone else. Just leave it all and start over.

I bit my lip and turned my face to the window, preferring to squint into the late-morning sun than let Key notice my anxiety. The houses we passed got bigger, then smaller, then bigger but older, then no houses at all, just green fields. I vaguely remembered coming out this way to pick apples in the fall, or maybe it was another little sideroad that looked like this. Crook's Falls was a small town, but there were still unknown places—as I was finding out.

I hadn't mentioned the dream I'd had last night, after Stella had filled us in on her research.

Safe in the pines, where I knew I should stay.

But it wouldn't let me.

The sun was high in the sky, but everything was drained of color. Everything was wrong.

In the meadow—

Key.

My feet took the first step forward, the first of many I wouldn't be able to stop.

A camera dangled from his left hand.

I couldn't stop.

I tried and failed.

It always ended the same.

I pressed my fingers against my eyes, willing the image away. Add another secret to my pile, because there was no way I was telling either Key or Stella about the new dream. I'd burdened them enough.

In the back seat, Stella cracked her gum and hummed some kids'-show earworm she'd gotten from Luci, each note grating on my already taut nerves.

"Okay." Key peered through the windshield of his dad's very sensible sedan. "This is Miller Road."

"Are you sure?" There was nothing but open field surround by trees in the distance. On the left, there was just dirt and golden bits of stubble. But to the right and ahead of us, the fields were seas of long grass, reminding me of something else. I clenched my jaw and looked away. Beyond the grass, I saw nothing but trees—although not like the forest trails; even from here I could see there was nothing but pure brush. No strollers getting through those woods.

But there was someone in the trees. As we passed, I could see a dark shape moving in the same direction, something large and dark headed to where we were going. I suddenly wanted to go faster, to make sure we got there first.

"Key?"

"Did you not just hear Siri?" He wasn't looking at me and was getting annoyed.

"Okay, but this guy can't live in the middle of a field," I muttered. If this turned out to be nothing, I'd be back to square one. Stella would be disappointed, Key would be upset, but I was the one with the dreams. I was the one who had to live with this.

"House!" Stella's arm snaked in beside my head and jabbed at the window.

"But is it the house we're looking for?" Key headed for it anyway.

"We can ask." I shrugged. "If it's not them, maybe they know."

The mailbox standing crooked at the end of the long narrow driveway we turned into bore no name and no number. Key drove agonizingly slowly, until a slight rise in the driveway revealed a small blue house sitting like it had been dropped from the sky between a single oak tree and a decrepit garage that had been painted white a long time ago.

The car lurched into a pothole, making us all hiss in sympathy.

"Oh my God," Key muttered. "My dad . . ."

As the car crept closer, I could see an old man sitting on the little porch, rocking himself on a swing, white hair lifting in the breeze like a fluffy halo. Key slowed, stopped, and turned the car off. Nobody moved.

"Well." Key jerked his chin toward the house but made no move.

The man on the porch gripped the railing in front of him and pulled himself to his feet. It was impossible to say how old he was, but old enough that if Key saw him shuffling across the street, he would offer his arm. The man stood on his porch and looked at me, setting off a flutter in my chest, like something had woken up.

"So, do we get out . . . ?" Stella undid her seat belt.

The man on the porch waved to us from the top step. Not "hello" but "come in."

"I think that's a yes." Key slipped his phone into his pocket. "But let's not freak this man out, right?" He swiveled around to look at Stella. "Starla."

Stella clutched imaginary pearls, offended. "I'm not the one— Hey, Ave! Wait!"

I was up and out of the car, halfway to the porch before they caught up to me. Whether he was Stella's F. Miller or not, he was who I was looking for. This man could help me. This man knew. I could feel it.

At the bottom of the porch steps, I stopped and looked up.

"Shé:kon. I'm Foster." He turned and opened the door.

An Elder. If I'd known, I would have brought something—a gift. As nervous as I'd been to talk to a stranger about the things that were happening to me, this latest development left me momentarily speechless, because even though Stella and Key knew me better than anyone, the prospect of exposing my cultural ignorance in front of them made my blood run cold. And I would have to. Even I, clueless Kanyen'kehá:ka that I was, knew that you don't just ask a traditional Elder questions and expect straight answers. Even before her mind started to crumble, Ihstá Lily had told me stories—lots of them—in response to questions. That was the way: ask a question and get a story with your answer embedded; it was up to you to figure it out. Sometimes I had understood the point; sometimes I hadn't. I hoped Foster wouldn't make me work for whatever he had to share because whatever I'd found in the forest was haunting me, and apparently the town I lived in was not quite normal. I needed help.

"Shé:kon, Uncle," I murmured. "I'm Avery."

"You a Green?" Foster squinted at me.

Kind of. My mom and Ihstá Lily were Greens, but my dad's last name was Ray, and his family had gotten here by crossing an ocean a long time ago. I'd always thought of myself as something caught in the middle. I shrugged, uncomfortable. "My mom is."

"Hmm." Foster turned to Stella and Key, who were scurrying to the porch, and waved me toward the door. I hesitated for an instant, and then stepped into a museum, or maybe back in time.

Foster's house had been cute at one point, maybe forty years ago. It had the wood-paneled walls that had been all the rage, delicate floral wallpaper now faded to the barest blush of pink. On every surface, on every available inch of the wall, were framed family photos, some no more than little snapshots like the ones Key made with his vintage cameras—adults gathered around a cake ablaze with candles, a child wrapped in a beach towel grinning up at the camera. Some were black and white, some were in color. I knew that if any of them were moved, a frame lifted from the wall would reveal the original vibrancy of the wallpaper; a frame nudged out of place on the side table would leave a footprint in the fine film of dust. It was the kind of clutter that came from being stuck. Foster's house wasn't a museum. It was a shrine—but to who or what?

And why?

"Sit." Foster emerged from the kitchen, motioned to the little sofa covered in faded yellow roses, and set out teacups on the low table in front of us. "Tea?" He set the teapot down. "You should pour. My hands . . ." He rubbed his wrist with withered fingers and sank down into the only other chair in the room, a blue easy chair, the armrests worn shiny smooth.

"Nyá:wen, Uncle." I wasn't used to addressing people like this, not even Ihstá Lily, but I knew it was right.

We all sat down and the tiny sofa responded with an ominous creak. Everyone in the room froze, but the sofa held, so we stayed put. Under his cardigan, Foster's faded red T-shirt featured a man with a single feather on his head, which seemed out of place. Why would a tiny old man who offered us tea be wearing a Mohawk Warrior Society shirt? I tried to picture him with his fluffy baby-bird hair, manning a blockade. And couldn't. But maybe this Elder wasn't what he appeared to be. Foster seemed to feel me looking and drew the sides of his cardigan together, covering the shirt and resting his hands over his belly. He gave the impression of having once been a larger, sturdier person who was now in the slow process of curling in on himself.

Each of Foster's teacups were white with different colored roses on them, oddly dainty for a man who obviously lived here by himself. The tea burned my hands through the porcelain and I suddenly wished I'd come here alone.

"It's hot." Foster nodded at the steam rising from his cup.

"I hope we're not disturbing you," Key said politely.

Foster chuckled and nodded, as if Key had made a joke. I blew on my tea for something to do. I hadn't expected an Elder. It had totally thrown me and now all the questions I'd rehearsed in my head on the drive over had vanished.

"That's beautiful." Key lifted his chin.

"It's new. Open-box sale. Got a real good deal." Foster nodded to the TV, one of the few shiny new things in the room. "Netflix has so many good baking shows. Have you seen the one where everything is cake? And you know"—he pushed back the cardigan sleeve to show us a pretty decent watch—"it sends notifications when new episodes drop."

"No." Key smiled. "I mean the—" Pointing.

"Oh." Foster sat up and turned, as if surprised by the colorful painting of a woman with long, black windswept hair seated on a turtle's back in the middle of an endless sea.

"Sky Woman," Foster said. "You know this story?"

Key and Stella shook their heads. I kept my eyes on the painting, because of course I knew it. Even a toddler would. Sky Woman's story was where our culture began. It was the one story Lily had told me many times, some details shifting with each telling, depending on her purpose. The painting on Foster's wall was pretty enough, but there was something unsettling about it—the woman stranded in the middle of all that water and no land in sight. The hole she'd fallen through was tiny, near the roots of a tree up in the very top corner of the canvas. It was a long way down through the bright blue sky to the dark ocean with no coast. I'd heard the story, but I'd never seen an illustration of it. The part I remembered best was all the animals that dove down seeking earth and came up empty. I'd never thought about her, about the fall. I tracked Sky Woman's path with my eyes. She must have felt like she was falling forever.

I shivered.

Foster nodded to himself again.

"In the sky world," he began, "they warned her not to get too close to the hole she dug. At the base of that tree." He pointed.

"But she couldn't resist. So curious. She had to see what was on the other side. She leaned in too far and fell." His crooked finger tracked her descent. "All the way down. Turtle lifted her out of the water, knowing she would drown without help. One by one, other animals dove to the bottom and finally one brought her mud so she could build on Turtle's back and make this place. That's how it came to be—Turtle Island. She made it for us. And here we are." He met my eyes, and for a moment he didn't look old at all.

"A creation story?" Key loved this stuff. "For North America?"

Foster shrugged. "You can call it what you want. For my people, we live on Turtle Island." He sipped his tea cautiously. Storytime was over, it seemed.

The little house was quiet but for an unseen clock ticking.

I studied the painting. A woman who couldn't resist trying to get a better look at the water. She had to see. And she fell.

Foster set down his cup and looked at me.

"Was it you?" he said, his eyes crinkling kindly, even as a jolt of shock went through me.

"I think so," I breathed. The skin on my scalp prickled and sent a shiver down the length of my body. He knew. He knew about the black water. He knew I'd been there. But how?

"I've been waiting," he said, "for a long time."

I was sitting on the love seat in that tired little house, sandwiched between Key and Stella and across from the old man. And I wasn't. I was watching it all from somewhere just above. My heart was racing, but my skin was cold. Every part of me expanded out and then rushed in, contracting into a tiny, hard kernel.

"In akhsótha's time." Foster clasped his hands. "My granny. It took twelve of the family. The black water." A sigh. "That's why you're here."

"How do you know that?" Key asked, not as a challenge; he was genuinely curious.

"I started dreaming of it again." Foster shrugged like it was obvious.

My whole body went cold. *Runningpineswaterdark.* I was curled in on myself so tightly, the touch of Key's hand made me jump.

Two taps on my leg.

You there?

I blinked, surprised to find that I was still sitting on the love seat, in one piece, next to Key and the eyebrows of concern he was giving me. Stella peered around me at Key, her eyebrows doing their own version.

"Have you seen it?" I turned to Foster, wanting all those searching eyes off me and ready to hear some answers. "You've been out there?" The tea was no longer scalding, so I swallowed a mouthful.

Foster picked up his cup and contemplated his tea for a moment before turning his gaze to the window.

"The Kanyen'kehá:ka, we've been here forever. The black water, it was here before that."

Okay, but not what I wanted to know.

Beside me, Key leaned forward, elbows on his knees but his eyes on me. Stella twined a golden strand of hair around her finger, over and over, the way she did when her mind was whirring. They were both full of questions, but looked to me for a cue. They weren't Kanyen'kehá:ka and they didn't know the rules. They thought I did. They both knew the disconnect I felt from the culture that was supposed to be mine, but neither of them knew how deep it went.

The truth was, I didn't even know half as much as they thought I did. They thought my culture was a rope, a guideline that I'd temporarily lost my grip on, but I'd never held it in my hand. I'd never felt the security of it leading me. I sat on the little sofa, at a loss for what to say next, every beat of my heart like a thundering drum.

As Foster talked, the sound of his voice washed over me, an unexpectedly soothing balm, like a lullaby I'd forgotten. "It wakes, and then it sleeps. People learn, but then it makes them forget. Or they're gone by the next time, as I could easily have been." Foster turned his eyes back to us and smiled. "I've been waiting a long time." He gestured to himself. "As you can see."

"So what should we do?" Stella asked. We. I loved her then. I could see it on Stella's face—trying to work the problem, tease it out like a tangled ball of wool. A dog with a bone, Key always said. Sometimes Stella's persistence drove Key and me up the wall. Now I knew it would work for me. Stella would treat this problem like it was her own. Which made me feel bad about how much I was still keeping to myself. I justified it because dreams weren't real, but none of this should be. And the truth was, I was scared; part of me believing that reality was affected by the words that I spoke or swallowed.

"Well, for one thing, don't try to find it again." Foster set down his tea. "Don't go out there."

Um, yeah.

"You won't find many people willing to talk about it." He glanced down at his sneakered feet. "And if they do, they'll spout stupid stories. The things they said about my family to explain it away . . ." He shook his head. "It's best to . . . just let it go because once it starts, you can't stop it," He turned the teacup in hands that looked just like my ihstá's.

I waited, but Foster seemed finished. Finding the black water again was the last thing I would ever think to do, but I needed to do something. I didn't believe it was just a story anymore, and I couldn't just let it go because it wouldn't let *me* go. What about Jackie? Something was happening. My pulse picked up once more.

"So, definitely not a sinkhole, then?" Stella prompted, frowning.

Foster shook his head with a bitter chuckle. "This town," he murmured. "Sinkhole." He snorted. Foster's watch buzzed. "Oh! A new episode of that Bake-Off just dropped." He patted his watch like it had done a good job. "I like that one." He smiled like he'd been saved by the bell.

Key patted his thighs and started to stand. "Okay. Thank you for talking to us, Mr. Miller."

Stella rose and turned toward the door, following Key's lead. "It was nice meeting you."

Key tapped the back of my shoulder, but I didn't move from my spot on the sofa. There had to be more than this. I wasn't going anywhere until there was.

"You said it'll sleep? Like, go away?" I asked. "When?"

Because if it could sleep, that meant I had woken it. If it took people like it had before, would that be on me?

Foster folded his hands in his lap. "It's old," he said softly. "No one really knows what it is or where it came from. The best thing to do now is ignore it. Don't feed it."

"Ignore it?" The memory of the water rising against my skin on the bus made me shiver. How could I ignore it? If anything, I needed *it* to ignore *me*. And "feed it"? I didn't like the sound of that.

Maybe Foster didn't know anything. Maybe he had nothing helpful to share, but that wasn't the vibe I was getting—there were things he wasn't telling me. Had I offended him by not bringing a gift?

Key was aggressively giving me the "go ahead, do it!" face, but there wasn't any point. Nobody had ever taught me anything other than a few words that made me *sound* like I belonged. A few stories I knew that made me slightly more knowledgeable than the average person. I looked Mohawk and technically I was. But I didn't *feel* it; I never had. And now that I needed to *be*, that I needed to navigate, I was clueless except for the fact that whatever Elders are going to tell you, they're going to do it in their own sweet time.

Which was fine, if you had time. I was afraid that I didn't. A curl of heat rose in my stomach, spreading up to my face. Foster and I sat, looking at each other, his face calm and open, my jaw clenched so hard it creaked, my pulse skipping faster by the second. Key and Stella silently argued about what to do until Foster gripped the chair arms and levered himself up. He didn't seem upset, so maybe he genuinely didn't know anything. I got to my feet and reluctantly followed Key to the door. Either Foster had answered my questions and I couldn't understand, or he didn't know the answers, either.

"Don't try to find it," Foster murmured behind me as Stella pushed the squeaky screen door open. "Don't listen to it."

I stepped out onto the porch and turned back to Foster, who was standing in the doorway.

"You had dreams," I pressed, desperate. "But was there . . . anything else?" Like seeing people who weren't there? Like almost drowning on a bus? Any of that ring a bell?

He looked placidly back at me, like I wasn't interrogating him. I saw Stella and Key out of the corner of my eye, and if it weren't for that, if they weren't there, I knew I would have told him everything I was still keeping from them—the things I'd seen, the dream I'd had last night. All of it. Sometimes it's easier to reveal yourself to strangers rather than the people who know you best, the people who are staring at you so hard you can feel it. My eyes snapped over to Stella and Key on the porch and then back to Foster. Did he feel the same way? If I were here alone, would he tell me more?

"You're not the first to find it; believe me," he said, "but if you're lucky, it'll sleep quickly. It'll stop."

My disappointment was a rock in my stomach. Whatever he was telling me, he might as well have been speaking another language. I didn't understand. And I'd never been lucky.

"Ó:nen ki' wáhi," Foster said softly with a little wave of his gnarled hand.

"Thanks, Uncle." I managed something like a small smile before woodenly marching down the steps to the car. Ahead of me, Stella and Key crunched across the gravel, talking too quietly for me to hear. I opened the car door and looked back at the little blue house, the front door now closed and the porch empty. But at the edge of the living room window, I could make out Foster standing, waiting for us to leave. Watching.

I slammed the car door and sat with fists clenched in my lap. If what Foster had shared was truly all he knew, I was in trouble. But he knew more than he'd told me, I was sure of that. As an expert at withholding information myself, I recognized it in other people.

There was information and he had it, but he wasn't sharing, maybe because I'd messed up.

Why?

"What?" I realized Key was talking to me.

"I said"—Key put on his seat belt—"why haven't you ever told us stories like that?"

"Like what?" Sometimes he jumped around so much it was hard to keep track of his thoughts. Especially when mine were all over the place.

"Like Sky Woman. That was so cool."

"Why would I?" I shrugged and turned away. "They're not mine to tell."

None of it was, but Key wouldn't understand that. His family tree was like a hundred-year-old oak, giant and sprawling. He'd known fourth cousins since he could walk. My tree was a skinny sapling. Not everyone had the ties Key did.

"You should have asked more questions," Stella scolded from the back seat.

"When you talk to Elders, they'll answer in their own time and in their own way," I said sharply. I felt like a fraud, explaining culture, and resented it. I didn't mention that I didn't understand Foster's way, and I was starting to feel like I didn't have time.

Key shook his head, like I was being unreasonable. I wasn't against stories, but I wasn't hearing the one I was most interested in. The muscles in my jaw clenched, and I kept my face to the window. Key put on some music, and Stella was quiet in the back seat. They both knew me well enough to let it go for now.

TEN

I'D HAD SO MUCH HOPE THAT I'D GET ANSWERS from Foster in the little blue house. I'd been buoyant and hopeful, but on the silent ride back, gravity had doubled, pressing down, like it wanted to sink me into the ground until I disappeared.

I was back at work with nothing to show for the trip but a growing dread, a rock in my stomach. Foster had said to ignore it. *Don't feed it.* Which begged the question—what did it eat? Could I really wait to find out?

I'd spent the day googling everything. Black water. Crook's Falls forest, Crook's Falls forest pond. I tried every combination of search words I could think of, and got nothing. I tried looking for drownings, or accidents in the forest, disappearances, and the only thing I got were search results about endangered species of songbirds and keeping cats indoors. So many chat groups about that.

I sat at the counter, staring at nothing, thinking about the piece of green paper taped to the window behind me. A new missing poster had gone up, just like Jackie's—but there were two pictures on this one.

A little white dog—Wilkie—laughing into the camera. A woman—Cara Messer—sitting in a lawn chair with a paper plate of barbecue on her lap, looking up with an indulgent smile, caught unaware but not minding.

Both missing.

I'd stopped to look at it on my way in, the dog and the woman who hadn't foreseen herself on a poster. I didn't know if Jackie and Cara knew each other, but they both knew me. A creeping sense of dread settled over me, so oppressive and heavy, my lungs found it hard to work against it.

But I was at work and had to sit here and pretend that my life was normal, I was fine, and reality was not splitting at the seams. The poster broke the late afternoon light streaming in the big window behind me, its shadow a palpable weight on my back.

"Not hungry?"

"Huh?" I straightened up.

Key nudged the snack on the counter.

"I bring you sustenance, and you let it sit there, getting cold and more and more likely to be eaten by an innocent bystander with every passing second."

"Thanks." I popped an egg and cheese bite from the coffee shop into my mouth whole. They were truly magnificent, especially for the sleep-deprived.

In the corner of my eye, the wind caught the edge of the poster like it was waving at me, trying to get my attention.

Remember us?

"Ave." Key waved his hand in front of my face.

"Hm?"

"I said, you sleeping any better?"

"Not really." I shrugged. "Kind of getting used to it, though."

"Still the same dream?"

I squirmed and gave him a half-truth. "Yeah."

Key frowned down at the counter. "That is so weird."

And here it was—the maddening part of my personality that just couldn't deal with Serious Feelings Talk. Sharing. Vulnerability. I couldn't do any of it, even when I wanted to. And I did. With him.

But just like my mom, I found sharing scary. Unlike her, I was basically a coward. As close as we were, there should be no risk in speaking the words. But saying things can make them real, and when they're real, they can be taken away. So for the hundredth time, Key gave me an opening, and I watched it drift past us.

"Don't worry, kid." I slapped his arm lightly. "It'll be fine." Pathetic.

Now Key was frowning at me, which was the opposite of what I wanted. He was looking at me for so long and so directly; he knew I was . . . not lying, exactly, but not being completely truthful. A knot of fear twinged in my stomach.

Key squared up to me and put his hand over mind on the counter. "I'm worried, Ave." His hand was warm and solid on top of mine.

I looked down at our hands and bit my lip, way out of my depth.

Key slid his hand underneath mine. I looked up, caught in his eyes. I was standing at the counter, at work, holding hands with Key. The sun was circling the earth, and piglets soared like eagles. The only place I existed was where my skin touched his, something buzzing through my veins that set my pulse racing and the *me* became *we*, which was infinite. I'd had no idea I'd been so tiny and singular before this. I wanted desperately to escape but also wanted to never, ever leave this space we were sharing. This moment.

"It'll be okay." He cradled my hand between both of his, smiled, and gave me the eyebrows of concern all at once. No one could be expected to withstand that. When he smiled like this, his eyes crinkled up at the edges, number two of Top Ten Things I Love but Will Never Tell. Something in my chest expanded to the point I thought I would burst open, and I could only nod in mute agreement. If I opened my mouth to speak, to say anything at all, I wasn't sure what would come out. I wasn't good at this, never had been.

I wished I was.

But Key knew all of this and released my hand before I vibrated out of my skin, leaving us on opposite sides of the counter, palms flat but eyes still locked on each other, and though words failed me as they always did, I let him see how scared I really was. He was the only one I could trust with this, the only one who knew me well enough to understand. I let him see, and he nodded.

"It'll be okay," he repeated, his voice soft and low.

I desperately wanted to believe that. I wanted to believe that there was a solution, that we would find it and things would go back to normal, to the way they had been before. Maybe better.

But the little voice in my head was back, whispering from a great depth. As much as I hoped and wished and wanted to believe, I heard the voice and knew it was right.

It'll be okay.

But the voice whispered back.

It won't.

"Very nice," Frank observed, startling us both as he pushed a cart half-stacked with books from the back office. "Bringing you a snack. That's a good boyfriend."

This was an old tease, but Frank wouldn't let it go. Probably because he knew I couldn't resist biting. When I'd come to work for Frank, he'd quickly decided that I needed a grandpa. And I guess with his wife gone, he needed a surrogate granddaughter. As a result, Frank was a little more familiar with my life than the average employer.

I drew my hands back and flexed my fingers. "He's not my boyfriend." Although technically true, my habitual response came out a little sharper than I'd intended. Key raised his eyebrows at the comment and pushed off from the counter. See? This is why words suck.

Frank smiled and shelved a history of grist mills in the area. Frank always made sure local authors had a space, and there were lots of them. Most of the books were self-published histories of the area, and there was no shortage of photographers. Old mill sites, bridges, birds, fall foliage: you name it, the creatively inclined residents of Crook's Falls went out and snapped it.

"You could do worse, you know," Key told me, crossing his arms, feigned indignance ruined by the smile flirting with the corners of his mouth.

"The question is"—Frank turned to the cart for more books, one finger raised—"which one of you could do better?"

"I mean, she's smart," Key conceded. "But I'm prettier. So . . ." He shifted his hands like a scale. "I think it balances out."

"Tell you what." Frank winced a bit as he bent to take a coffee-table-sized collection of waterfall photos off the cart. "Bring in a couple boxes from out back, and I'll make us all a nice espresso."

"Deal!" Key slammed his hand down on the counter. "You make the best espresso. You also drink more of it than anyone else I know."

"It's the fountain of youth." Frank shrugged, acknowledging a fact.

Key disappeared into the shade cast by the tall bookcases, like he was walking down an avenue of huge trees, disappearing once the shadows at the back swallowed him.

"Make sure you announce yourself when you come in, though," Frank called out as he straightened some misaligned spines. "This one nearly took my head off with a five iron the other day."

I cringed. Internally, externally, every way you can cringe. That had not been one of my finer moments.

"What!" Key was striding back out of the darkness, toting a box on each shoulder. Show-off. "Well"—Key put the boxes on the floor and rubbed his chin—"she's been a bit twitchy lately." Key was steadily looking at me in a way I couldn't read. "She had a scare."

I stared.

"Right, Ave?"

What was he doing?

"What? What happened?" Frank put both hands on the counter and searched my face for clues.

Unbelievable. I was going to kill Key later. Seriously, blabbing my business like this? What was he thinking? And now he had Frank all worked up.

"I just got lost." I smiled and gave an "oops!" shrug. "I just . . . got lost and it freaked me out."

"Oh." Frank placed his phone on top of a pile of flyers for a book signing and nudged them all into alignment. "You got . . . lost."

"Yeah."

"In the forest?"

"It's a big one." I nodded, wanting this conversation to end.

"It sure is," Frank mused. "It sure is." He drew a perfectly manicured finger along the edge of the worn wooden counter, inspecting nonexistent dust.

The air conditioner out back kicked on, eliciting an answering rumble in the vents. Frank looked up at me and smiled. "Where?" he asked, way too casually.

"Where what?"

"Where did you get lost in the forest?" Frank was still smiling, his fingers now picking at the hem of his cardigan. "You must have left the trail."

I threw a look at Key, but Key was watching Frank.

"Yeah, I did. I was looking for more of a challenge."

"That sounds like you." Frank nodded. "But where? Off the main loop? Near the headwaters? Where did you leave the trail?"

This was uncomfortable. It felt like he was . . . digging. Like you meet someone at a party who offers you a ride home. At first, it's cool, but then the questions get creepy. Where do you live? What's the address? What apartment? Do you live alone?

"Um, it was off the loop." But now that I thought of it, it was kind of hard to picture exactly where I'd been, like the details of a dream that had started to dissolve at the edges.

Frank nodded and produced a smile I had never seen. It was stretched and wrong. He wagged his finger at me. "You shouldn't leave the trail. Didn't your parents ever tell you that?"

I stared, speechless, because I didn't know the man in front of me. And yes, they had. Was this a product of the urban legend, or did everyone know more than they were saying? Just how weird was this town?

Why was he being so odd, and what did he know? "What's out

there, Frank?" His face paled a bit, but he just shook his head with that same stiff smile. Now he was the one trying to change the topic.

Frank patted my hand mechanically, his eyes lighting on everything but my face. "It's just dangerous out there all alone."

I leaned closer. "Have you seen the black water?"

Frank went completely still, his green eyes flat and hard. "That's just an old story, Avery. Everyone knows that."

Which wasn't what I'd asked. Behind Frank, Key raised his eyebrows—a micro-expression that only I would notice.

Frank closed his eyes like something pained him, wrung his hands, and then gave his head a firm shake, steeling himself to say something. I held my breath.

And then the bell over the door jingled.

"Excuse me," said a very tall, very thin white woman who stepped up to the counter. "Do you have the new Paul Tremblay?"

I'd never been so angry to see a customer walk through that door.

"Yes. It's in the New Releases section, right over here," Frank said, moving away from the counter to lead the woman to the shelf dedicated to new books, like he couldn't get away from me fast enough. Out of the corner of my eye, I watched Frank as he found her book and then walked back through the rows and into the office, closing the door behind him.

"So, that was weird." Key was back at the counter after I'd slipped the Tremblay book into a paper bag—one of hundreds I'd spent hours hand-stamping with the *Frank's Books* logo—and waved the customer out along with several browsers, early to the cinema.

I was pissed at Key for telling Frank anything. Yes, Frank probably deserved some kind of explanation for the five-iron incident, but it was not Key's story to tell. He knew me better than that. I was a prickly cactus when any of my many boundaries were breached.

But Key was right. That had just been bizarre. It was like suddenly I was talking to someone who looked exactly like Frank but wasn't. I'd worked at the store for two years, and he'd gone from his predictable Frank brand of concern to creepy stalker in nothing flat.

I tidied everything there was to tidy on the counter before I finally acknowledged Key. That's right, sometimes I was a bitch. Sometimes I used the silent treatment. I couldn't help it. Maybe I was also just mad at myself for not pressing Frank.

"Look, I'm sorry. Everyone's heard some story, but maybe the senior crowd knows even more." Key gave me prayer hands and puppy eyes. Just as manipulative as the silent treatment, really.

Which meant that he had to break first. I gave him my best blank face to let him know it was on.

"Foster wasn't exactly a goldmine of information," he tried again. "Frank's lived here forever *and* he's Mr. Local History. But you haven't mentioned anything to him, have you? God forbid you actually *share*. You'd rather die from sleep deprivation than ask for help."

Possibly true. I wouldn't have asked Frank for help on my own. But that wasn't an excuse. If Key knew that, he should also know how much I hated him blabbing my business. I folded my arms across my chest and kept my face stony.

Key sighed dramatically. "Fine. Yes, I'm an ass." He slipped his phone off the counter and into his back pocket. "But I'm also getting kind of fucking worried about you." He stepped back from the counter. "You don't seem to get that."

"*You're* worried?" Jaw-dropping self-involvement, that's what that was. Who couldn't sleep at night? Who saw things that weren't there? Who was that? Not Key.

He took a deep breath, as if I were trying his patience and not the other way around.

"Okay." He nodded. "Okay. I'm going to go."

Not okay. "You're not going to walk me home? You're that mad." I could hear the edge in my voice, the one that crept in right before I said something meant to hurt.

"I'm not mad." Key shook his head as he pulled the door open and stepped through. "But I'm also not your boyfriend." Throwing my own words back in my face.

The bell over the door wouldn't shut up as people followed Key out, heading for the movie theater. I stood there, both hands gripping the edge of the counter like I was about to hop it.

He was mad. Had to be. He'd never slapped me down like that before. Never. The feel of his hand on mine seemed like another lifetime.

I turned to the big front window, but the light outside had changed, and around the posters, I couldn't see anything outside. The window had become a mirror, showing only myself. Anything could be lurking out there.

Or in here.

I froze like an animal scenting danger, staring out at the shelves. I had no idea how many hours I'd spent in the bookstore, but it was a lot. Enough that I was familiar with the shadows the freestanding shelves cast at every hour of the day, the soft rumble of the furnace coming on in winter and the clatter of the air conditioning starting up in summer. I knew the creak of the floorboards and the quiet whoosh of the big wooden door closing behind a customer.

But that wasn't what I heard now.

The sound was very faint at first. I tilted my head, watching my reflection in the window. I tried to slow my breathing, closed my eyes, and listened. Water, trickling, like someone had left the tap on in the sink in the back room. Except we didn't have a sink in the back room. And the only someone here was Frank.

I turned slowly, my gut telling me not to draw attention to myself. At this hour, the shelves formed an orderly forest illuminated only at the ends, the rest shrouded in impenetrable shadow. Three aisles in front of me, three dark doorways through which something dripping could emerge. My eyes darted between them. I stared into the dark, listening to the water *trickle, trickle, trickle.* And stop.

I held my breath long enough for the blood to start pounding in my ears, then shifted my weight forward, pressing my fingertips to the counter, waiting. Nothing. No more water, but no familiar sounds, either. I took a single step toward the open end of the counter, and a new sound stopped me in my tracks. *Sshhhickk!* This was not the noise of cup on saucer, number eight on my Top Ten Things I Love but Will Never Tell. This was the sliding, scraping sound of something not used to walking.

"Frank?"

Who else could it be?

Sshhhickk!

"If you're making espresso, don't make one for me," I called. "I need to sleep tonight." I meant it as a joke, but my fingers gripping the counter edge told the truth.

There was no answer.

Sshhhickk!

The terrible sound of that dragging, rasping movement again, but now I could see the source. The shadows shifted around something approaching.

It was Frank who emerged from the black gaping area between the shelves, coming up the aisle toward me. I sagged against the counter and let the air threatening to burst my lungs out in a rush. Thank God. I plastered on a smile so he wouldn't see how freaked out I'd been two seconds ago by absolutely nothing.

But just as quickly as I slapped it on, my smile faded. Frank's steps were oddly measured, as if he suddenly wasn't sure of the floorboards he'd walked over every day for years, his left foot dragging as if unwilling. He walked like a windup toy, his gait mechanical and jerky, arms straight at his sides, hands fixed open with his fingers straining for the floor.

I squinted. "Are you okay?" Because that was the most likely scenario for a man his age, a stroke or heart attack—all that espresso caught up to him. "Frank?"

Fully out of the shadows, Frank reached the end of the counter—my only escape route—and stood, staring not at me but *through* me. I stared back, hands clenched at my sides, still as a stone but screaming inside. Something wasn't wrong with Frank. Frank was wrong. We stood like statues, the sound of my own breathing loud as thunder.

As I watched, a single drop of dark water appeared from under the cuff of his cardigan. It meandered down his wrist, slipped onto his index finger, and fell to the floor. Frank had no reaction. I bit my lip against the crushing pressure in my lungs but couldn't move.

Over the end of the counter and out the door.

My body wanted to run, but I was frozen. The first drop of water was followed by another and another, each hitting the floor with an unnaturally loud *thud*, as if the water had much more weight than it should. I watched the dirty water run from his fingers and track down his face, over unblinking eyes, until he was dripping wet, like he'd been dunked into a pond—*you know the one.*

"No, no, no." I whimpered, eyeing the puddle that formed at his feet and crept out in every direction like spiders from a nest. Panic tightened its grip on my chest, forcing tears into my eyes. *Ignore it. Maybe it will go back to sleep.*

How? How was I supposed to ignore *this*?

A smile spread across Frank's face that was a thinner, sharper version of the Frank I knew, his mouth a rictus taut and ready to snap. His eyes changed, becoming shadowy and indistinct, blurring and sinking into his face like dark pits, like someone had driven their thumbs into his eyes. I gasped and backed up against the window, seeing the shadows the poster cast across the thing that looked like Frank.

"Frank," I whispered, trapped between the counter and the posters looming behind me. But it wasn't. It couldn't be. Whatever this thing was reached out for me with one dripping hand and my body took over. With nowhere else to go, I spun and vaulted over the other end of the counter closest to the door, but not before I saw Frank burst, exploding with a splash of fine spray that hit the side of my face.

I landed hard, catching myself with my hands braced against the floor and popped back up, ready to run for real, to tear the door open and just go—down the sidewalk at top speed and never stop.

There was nothing. There was no watery version of Frank at the counter. Even before I looked, I knew there would be no water on the floor. Just like the bus, I'd seen things that were not there. The black water was poking around in my head looking for things to scare me.

And it was doing a really good job.

For a moment, my ragged breathing was the only sound. Then the air conditioner casually clicked on. I pressed my palms onto the counter for support. Anything to hold me in this world, the real world, where my friends didn't dissolve in a splash of brackish water. I gave myself the length of one long, shaky breath drawn in to think of something to say. I wanted to call out to Frank in the back, to have him answer and have everything be fine. But I couldn't get any words through my tight throat, still afraid of what they might summon.

I crept around the edge of the counter, peering down at the floor.

As expected, it was dry, which actually didn't make me feel better. Other Frank had been there. I'd felt the spray of water on my face. I'd heard the water hit the floor. That thing had radiated an absolute, seething malice. It hadn't been real, but it had been here. How could that be?

"Did he leave?"

I startled so hard, my feet left the floor.

Frank came stepping carefully down the aisle with an espresso in each hand and a third balanced on top, in the middle. He looked like a third grader balancing an egg on a spoon, right down to the tongue sticking out for better focus. This, this was my Frank, no doubt about it, the certainty slowing my pulse just a fraction.

"Yeah." Hearing the tremor in my voice. "He had to go." Watching him carefully, I stepped around the counter to relieve him of the third cup and then pulled up both stools.

"Ah." Frank sat with a sigh. "Sorry, you're not going to be able to sleep tonight."

"Doesn't matter." I wasn't expecting to sleep anytime soon; didn't even want to try anymore. I took a sip. The espresso was bitter and dark and perfect and allowed me to blame my trembling hands on caffeine.

"I putter around the house until all hours, so it's of no consequence to me." Frank was already looking at the lonely third cup; no way he'd be able to resist. "I forget that other people do sleep. And don't have my tolerance for caffeine."

We sipped in silence.

"Biscotti?" Frank nudged the plate my way.

As if that were a question.

"You run so much." Frank sighed. "I do worry about you."

"They don't give scholarships to slowpokes."

Frank frowned, as if the concept of tuition had never occurred to him before, but he'd never put kids through school, so maybe it hadn't. "Hm."

I nibbled on my biscotti, wanting this little island of feeling okay to last far longer than I knew it would.

"I had a twin sister, Margot." Frank smiled and slowly rotated his cup on the saucer. "Did you know that?"

I couldn't imagine Frank as a young man, let alone a twin. "Did you have a secret language?" I nudged him gently with my elbow, relieved to find him solid.

"Not exactly. But it's true that there's a connection, something different than we had with our brothers."

That seemed to be all he was going to say. The store was quiet, and Frank was Frank again, tapping the edge of his cup. The espresso had warmed me, and I wasn't ready to go home yet, so I stayed still and quiet, hoping he would continue.

"Margot had a friend. A boyfriend." Frank raised his eyebrows at me. "A boyfriend named Frank."

"No. Eww."

Frank nodded. "It was unfortunate. To differentiate us, Margot started calling me Franco, and I have to say I didn't like it." He looked down at the counter and lowered his voice, like he was talking to himself. "He was nice enough, but I guess I resented that he'd taken my name. If anyone had to change, it should have been him."

I looked down at the counter, too, because Frank seemed to be seeing the past there, projected like a movie.

"He was nice enough, but not . . . enough." Frank sighed, straightening his back. "His family wasn't—well, my parents didn't approve. But Margot . . . One night, she asked me to walk her to the cinema so she could meet him, and, I don't know, I'd just had it." He frowned. "I told her that if she couldn't be above board, then maybe she needed to rethink what she was doing with him. I was just afraid of losing her, really, of this other Frank taking my place."

"Did she go?" I leaned on my elbows, hunched over the counter, and pushed back against the image of the other Frank I'd just met.

Frank smiled at me sadly. "She did. My parents were furious, but she walked to the cinema with that boy and neither of them ever came home."

My skin went cold.

"The last thing I ever said to my sister was that I didn't care what she did anymore."

I felt like a stone, cool and still. "I'm sorry." I patted his wrist.

Frank turned to me like he'd just woken up. "I tell you this because people think small towns are safe, but bad things, terrible things, still happen." Frank put his hand on my shoulder, pressing down. "You need to be careful."

"What do you think happened to her?" I asked dully. If Frank really didn't know, I had a pretty good idea.

Frank patted my hand back and left it there. "I still think of that night sometimes. More often lately. It was early fall, still warm. After all the ruckus with my parents, I watched her walk down the street with him from my bedroom window. It was a beautiful evening." He smiled and patted my hand again, looking out into the expanse of the store at something I couldn't see. "I hope they had a nice walk."

The hands of the big clock thunked into place, announcing it was time for me to venture out into the evening, with Frank to see me off—just like Margot.

Frank smiled sheepishly and reached for Key's cup. "He won't mind."

"Fountain of youth," I murmured.

"Exactly." Frank raised the cup to me and downed it.

He put his cup on the saucer with the soft clink that I loved, and we sat in companionable silence. I'd leave him to ride out the end of the evening and close up on his own. I'd walk home in the cool night air, have a shower, and crawl into the fresh linen my mom had put on my bed. Maybe I'd even sleep.

Frank began piling our cups so I slid off my stool and turned, resting my back against the counter and taking a long, slow breath, trying to quiet the buzzing just under my skin. My eyes settled on the window, the green paper edges flapping in the breeze. Jackie and Cara were missing. The black water was poking around in my head and pulling nightmares into my waking life.

"You really shouldn't go off the trail, Avery." I wasn't surprised to hear the quiet words behind me, but it was Frank's reflection in the window that moved. "You must promise me that you won't do it again."

"I promise." There was no other answer.

ELEVEN

THE SCENT OF THE PINES WAS CALMING. BUT IT didn't last. It never did.

> I was back in the meadow, the rank odor of stagnant water enveloping me.
>
> Frozen yet still moving closer to the pond.
>
> Key was there, smiling.
>
> I tried to speak, to yell—he was so close to the edge.
>
> The water.
>
> I didn't know what it was, but it was danger, dark and hungry.
>
> It pulled me closer, even as I tried to run away.
>
> Key smiled and stepped into the water.

Another night, another dream, each one worse than the one before. A good long Sunday run would clear my mind and give me a chance to think without the well-intentioned but ultimately unhelpful input of Frank, Key, or Stella.

This time, I was up way before Mom and left a huge note to prevent another freak-out—black Sharpie on a full sheet of lemon-yellow paper.

> **I, your daughter, Avery Ray, have gone for a run. I shall return before 9:00 a.m.**

I signed it with a flourish and left it on the kitchen table. Mom would see it before she left to see Lily; maybe it would make her laugh. Maybe not. I never knew these days.

I still didn't take my phone; I hated carrying it. I couldn't run with anything strapped to me, so out the door and down the street I went—just me in my new shoes, compression shorts, and favorite ratty tank.

When I raced, my mind was sharp, focused on every step, every muscle working in unison. Long runs left me feeling cleaned out, tired from the inside in a very pleasant way. I had the kind of brain that never really stopped. Even when I was asleep. I'd roll over in bed and then thoughts would invade. Was I ready? Were my notes good enough? What would I do when the cat died? What would I do after university? Stuff I really didn't need at 3:00 a.m. But on a long run, it all went quiet and still, a lake on a day with no wind.

This had not been that kind of run.

I'd hoped a run would clear my head, give me a moment of peace. With no desire to go back into the forest, I had followed the perimeter of town, and the whole time, I'd struggled to find the rhythm, to let muscle memory take over so my mind could check out. It never happened. I just couldn't get into it; I wasn't a road runner. Cracks in the sidewalk, cars on the road, people walking dogs, Key, Jackie, Cara—I was right there, fully conscious every step of the way, and it sucked. I slowed to a walk and checked my watch to confirm that fact.

I couldn't do anything about traffic or the weather, but I could do something about whatever had gone wrong between me and Key last night. That was more important than any run. We'd had minor disagreements before, but this time, I wouldn't wait for him to reach out; I would suck it up and make the first move.

Yeah. I could do that. I'd just text him to see if things were okay. And if they weren't—I'd fix them, like someone who believed that he valued our whatever we had as much as I did. I could do that. This was New Avery.

This run wasn't getting me anywhere, but I needed to work up some endorphins to get the nerve to text him. There was always the community center; I wasn't much of a swimmer, but there was the little gym. I could do the strength training I hated. It would do.

I headed toward home at a trot, a warm wind at my back urging me on. After a workout, I'd talk to Key and start the summer fresh, the thought bringing a soft smile to my face. I'd had a rough few days, but I'd smooth things out with Key, we'd have fun at FallsFest, and I'd start the summer I'd been dreaming of. Turning south toward home, I was determined to make it so. Things were about to get much better.

But by the time I'd gotten home, changed shoes, and headed out the front door with my backpack, my optimism slipped, and I found myself glancing over my shoulder like I'd forgotten something, unease a stone in my stomach.

Striding down the sidewalk toward the community center, I couldn't wait. I pulled out my phone to text Key—Operation Make Up. I'd just make sure he'd be walking with me to the bookstore later, not a big deal, something I'd normally do. Things might be weird after last night, and if things between us had shifted or changed, I needed to know how much and in what way as soon as possible so I could try and smooth it over. Especially after what had happened, what I'd seen, I needed Key with me. My first message didn't make the cut, got erased, replaced with Option 2, which got deleted in favor of the last resort. I was used to agonizing over communications with my dad, but never had I spent so much time on a single text to Key.

Hey.

That's what I came up with. Truly inspired, Ave. I rolled my eyes at myself and slipped the phone into the front pocket of my backpack, mourning the fact that women's clothes never had pockets big enough for phones. Why did my pockets have to be stylishly decorative, when Key's were actually functional? But it was a big deal that I was texting first, so, really—yay, Ave?

Halfway down the block, I still hadn't gotten a ding, which was odd. Maybe I just hadn't heard it? I stopped and pulled the phone up far enough out of the pocket to see that, nope, nothing yet.

I stopped short, pressing my bag against my chest, getting more anxious with every second that Key didn't answer. Maybe smoothing things over was going to be harder than I thought. Two blocks ahead, a tall, lean figure stood in front of the bakery. A man in profile, leaning against the wall, doing nothing. I started forward again, walking toward the man, but kept my bag where it was. At the end of the block, I looked both ways twice. I was stalling, and I couldn't say why.

And then he turned. I couldn't see his face, but his head definitely turned, looking right at me, sending a jolt through me like I'd touched a live wire. I'd taken a self-defense class once, mandatory for all the runners at school. The instructor had told us to be aware when we were afraid. "Fear is your friend. If you feel it, there's a reason."

I couldn't name the reason right then, but there was one, I was sure of it. Continuing on to the next block didn't feel like a great idea, so I crossed to go through the town square. I headed toward the fountain, intending to cut across, and take the scenic route to the community center. Nice weather. Fresh air. Sure.

It seemed like a good idea until I realized that, by going through the square, I was leaving all the other pedestrians behind. I trotted along the pea-gravel path through the empty square, the sound of my footsteps oddly amplified despite all the activity on the other side. Ringed by the big trees on the square, the ugly, inoperative fountain was the showpiece or eyesore of downtown, depending on your opinion.

The safety of open space pulled me on, just as much a lie as the moth heading into the flame. Yeah, there were no big trees here for creepy people to hide behind, but there was nowhere for me to hide, either. I bit my lip and sped up, unsure if the thudding I heard was footsteps behind me or my own heart thumping away.

I was so intent now on avoiding the man by the bakery, that I didn't immediately notice the woman on the park bench. My steps stuttered and then evened out, slower but not stopping even though I wanted to. She sat facing the dry fountain, everything about her gray and insubstantial, wavering slightly like an old movie being projected onto a bedsheet. Her dress had long, tight sleeves, and she was leisurely spinning a small umbrella—a parasol—over her shoulder. She gave every impression of sitting and enjoying a sunny day. The breeze carried the sound of water gurgling happily, but the fountain was dry like it had always been.

I slowed further, not trotting anymore, barely moving forward at all. Each step was a conscious decision, me forcing myself to advance toward something I just knew I didn't want to see. I knew the fountain was dry, but I dared a glance at the basin to make sure. Cracked concrete. Not a drop. The parasol slowly twirled around and around and then . . . stopped. So did I.

Chirrrp!

My clenched fists felt like they belonged to someone else. I wanted to walk away, I wanted to run, but my legs wouldn't obey. I kept my eyes locked on the woman.

Water trickling, splashing from a height.

This wasn't what it seemed.

The parasol wouldn't move. Nothing would happen.

The parasol tilted back, and I made a quiet sound against my will.

She had only an approximation of a milky face, the nose and mouth recognizable attempts, but the eyes just depressions, thumbs pressed into clay. She was a creation incomplete, unfinished.

The woman turned that face to me, and I fell back a step like I'd been slapped. She slowly rose, giving off an air of simmering anger, of wanting something. Of *needing*. I squeezed my eyes shut. This woman was not real. She was not there and not real. But if I had been betting the woman would disappear, I lost. When I opened my eyes, the woman snapped the parasol shut. Maybe not real, but definitely there. Her unfinished face still turned toward me, she took a step forward.

Chirrrp!

No shit.

I jerked back, heard gravel crunch behind me, and froze, a mouse sighted by a cat.

I had nowhere to go. The woman was in front of me, but there was something worse coming from behind. My eyes skittered over everything, looking anywhere but at what was in front of me. My heart was pounding but my body felt far away. I had to *gogogo*, far away and fast. Real or not, I didn't want to be here another second.

Trapped between the faceless woman and whatever was behind me, I grabbed the lip of the fountain basin, hopped in, and lunged for the other side, hearing twin footsteps in the gravel as I tried to pull myself out and over the other side of the basin. My shoes squeaked, losing traction against the smooth concrete for what felt like an eternity before I pulled myself up and over, one foot catching, and landing on my knees. My mind was a blank, my body taking over with no fight, only flight. I scrabbled in the gravel, dug in, and took off like I had heard a starter's pistol. North through the square then across to the cinema, two blocks more and cut across the baseball diamond, where the community center stood beyond, the blue barnlike structure a welcome sight. Heart racing, pulse pounding, right up the steps, and finally, finally bursting through the double doors.

Half-crouched against the wall, still clutching my bag, breathing hard and staring at the metal doors, I counted to five and then crept closer. Keeping one foot back, ready to run, I peered through the window in the front door of the center.

Nothing.

Nothing on the other side, no one coming after me. I blew out a long breath and pressed my palms and forehead against the cold wall. At the end of the hall at the office window, a line of people were waiting to sign up for summer programs but no one looked my way. Something was happening to me. I needed Key and I needed to be honest with him. I had to be Real Avery. I needed help.

Key still hadn't texted me back, which was not normal. He must actually be mad, but I needed to talk to him, no matter what he said, no matter how awkward things might be after last night. This was well beyond what I could handle on my own—I was willing to admit that now. I'd tell him everything and do whatever he suggested. I just couldn't take this anymore. It was—it was too much. The center on a Sunday was bustling with kids newly freed from school, people taking exercise classes and parents with toddlers, the vibe the particular brand of chaotic giddiness that the start of summer always brought. I straightened up, self-conscious about my grand entrance and my nerves stretched raw, but nobody noticed, too engrossed in their own little dramas.

"Stella." She taught water aerobics in the outdoor pool during the summer. It seemed like too much to hope for, but she might be here. I made a beeline for the changeroom, dodging bodies, towels, and backpacks in the hall before ducking into the women and kids' side, scanning the maze of lockers. I spotted Stella in her usual uniform—sneakers with no socks in case it was hot, baggy shorts, and a T-shirt with a sweatshirt draped over her arm in case it was cold. She reached into a staff locker and pulled out a massive water bottle with lemon slices floating inside and considered a granola bar before rejecting it in favor of reapplying lip balm. Ever prepared, and that's what I was counting on now. I hurried over to her. "You seen Key?"

Stella turned and looked at me like I was doing something weird. Maybe I was. Maybe I was trembling slightly. Who could say?

Stella capped her lip balm sporting a tiny frown. "He's usually with you," she said.

Usually. I took in one long breath to try to pull myself together. I'd heard the expression a million times but had never fathomed that it was possible to feel like you were actually coming apart. Like there were seams in your body and mind that you'd never been aware of until you found out how fragile they were.

"I know, I know." As close to an explanation as I could get, aware of my right knee bouncing like I was about to spring away. "But he hasn't texted me back. And now I'm worried." I hooked both hands into the backpack straps and twisted until the webbing cut into my skin.

"One missed text is not an emergency," she said, closing the locker.

Not for most people.

"Okay," she said over the brain-splitting shrieks of a child unwilling to change out of her bathing suit. "We can talk after my summer orientation, okay? Big changes in the world of water aerobics." She rubbed her hands together in mock anticipation and blew a kiss my way, oblivious to my frazzled state.

I stood back against the wall and watched Stella thread her way through the chaos of the changeroom, part of me wishing she'd noticed something was wrong. I guess I wasn't the center of the universe after all. Mom was right.

For lack of a better idea, I'd wait for Stella.

My phone still told me that no, Key had not texted back. What were the possible reasons for that? Where was he supposed to be right now? I couldn't remember exactly, but my head was still kind of buzzing from my unexpected run here. I set my loaded backpack on the floor, keeping my phone pressed against my chest like I could will it to ding.

Okay, maybe he was mad and maybe he had reason. But once he was here, he'd be all serious and share-y and for once, I was going to show my proverbial cards. I'd apologize. I'd acknowledge that I hurt his feelings. Pressing my back against the wall, I gnawed on the edge of my thumb, envisioning it all. It would be fine.

When my phone rang, I jumped and juggled it as I scrambled to answer. *Key's home phone!* He'd either lost his phone or dropped it in the toilet, or maybe his dad had taken it away. Relief flooded my body like a tide. Whatever the reason, I would never let him forget this. This would be my comeback to his flashlight story.

"Key," I said immediately.

"Avery? Avery, honey, it's Michael Rogers."

The chatter of the changeroom turned to a steady, high-pitched ringing, answered by a tingle in my fingers. Key's dad. He'd never called me before.

"Are you there?"

"Yes," I stared at a locker across from me, hanging open, recently vacated. "I'm here."

I felt like I should sit down, like what he said next might drop me to the ground anyway.

"Key didn't come home last night. Do you know where he is?" A hint of desperation, fueled by the knowledge that if I didn't know, no one did.

"No." A single breathed syllable.

"Are you sure? He was with you, though?"

"No." I could barely process what he was saying, let alone give a better answer around the tightness in my throat.

"Did something happen? Did you have a fight? Or maybe he's upset about something else. You can tell us, Avery. We—we won't be mad. He's not in trouble."

I could see Key's dad, standing in the middle of the spotless yellow kitchen where Key's family seemed to spend all of their time. He'd be dressed for work; his "corporate costume," he called it. Jeannie would be at the table, scrolling through her contacts and pausing to write down numbers on a pad with her real estate agency's logo and her own face. But they'd already called the only number that mattered.

"I was at work until eight. I didn't see him at all after . . ." I said evenly, the unreality of what was happening swirling around me, tightening its grip and ready to pull me under. Jackie. Cara. Posters in the window. "After he left." My last words were a whisper.

Then silence, because that was all I could manage. My body was cold and numb, like it was someone else's, like I wasn't really there in the hallway at all.

"Avery. Are you there? This is serious. Tell me what I need to know. Please."

I finally let my legs do what they wanted and slid down the wall onto the floor.

"Everything was fine," I said. "I texted him this morning, but he never answered. I thought Stella might have seen him. . . ." My voice trailed off into a whisper and then into nothing. Like my hope.

Jeannie's voice in the background.

"Do you know where he could be? Anywhere he might have gone?"

No.

And yes.

I knew exactly where he'd gone and why. My whole body went cold, the certainty of knowing Key as well as I did leading to only one conclusion. He'd do anything to help me, and since I wasn't finding answers on my own, he'd gone looking on my behalf.

"I think"—I could feel the sudden surge of hope on the other end but felt no answering echo in myself—"I think maybe he went into the forest."

TWELVE

THE REST OF YESTERDAY HAD BEEN A BLUR, and now I was sitting in the back seat of my mother's car, waiting for her to come out of Dr. Liu's office with Ihstá Lily. I couldn't quite feel my body on the seat, like I was wrapped in a fluffy comforter or cocooned in soft, cushy layers of shock. A shock burrito. Even the proximity of the town square didn't faze me. I didn't know how long I'd been in the car waiting, and I didn't care. Key was in trouble, and now there was a pigeon toddling at the very edge of the sidewalk, just looking around. Cars were so close, the bird had to feel the whoosh of air. There was no way he could not know that four-wheeled death was inches away. Yet he continued to sit.

I let my head rest against the window and watched. I'd started watching him and he hadn't gotten splattered yet, so if I continued to watch, he'd continue to be okay.

The bird hopped off the curb and onto the street, a city garbage truck grumbling toward him. I gripped the driver's headrest. I filled my lungs in one sharp gasp as the truck roared past. If it was mortally injured, should I kill it and end its suffering? How would I know if it was mortally injured? Or if it wanted to live? I wasn't an ornithologist, and I couldn't even kill the pale green spiders that showed up in the bathroom. It wasn't fair to have to make decisions based on nothing but your gut feeling.

When I dared to look again, the bird was still there, looking at me. He twitched his feathers for a moment and hopped up onto the sidewalk, then the fence circling the square. I let my head fall back, overburdened by the weight of micro-disasters like pigeons narrowly escaping death. I had bigger things to deal with.

Like me sitting in a tiny gray room that smelled of stale coffee and despair beside Key's parents—his mother still and quiet, his father methodically shredding the label on his water bottle—waiting for hours and then telling two white cops who didn't seem that invested about the last time I'd seen Key.

The last time. As if they didn't believe there'd be another.

"You had a fight?" The officer typing notes had iridescent pink nails, didn't appear that much older than me, and had yet to look directly at me. She latched on to the word that had never actually come out of my mouth, and I instantly knew that would be the story—"argument with quasi-girlfriend."

"No." I tried to backtrack. "Not a fight. I was just ticked because he . . ." Everyone was waiting—Key's parents, the officer in a uniform a size too big for him casually leaning in the doorway, and now the notetaker, waiting, fingers poised over the keyboard. "He talked about me. To someone else."

"Hmm." How could she type that fast with nails that long?

"Not like that." My hands went up like I could stop the keystrokes. *Fight with girlfriend.*

There was no way around it. They were headed down a dead end, and I had to get them back on track. I drew in a painfully deep breath and told the absolute truth. "I got lost in the forest. I found a weird pond that Key thought might be the black water. I think he went to find it. You know, the black water. The story?"

Silence and absolute stillness.

Blank faces and empty eyes, like I'd seen on Frank.

My eyes darted from one face to the next, convinced for a moment that I was the only person still breathing in the cramped room, the other four not human at all but extremely lifelike replicas.

And then the notetaker blinked.

"Ah. That forest." She nodded, unsurprised, throwing a look over her shoulder to the sloucher in the doorway.

"He could have fallen, broken an ankle," Key's mom theorized to herself, then looked to her husband for confirmation.

"It happens all the time," the sloucher drawled, adjusting his angle before letting the doorway take his full weight again.

What?

"I . . . also talked to Jackie the other day." Giving up even more details, because these people were not taking this seriously.

"Maybe he was upset after the fight." Ignoring what I'd just said, the notetaker was forming her own theory. "Got turned around in the dark."

"You'll search for him." A question Key's dad stated as fact.

"Of course." The sloucher nodded, hooking his thumbs in his belt like he had nowhere special to be anytime soon.

What was happening? Key's parents couldn't possibly believe this, but watching them murmur to each other, I realized they did.

"And Cara Messer," I said to anyone who was actually listening, hearing more than a hint of desperation in my voice. "I met her, too, right before she went missing."

"Heard there was trouble in that marriage." The sloucher tapped the side of his nose.

"What was he wearing?" Pink nails poised over the keyboard. "When you fought?"

"We didn't fight!"

Finally, four pairs of eyes locked on me, the girl being so unreasonable and stubborn. I felt like I'd fallen into an alternate reality, one of the other timelines Key was always talking about. It had to be that. Because nothing about this was right.

"It's not your fault, Avery." Key's dad reached across his wife to pat my hand. "They'll find him, and then you can make up."

From the fight we didn't have.

"We've found lots of hikers in that forest," the notetaker assured me, not taking her eyes off the screen as she wrapped up her report. "I mean, not lately, but . . ."

Ever?

"We will search that forest." The sloucher gave me a half-assed salute. "We'll do our best, anyway."

But I knew I'd just seen their best. They weren't really hearing me.

"We should go, in case he comes home on his own." Key's mom patted my shoulder, stood, and gathered the leather tote at her feet.

I wrapped my fingers around the edges of my gray plastic chair. There had to be more.

"Your mom is out front for you." The notetaker finished typing with a flourish and stood. "You can go."

I shuffled down the gray hall, a fluorescent light ahead flickering and then steadying, casual conversation and the sound of a file cabinet slamming shut behind me. No flurry of activity, no call to action. I'd told them about the black water, but they hadn't heard, or hadn't been able to, and now I knew. This was how it happened. This was how so many people disappeared so quietly over the years. "It makes them forget," Foster had said. Assuming they'd ever cared.

"Avery." Mom rose from the wooden bench along the wall and wrapped me in the biggest hug in years before pulling back and looking into my eyes. "They'll find him."

Searching her face, I found nothing but genuine belief, which should have made me feel better. But just like everyone else around here, she believed in the wrong thing.

"Now." Two solid pats on my shoulders, and Mom smiled grimly, glancing around at the uniforms. "Let's get the hell out of here."

The passenger door flew open, startling me back to the present. Ihstá Lily's small round face dipped down, saw me, and smiled.

"Sorry. Can I help?" I pushed the pigeon's near-death experience and everything else out of my mind and reached over the seat to hold Lily's elbow, getting mostly sleeve and not being very helpful at all.

"Oh, don't trouble yourself, dear," Lily said without a trace of sarcasm.

Mom covered the top of Ihstá's head with her hand and lifted Lily's feet one at a time into the car. She made sure the edge of Lily's pale blue cardigan wouldn't get caught in the door and then stood, blowing loose strands of dark hair out of her face. She looked tired, but was that new, or had I just never noticed?

"That cortisone shot should help," Mom said. "If it does, you can get one regularly, like the doctor said."

"For my knees?" Lily's words were shaky, as if confusion had a voice.

"Yes, Ihstá." Mom buckled her aunt in with a smile, but I could see the sadness. Lily's memory was not what it had been even a year ago, like her mind was being siphoned off, shunted somewhere else. Not much to do, the doctors said. Just don't make her feel bad about it.

I knew Lily was important to my mom, maybe just as important as the grandma I'd never met had been. I sometimes thought about the fact that someday, Mom and Lily wouldn't exist anymore, that I would be alone in the world. I didn't think of it often, and not for long when I did. It was just a ridiculous concept, impossible to grasp. But now Key was missing. Suddenly anything was possible.

Lily twisted in her seat and fixed her watery eyes on me.

"Avery, you look tired, dear. Trouble sleeping?"

Mom had buckled herself in, but I saw the twitch in her posture.

"A bit," I said hesitantly.

"Avery. Seat belt." Mom started the car.

"And how is school, Avery?" Lily smiled sweetly.

How could I even answer that?

"Ihstá." Mom stepped in to spare me. "Avery's friend Key is missing. They think he got lost in the forest last night."

"Oh dear." Lily shook her head, her hair perfectly coiffed even as the rest of her crumbled. "That forest," Lily murmured to her reflection.

"The forest is dangerous. You stay on the trails," Mom said to me firmly over her shoulder.

It's nothing, Avery, just your imagination. Stay away, though.

From the nothing. That you're imagining.

"But what if he went looking for it?" I pointed out. "Maybe that's how he got lost."

"They're going to find him, Ave." My mother looked at me in the rearview mirror. "He got turned around, and it got dark. He's not the first. Like that time the same happened to you. We had to go out with flashlights. And you've told me a million times you can't get a signal out there."

She sounded so sure, and I wanted every word to be true, but everything my mom was saying sounded just like what I'd heard in the little room with the cops and Key's parents. Nobody in this town seemed to be able to think straight about the black water. Was I the only one?

"I know it's hard," Mom continued, "but the police are out there. We just have to wait for them to search and find him. It's what they do. You already told them everything you know, right?"

I had. But they couldn't hear it.

"Nothing is going to be helped by you going out there," Mom insisted, as if she could read my mind, which wouldn't surprise me.

I let my forehead bump against the cool glass.

"Don't worry, Mother," I said quietly. "I won't go back."

Why had Key? What had he thought he could do?

"You only find it if it wants you," Lily said to the window. The words sent an icy finger skating up my spine.

I had. It did.

"What if it does?" I leaned up close, lowering my voice and speaking into the small space between Lily's head and the window. "If it wants you, what happens?"

"Oh, it calls to you." Lily raised a trembling finger, the knuckles swollen like knots on a tree. "It gets in here." She tapped her temple lightly, nodding. "It calls."

"And what if you answer?" I tried to keep my voice even, but my fingers gripped the back of Lily's seat.

My mouth was right next to Lily's ear; for a moment she was silent. I stared at her hands folded in her lap, and I was almost ready to admit that she'd forgotten the question.

"It takes you," she said quietly, her voice steady and sure now. "That thing takes you away into the dark."

"And how can you come back?" I whispered the words I wanted to scream.

"Back?" Lily half turned her head toward me. "Well, that's hard."

"But there's a way," I pressed.

Lily pursed her lips and frowned. "There's a way for most things, I guess."

"The way would be to let them search the forest and find him," my mom broke in loudly, turning to catch my eye. "He's in there somewhere, and they'll find him."

I slumped back in my seat.

"They'll find him, Ave," my mom said a little more gently.

Lily looked out the window and said nothing.

I waved to Lily through the window as the car pulled away from the curb. By the time Mom got her back to the retirement home, Lily wouldn't remember any of this. I wished I could just go home and not remember that Key was missing and that no one was taking it seriously but me.

I watched until they rounded the corner and then faced the big glass door. What were the chances that something dark and dripping would be waiting for me inside the bookstore?

But where else did I have to go?

I bit my lip, gripped the brass handle, and pulled. Frank looked up at the sound of the bell, his face tightening when he saw me.

"Avery, sweetie." He rushed around the end of the counter to me. "You know you don't have to be here."

So my mother had gotten to Frank. He knew. I bit back whatever had been on the verge of escaping my lips and let the wave of irritation flood through me. I'd just wanted to come to work like always, like it was any other Monday afternoon. Price books, stock shelves, ring up sales in a store where nothing terrifying happened—just a normal day. Maybe, if it was normal enough, if I really believed it, Key would saunter through the door, just like always.

At the same time, I was glad I wouldn't have to explain anything, wouldn't have to face Frank when he asked where Key was. Basically, I didn't know what I wanted.

He looked into my eyes but his smile was a hastily constructed thing. "They're looking for him."

If one more person said that, I was going to scream.

None of this made any sense. How could Key not be here? The thought made my life flash before my eyes—not my past but my future. I'd get a scholarship and go to university. I'd study kinesiology or maybe sociology. I'd try out for the Olympics—but why? What would the point of any of it be without Key there to share it and knowing that his absence was my fault? My pulse sped up even as my skin went cold. Life without Key. Who would be next? My hands tingled, and I started to feel floaty, like part of me was coming loose. I had never noticed that Frank's eyes were really green. How could I not have seen that before?

"Your eyes are really green," I murmured.

Frank patted my arms and steered me back to the counter.

"Okay. Okay. Let's get you situated."

Once Frank had me seated at the counter, he seemed to have come to the end of his plan. He snapped his fingers.

"I'm going to make you an—maybe not espresso. I don't think caffeine would be good now. But!" He pointed toward the ceiling like he'd discovered the secrets of the universe. That would be nice. He pressed his hands onto my shoulders, like he was trying to stick me in place, then hurried down the aisle toward the office.

In Frank's world, good news, bad news, shock—they all required a beverage of some kind. In this case, noncaffeinated and definitely nonalcoholic. He firmly believed that if you knew what you were doing, you could increase joy and soothe any hurt with the right beverage choice. On my stool at the counter, I sat with my hands in my lap and waited, because I didn't know what else to do.

The job at Frank's Books had been a blessing. I could make some money in my own personal library; entire shifts spent with my feet hooked over the rung on my stool, a book open on the counter in front of me, so lost in it that a few of the regulars apologized for disturbing me with their purchases. Frank didn't even really need the help—the store was a hobby for him, not a source of income. He could have staffed the store on his own with shorter hours.

But Frank had rattled around alone in his bungalow since Louisa died, and traces of my dad lingered in our house no matter how many times Mom repainted the walls or bought new throw pillows. Frank and I both lived in houses with ghosts, so it was nice for us to come to the store where everything was as it should be—warm, cozy, and exquisitely organized.

Running and books were very similar for me—both offered the opportunity to leave my body and send my mind somewhere else, somewhere I was not the main character with decisions to make and problems to solve. Key's understanding of my running came through that comparison because he loved books, too, although our tastes differed; unlike his photography, which was usually quotidian, in books he tended toward the fantastical and heroic, whereas I was drawn to the gritty darkness of twisty thrillers. Still, he understood the benefits of untethering your mind for a little while. He liked to escape, too.

At my station in the front, I willed it to happen, waited to see if the floaty part of me really would detach and just keep going, drifting up to the old plaster ceiling, maybe right through the roof and up into the sky. But when I closed my eyes, I felt nothing at all. Coming to work was maybe not such a great idea. My fingers twined together in my lap.

The urge to check my phone was overwhelming. I had enough trouble keeping my hands off it at the best of times, but seeing the text still unanswered wasn't something I could face. I put my phone face down on the counter, promising myself that I'd look at it in . . . twenty seconds. One thousand one, one thousand two, one thousand three . . . Wait—was that too fast? Should I start over? Maybe just add another ten seconds on, just to be sure. Okay. No, just start over. One thousand one, one thousand two . . .

My phone case was clear with pink sparkles, the kind of thing you'd get a nine-year-old. Key had given it to me for my birthday, as the joke gift. We always gave each other a real gift and a joke gift. His real gift that year had been—I exhaled sharply and wrenched my eyes away and around the store. Books, books, books. Look at all the books. Don't think about that.

Frank rattled around in the back, making reassuringly Frank-sounds. There was no dripping, no trickling, no puddles coming my way, slip-sliding across the floor so quietly I'd never know they were there until they slithered around my ankles. The image made me squeeze my eyes shut hard enough to see bursts of light. I needed to pull myself together. How many seconds had it been? Still not enough.

I spun around on the stool to face the big window and put my back to the store and the path Frank would take when he came out of the office. It was an old storefront, like most of downtown. Frank had mentioned it was a general store at one time, in his lifetime but not mine. The windows were almost floor to ceiling, and the ceilings in here were high. All that glass sometimes made me nervous. Windows breaking. But if they broke, you could take them out. Put new ones in. What were my options? Nothing could replace Key. I drew in a breath so big it hurt, held it as long as I could, distracted by the pressure of my lungs burning. As long as I didn't look at the phone, I wouldn't see it unchanged, and if I didn't see it, it wasn't true. Simple as that.

My lungs had to empty sometime, and when they finally did, I looked across the street to the square, remembering with a shiver the woman I'd seen and run from. The sidewalks now weren't crowded, exactly, but there was a steady stream of people filing past the window, almost all of them carrying some variety of coffee cup. A little white girl moved into my field of vision, moving slowly, differently than everyone else, her steps measured and careful, arms held stiff at her side. The longer I watched, the more I could see something not quite right. Her long, washed-out hair was ratty and tangled, her summer dress had no color, and the girl had no substance. My heart sped up. It was happening again.

I shook my head.

"It isn't real."

The girl stopped just at the edge of the window, as if she'd gotten to the end of a leash.

Chirrrp!

I slapped my hand over my watch to muffle the alarm, but the girl cocked her head.

Chirrrp!

The girl started to turn her head, and I squeezed my eyes shut. I didn't want to look. I should never have looked. If I'd refused to see, none of this would be happening.

"What isn't real?" Frank said, placing a tray on the counter with a frown. "Avery?"

I spun away from the window and gave my head a tight shake, because what could I say? I see people who aren't there and maybe they have Key?

"Avery, what is it?" Sitting beside me now, his hand on my shoulder a vague, distant pressure.

Frank's face shimmered in the tears I blinked back. I wanted to tell him everything, but I couldn't bear to see his face go blank and empty. Not again.

Frank glanced at the window behind us, seeing nothing unusual, and then back to me.

"Sweetheart." He patted my back, prompting me to stand and put my bag in my hand. "You really should go home."

But I didn't want to go home, not with whatever I'd seen waiting for me outside. I wanted answers. I wanted information. I needed to know how to stop this, because I wasn't safe anywhere and neither was anyone else. I swiped at my eyes and sniffled but didn't move.

"Look, Avery." Frank sighed. "I know you feel like you need to do something, but . . ." He leaned forward and met my eyes. "A lot of people have driven themselves crazy trying to figure out the forest."

I didn't blink.

"My advice is to let them search. They'll find Key."

Like they found Margot?

We stared each other down.

"But"—he sighed and straightened up—"I know that's not what you want to hear."

I let my hands fall open onto my lap, palms up like I was ready to catch any answer to this insane situation that fell from the sky and looked up to find Frank watching me.

"Now." Frank gently tapped my arm to get me to stand. "Off you go. Home."

Home, staring at my phone, waiting for a ding that wouldn't ding? But I nodded.

"What kind of ogre would I be—making you work at a time like this?" The concern on Frank's face was an echo, a look that

I'd last seen on Key that I had to turn away from now. I picked up my backpack like any of this mattered and edged out from behind the counter.

"Okay." I pointed a finger gun at him in the best impression of Normal Avery that I could muster. "But I'm working tomorrow." I pulled the door open.

"Avery." Frank's voice, soft behind me. "Try not to worry. It's probably nothing."

But he hadn't thought it was nothing when I got lost off the trail, and he'd had a sister who never came home. I turned back to see his face, needing to see if he believed what he was saying, but the lettering on the window cast his face in shadow, only the suggestion of his features visible.

I stepped out onto the sidewalk and let the door swing shut behind me.

THIRTEEN

MY FEET STEPPED OUT ONTO THE SIDEWALK, headed home, and I went along for the ride.

Left, right.

Left, right.

A last resort technique for the worst runs. One foot at a time will get you across the finish line sooner or later.

I watched my shoes hit the pavement. Feet attached to legs attached to someone not me, someone very far away.

Left, right.

Left, right.

How many in Foster's family had gone into the forest and never come out?

Whose family would be next?

This was not something I could handle. Panic uncoiled like a snake that had been hiding in my chest. I needed Key for something like this.

Left, right.

Left, right.

Left, right.

And then I saw him.

Foster was sitting on a bench, cane braced between his knees, his fine white hair messy from the blue baseball cap that was next to him. Even in the heat he wore the same cardigan he had when I'd met him, but he had on a white T-shirt, rumpled khakis, and white sneakers. I stopped and we stared at each other.

"Shé:kon." He moved the worn blue ball cap beside him onto his lap to make room for me to sit. "You work for Frank?" Foster asked, trying hard to control his scoop of rainbow sherbet in the heat.

"You know Frank?"

Foster nodded, squinting at the store across the street. "Since a long time ago." In danger of losing his battle against the melting sherbet, Foster broke the unspoken law of frozen desserts by taking an actual bite.

I waited for more, but Foster was locked in a race against time and sherbet. Crook's Falls wasn't so small that everyone knew everyone. Still, it struck me as odd that Foster knew Frank, but I'd never heard of Foster. And another thing . . .

"He knows. About the black water." I was sure of it. Frank had spouted the same tired theories about what happened to people in the forest but he'd also told me about his sister. Maybe that was the closest he could get or all the black water would let him say.

Foster tilted his head. "Everyone knows something," he allowed, popping the end of the cone into his mouth. "Some of us know a lot, and others just have a feeling." He shrugged. "Maybe they sense there's danger in the forest. Everyone knows something. But there's knowing, and there's *knowing*."

I had to agree with at least part of that. I knew I hadn't caused my parents to split up by asking a single question. But at the same time, I *knew*. Some deeper part of me had more, better knowledge. And that part knew that I'd enabled the fracturing of my family with the words that passed my lips. If I'd kept my mouth shut, it might never have happened. They might never have had the courage to do it if not for the door I'd opened. And now I'd gone for a run and opened another door. I needed to know how to shut it, to lock it and seal it up forever. But I also needed to know what was on the other side.

The late-afternoon breeze swirled up around us, tasting like the end of the day and lifting strands of Foster's wispy hair like a mother ruffling her child's head. Foster closed his eyes for a moment, as if enjoying the caress. Maybe he had a Top Ten list as well.

"So you came all this way for sherbet?"

Foster shook his head, frowning like it should be obvious. "New book-club book." Nodding in the direction of the store.

My jaw actually dropped.

"You're a member of the Crooked Book Club?" I'd just unpacked the club's current selection, a historical rom-com that Frank had described with raised eyebrows as "racy." I hadn't thought Foster could get more mysterious. But here we were.

"You can only watch so much Netflix." He shrugged. "And books—good for the brain." Tapping his temple.

Huh.

There was really no way I could have seen this coming. I had never conceived that I would one day be sitting on a bench with an old man eager to begin reading *Corseted Desires* while Key was—I took a deep breath, wishing the breeze would return.

"You pick up a book every month?" I narrowed my eyes. "I'd have met you before now."

"I don't." Foster admitted. "I usually get Cara Messer to pick one up for me."

The name stung me. "But you came yourself this time."

He nodded. "I have a reason."

Cara wasn't going to pick up his book this time. A wave of fatigue flooded my body. I was tired. I wanted to sleep, didn't want to sleep, needed to find a way to fix all of this but couldn't stand to think about any of it a single second more.

Foster cleared his throat and looked up at the sky. I leaned forward, ready to rise and head home.

"You may think you started this, but you didn't. Don't think you can fix this by yourself—or at all." Foster smiled, and my heart melted a little. His eyes looked like Key's just then.

There was a message in Foster's face that I couldn't read. He was telling me something, but it was in a language I didn't speak. "I know it's hard," he said quietly. "I know. A long time ago, I was you. Take the advice I didn't and let it go." He opened his hand, like he was releasing something to the wind.

Let it go? I was supposed to just accept the creeping, invasive darkness that had taken over my life and stolen Key away? Like Foster had just said, there was knowing and there was knowing. And I *knew*. He hadn't dragged his old self all this way to sit on a bench and eat sherbet. He'd been waiting for me. He'd come to tell me something, and I wasn't getting it.

Foster's fingers tapped the top of his cane.

"It'll be dark soon." He sighed, looking up at the sky. "I'd like to get home before then."

Wouldn't we all. Except the dark follows some of us. Home, away—it wouldn't matter where I went. The dark was everywhere these days, all the time.

My skin tingled, over my arms and down my back.

Foster brushed off his pants and put on the cap. "Time to get my book." He rose carefully. "And see the old fart." He flapped his hand at the store.

I stayed where I was, wanting to believe he was trying to help me, trying to shut up the little whisper voice. He was speaking in code, and until I understood it, I was lost.

"Wait." I tugged at his sleeve. "You remember Key? He was with me? He's gone. Missing."

Foster stilled, his weight shifting almost imperceptibly back onto the bench.

"And a girl I go to school with."

"I've seen the posters," he said dully, looking out onto the street, his mood suddenly changed—gone was the kindly old man, switched out for a resigned, dimmed version.

"I need to find him," I said quietly. "I need him back."

Foster sighed and drew one hand over and down his face like I'd spoken the words he had least wanted to hear. "It's always the same," he said, voice low and urgent. "If there were a perfect fix, don't you think someone before us would have found it?"

I kept my eyes on my hands, twisted together on my lap. My question had agitated him, but Foster's irritation didn't seem focused on me. I had the feeling he was upset with himself.

"I'm very sorry for your friend." He shook his head. "But I can't offer any help. You have to understand, this is how it's always gone. We're facing something much bigger, much older, and far more powerful than you know."

I took a moment to process this, because underneath his

prickliness, gliding just under the surface of his words and sharp tone, I heard fear. Based on what Stella had discovered about his family, I couldn't blame him. Maybe he wasn't ready, because of what had happened in the past. Losing a chunk of your family—that had to leave a scar. It had for me. I took in everything he was telling me now, but it might be just that—what he was telling me *now*. Maybe there was a point in the future when he'd be braver. But could I afford to wait?

"Is there . . . anyone else?" I tried to phrase it carefully. "Who knows?"

Foster shot me a sour look that I definitely deserved and snorted. "I'm not good enough?" He stamped his cane on the ground. "You don't like what you're hearing."

I didn't.

"The only others left who know . . . they're just as old as me and they'll tell you the same thing." He turned to look at me. "Or worse."

"Okay." I nodded, accepting his "now" answer.

Foster squinted at me, clearly suspicious of my non-reaction. We studied each other for a long moment, like two poker players searching for a tell.

"I really do need to go."

I held his elbow to help him rise.

"Okay." I gave a little wave. "Ó:nen ki'wa'hi."

Foster smiled and nodded. "Ó:nen. Just . . ." Foster rubbed at his mouth and I could see it, could see the braver part of him, the part that wanted to break from the past struggle, wanting to tell me everything. "We have to be careful."

He tapped the brim of his cap and stepped carefully off the curb.

I watched him do the old man hustle across the street, throwing a little wave over his shoulder. He hadn't given me the answers I'd been looking for, but he had dropped one little word that gave my stubborn heart hope.

We.

One of the things I loved about Stella was that if I texted her and asked her to come over, she would. No questions. Which was good because I didn't want to be alone. With everything that was happening, solitude felt like an invitation. If I didn't provide company for myself, the black water would step in and oblige, especially after Foster's parting words. If I was one of the few who knew what was really going on, I couldn't afford to become careless and mess up.

The clink of utensils on plates and Stella prattling about the horrors of driving her little brother and his friends to a music store swelled and flowed around me. I was a rock in a steady, slow-moving river. Sitting at the table, I closed my eyes, hearing the pause and slight gasp as Stella gripped the pan handle and flipped the grilled cheese.

"There's a spatula in the drawer." I opened my eyes and smiled.

"Unnecessary. I make this for Luci all the time." Tongue peeking out, eyes locked on the sandwich, Stella did it again, and the sandwich stuck the landing. She beamed.

"Practice makes perfect."

Maybe I was just hungry. I hadn't been eating regularly even before Key disappeared. So maybe it was just that. But the sandwich Stella had flipped was the most delicious thing in recent memory. It was greasy, cheesy, warm goodness that hit the spot. It's called comfort food for a reason. Stella brought her creation out to the dining table and sat next to me.

"Mm" was Stella's emphatic comment on her own culinary skills. "When was the last time you ate something like this?"

Something like this? Or anything? I couldn't answer either question.

"So good." But my eyes were on a third sandwich, sitting on a plate in front of us as I popped the last bit of corner crust into my mouth. A lonely sandwich, getting cold.

Stella followed my eyes and chewed slowly. "I . . . guess I made . . ." She swallowed, aware that all of her hard work distracting me was undone by the sight of a sandwich with no owner. Then she recovered. "I made that for us to split! I knew one wouldn't be enough!"

She turned a dazzling Stella-smile on me, cut the sandwich in half—diagonally, as is the law—and slid a half onto each of our plates. She picked up her half, offering to toast.

"Here's to the third sandwich," she said.

Stella's face got a little watery then, with me missing the third sandwich so much. I blinked away a tear that threatened to fall and raised my half.

"To the third sandwich," I whispered.

Stella's hand on the back of my neck brought our foreheads together for a moment, but only just, because like Key, Stella was aware of my limitations. It was there though, Stella's intent, and I felt it. But I didn't do mush, so as Stella sat back, I nipped at the corner of Stella's half.

"Hey!" Mock outrage on Stella's face.

I wiped my greasy hands on a napkin—really, when was the

last time I'd eaten anything containing that much butter?—and chewed the ridiculous amount of sandwich in my mouth until there was nothing left, putting off the moment, the reason I'd asked her here. It was more than not wanting to be alone. I needed help and after today it was clear that I wasn't going to get it from the cops or Key's parents or my mom. Or Foster—yet.

"I didn't find much online, but thought you might have," I said.

Stella nodded, as if coming to her for help was an obvious avenue. I reached across the table and grabbed my iPad.

"What did you search for?" Stella went to the sink and started washing her hands.

"Uh, everything I could think of." I didn't really want to reveal either the depths of my ignorance or the increasingly desperate measures my searches had become. I had literally searched anything that could even possibly yield any information about the black water, but Crook's Falls was an insignificant blip on any map, and why would there be information on a topic no one in town seemed able to acknowledge?

Stella came and sat next to me, drying her hands on a dish towel.

"You have to optimize your search terms, Ave."

Which made me smile. "Do the theater kids know you're a nerd?"

"Theater kids are just a different kind of nerd. Besides, I'm not the nerd here," Stella said archly, before biting her lip.

My chest tightened, because there it was again. It was true. Stella wasn't the nerd. The nerd wasn't there. And whose fault was that?

"Try." Stella nudged me with her elbow. "Try Crook's Falls plus Miller."

I felt an irrational giggle bubbling up, because this was a bit of a different dynamic than usual. I couldn't remember the last time Stella had issued orders like this. Key, sure—take your rest days, don't skip your cooldown, eat enough protein. Even though he didn't really know what he was talking about, he'd read enough to know these things were important.

My fingers stilled, and in the single second it took for the internet to do its work, I realized—he'd researched all that. He'd looked up running stuff because although he didn't care about it, I did. I held my bottom lip between my teeth. And I'd never bothered to learn the origin stories of all of his favorite superheroes.

"And?" Stella leaned in, her curls grazing my ear, tickling me.

"Well." I was surprised to see so many entries about Crook's Falls, frankly. But they were all in relation to . . . grist mills?

"What's a grist mill?" Stella scrunched her nose. "Like, in meat?"

"What?" I turned to her and got a face full of curls.

"Grist." Stella repeated, the puzzled nose scrunch transforming to the "ew!" nose scrunch. "The part of a steak that's like . . ." She mimed vigorous chewing.

"So the mill would—"

"Grind it."

"Into what?" I spread my hands. "And why?"

"How could we not know this? That we live in Meat Town?" Stella mused, peering at the screen. "So many."

We were getting way off track.

"That can't be right." I typed a new search. "Gristle! You're talking about gristle, Stell." Mildly relieved that we didn't live in a town known for its meat grinding, I went back to my original search page and waited for instructions. "What now?"

"But what's a grist mill?" Stella screwed up her face.

"Stell, who cares?" I sighed, because this was really not the time.

"Well, now I want to know!" Stella insisted, wide-eyed.

"Key would know," I said, my voice low, my eyes on the screen.

I hadn't meant to do that. Okay, maybe I had, but as soon as I saw the stricken look on Stella's face, I regretted it. Stella was here, trying to help, and I had slapped her down in the most hurtful way. I just wanted to get us back on track. I hadn't meant . . . I could be such a bitch sometimes.

"Okay." Subdued now, Stella put her hands flat on the table and narrowed her eyes at the screen. We were just going to carry on, then, pretending I hadn't said what I'd said. Because this was how my friends always accommodated me: pretending that the things I couldn't say weren't important. "Try Crook's Falls plus Miller plus forest."

"Does Miller need a capital?"

"It doesn't matter." Stella shook her head, still not looking at anything but the screen.

I dutifully typed. "Sorry, Stell," I said quietly.

"It's okay." Just as quietly.

A second search, the same result. So many grist mills. Which, as an olive branch, I quickly found out grind grain, not meat.

"Hm." Elbows on the table, Stella pursed her lips and tapped them with her fingertip.

I waited.

"Okay. Try Crook's Falls plus Miller plus family plus water. Try that."

One more search. Very different results.

Not very many, mostly birth and death records. But there was one that I clicked on and Stella pointed to simultaneously. It took us to a website.

Lost Voices of Crook's Falls. An archive with old audio and video recordings of residents and historians, recounting the founding, building, and history of the town.

"Frank would love this," I breathed.

Again, a fair amount about mills, but one entry—a video titled "Maxine Miller Excerpt"—was what I settled on. It took a moment to load, and Stella moved even closer, practically sitting in my lap.

"Stell, hair," I whispered.

"Sorry." She pulled it back.

I plugged in an earbud, handing one to Stella. We hunched over the table, waiting.

The clip started with a blank screen, then numbers counting down. It had clearly originally been actual film. Then there was a tiny old lady, brown and wrinkled, dwarfed by the easy chair she sat in, in a small room that I recognized with a start as Foster's house. She picked at the front of her blouse and touched the silver turtle brooch on the purple shawl draped around her shoulders. Her white hair was carefully curled and coiffed, a very elderly but perfectly put-together lady. She reminded me of my ihstá. At a cue from off-screen, she looked at the camera, pursed her lips, and folded her hands in her lap.

"My name is Maxine Miller," she began in a reedy voice. "I'm Turtle clan. My family, my people—the Kanyen'kehá:ka—have been here a lot longer than yours." She nodded to whoever was filming. "The black water, it's been here longer than us."

Turtle clan. The same as mom and Ihstá Lily. The same as me. My fingers rose to touch the turtle at my neck, my chest tightening with anticipation. This might be what I needed. Excitement bubbled up, quickly tempered by the fear of being disappointed again about something so important. My hands curled into fists on my knees.

"When I was a little girl, just a small one, my granny told me a story." Maxine nodded, looking at her hands in her lap. "A long time ago, a man came to the people. A white man who wasn't white, who looked like he'd been dragged through ash, looked like bread taken from the oven before he was finished."

Every part of me went still.

Unfinished.

"The Ragged Man, the old people called him. Into the water he'd take you, into an endless nightmare. Walk with him, and you don't come back."

I held my breath, heart beating fast. An endless nightmare—that's where Key was. The thought triggered a high-pitched ringing in my ears.

On the screen, the old woman paused, then looked up in response to a question I couldn't hear. The film was grainy and the audio full of staticky pops. Stella squinted and pressed the lone earbud into her ear.

"It's always been there." The woman shook her head. "But it hides. It's smart." She raised a finger and tapped her head. "It takes what it wants and then goes back to sleep. It waits until we forget. Then it gets hungry and starts over." She shook her head, twisting her hands together in her lap. "Just gone."

Forever?

Maxine looked into the camera, the hint of a smile on her thin lips, a glint of something fierce in her eyes. "We've tried to warn you before, but that thing stops up your ears. And you don't listen anyway. You think I'm a foolish old woman full of old stories." She nodded, looking straight into the camera, into me. "You do. And you will. Right up until it starts again, right up until it's too late."

Another inaudible question. Maxine shook her head again, this time impatient. "No one knows. It's not on any map." She looked into the camera. "You only find it if it wants you."

A phantom breath on the back of my neck. I shivered.

The screen went black.

Stella let out a long breath then drew one in, preparing, I knew, to say something comforting. Key was just lost. This lady was crazy. Everything would be fine.

I waited.

But Stella had nothing.

What were we going to do?

Hours later, Stella had yawned so big her jaw cracked. I'd offered her the living room sofa, but Stella had insisted on rolling out her sleeping bag on the floor beside my bed. While she brushed her teeth and went through her multistep skin care routine, I sat on the edge of my bed, as far away from sleep as I'd ever been.

You only find it if it wants you.

Isthá Lily had said the same thing in the car.

Unfinished.

The man at the bus stop.

Gone.

Key.

I sat down on the edge of my bed, gripping my hands together to keep myself from flying apart.

"It could still be nothing."

I startled to find Stella in the doorway in pink plaid sleep shorts and a T-shirt covered in pandas, cradling Buttons. He hated being picked up, yet there he was, eyes half-closed, drooling in Stella's arms as she stroked his head.

"People go into the forest every summer," she continued gently. "Sometimes they fall. Sometimes they get lost. Remember that time"—she perked up—"you got lost, and your parents had to go out—"

"With flashlights. Yes." God, would no one ever forget that!

"I'm just saying, Ave." Stella scratched Buttons behind his ears. "They've closed the park. They had search teams out there all day."

I'd heard about that. Mom had told me the same thing—the park was closed, the parking lot full of emergency vehicles and a base camp for search teams. Which was great, that it had all come together so fast. It should be comforting, but I'd seen the blank faces at the police station, I'd heard multiple people in town parroting the same lines. They wouldn't find Key. The black water wouldn't let them.

Buttons had had enough. He dropped to the floor and hopped up beside me, curling up into a cat sphere, purring. If Stella went this way, the "he's just sprained an ankle or gotten lost" route, I would really be alone. And Key would have no chance.

"Do you really believe that?" I asked. "That it's just a story? That he got lost?"

She stared at me for a moment, arms crossed. Finally, she pursed her lips and gave a tight shake of her head. *No.*

I stood up suddenly, making Buttons squawk. The clip of Maxine was all we'd found online, but I had a feeling I was looking in the wrong place. Foster hadn't said he was the only one—he'd said the others would be just as old as him. If Foster wasn't ready to be brave and help me, there was someone else I could talk to but it wouldn't be easy, for either of us.

Stella spread out her sleeping bag shaped like a shark, with the teeth for a pillow. Great to know I would be waking up to the sight of Stella being consumed by Jaws. I drew the curtains across the window so the neighbors didn't have to witness it.

I wasn't ready to give up on Key. Not yet. Not ever. If it was a twisted ankle—great. If he was lost, I'd never let him forget it. But those search teams could look all they wanted. They would never find anything. Key would just be gone, like Maxine Miller's family.

"Stell." I turned to find Stella willingly climbing into the shark's mouth. "Thanks."

Stella smiled and pulled the teeth up over her shoulders, a truly unsettling image.

I knew I was lucky to have a friend who didn't make me say it, who knew what I wanted to say but couldn't. I was lucky to have a friend like that.

But I used to have two.

FOURTEEN

I'D BEEN SITTING ON THE SOFA LONG ENOUGH to watch the light move across the room like a searchlight. Which is what I needed now—a light as bright as the sun, to find where Key had gone. On any other day, I'd be diddling around on my phone like a normal person. But today, that was the last thing I wanted to do. Social media was now unbearably stupid, all of it. I didn't want to see any hopeful messages from Key's parents. I didn't want to see or feel or know anything. It felt right to be surrounded by silence.

My mother still wasn't home from work, Stella had left, and now I was finally alone. Which wasn't great. Stella and I had spent most of the day searching for more information, but the one clip of Maxine was the only thing that came up. There was still one avenue of possible information open to me, but I'd spent the day finding reasons to put it off.

Beside me, Buttons crouched, content. I'd always wanted a dog. They didn't ask for explanations. Buttons had been my parents' compromise—a furry creature that didn't need to be walked every day. Although Buttons had his own demands—sleeping curled up behind my knees every night, hovering beside my pillow in the morning so he could flop down in my spot the moment I got out of bed, and using feline mind control on me to get a few extra treats. I rubbed my finger behind his ear and was rewarded with a deep rumble that always made the tightness in my shoulders loosen. I loved Buttons in a way I loved few people.

At the thought of his name, he sat up, looked at me for a moment, stretched languidly, and then pointedly turned to look toward the kitchen.

"You're so weird."

But I obeyed and got up. It wasn't a bad idea. The only thing I'd eaten lately was toast this morning and the sandwich and a half Stella had made yesterday, and my body was used to a lot more calories than that in an afternoon. I poured kibble into his dish and got a bowl out for myself. Cereal? I poured in the last of the almond milk and started crunching my way through the bowl of granola, standing at the sink. Looking through the window at the backyard, I spotted Mom's "lawn shoes." That's what she called them, with audible air quotes. They were actually a pair of my old running shoes, discarded once the midsole began to show wear. I usually dropped old shoes in the donation bin at the running store, but this pair mom had rescued and claimed. The grass had tinted them a surprisingly pretty shade of green and the laces were permanently tied for easy on/off. Lawn shoes.

It was a dig at my dad. Or me. Some variation of Mom's complaint that she had to do everything around the house. Which she did. She didn't trust me to do her laundry, and she didn't like the way I cleaned. I felt bad about that, but she said I had school and running, and Dad wasn't around to have the lawn shoes in his face to feel guilty about. Mom hadn't ever mowed the lawn before my dad left. But she hadn't done a lot of things that she did now. She had to. Her situation changed, so she'd changed with it.

I was the same old Avery.

I squinted through the door, and then pulled it open, happy to breathe fresh air. The sun was still up, but the air already felt like night. No one was there, but there was something, a palpable density.

This wasn't a feeling. It was a presence.

"Key?" I whispered, then said louder. "Key?"

A five-second fantasy swirled through my head. Key came striding through the yard, walking straight to me, apologizing all the way. The images blew through my mind like a tornado and were gone.

That's when I spotted something.

I slipped my feet into the lawn shoes and went down the steps. The grass was growing up around the legs of the rickety picnic table where Mom couldn't get the mower close enough, and the table wasn't stable enough to move. One good yank and the whole thing would fold. So it stayed where it was, and the grass grew, and the table looked like it was slowly sinking into the yard.

Halfway there, I slowed and started to creep cautiously. Then stopped. I whirled around, scanning the fence and even up into the trees.

"Key? Key!"

I had been meant to find it. Two years ago, Key's birthday had been approaching fast, and I'd not had a clue as to his "real gift." The joke gift had been easy—Superman knee socks. Because Key loathed Superman. He could go on at length about the many reasons why Superman was unimpressive, if you were clueless enough to ask. And also—socks. Quantifiably the worst gift for any occasion.

But the real gift, that had been a problem. It had to be relatively inexpensive (a.k.a. cheap) because Frank wasn't paying me in doubloons. I was clearing out the storage upstairs at the bookstore when I found the camera. It was old and heavy and perfect.

Frank had sold it to me for the bargain price of one smile. Seriously, he was so corny when he was all hopped up on the bean. It had cost twenty-two dollars to get the thing in working order, and it was the best money I'd ever spent.

Key had flipped when he'd unwrapped it. It had been the best real gift ever.

And now it was sitting on the picnic table. Nothing else: no backpack, no phone, no Key. Just the camera, in the middle of the table, like it had come home.

I stared at it for a moment before picking it up; it was heavier than I remembered. I wrapped both hands around it and brought it close to my heart, closed my eyes, and tried to find him. If the camera was here, where was he?

Nothing.

I opened my eyes and turned the camera over in my hands. The strap was damp and there was a small chip on the bottom corner of the casing that I didn't think had been there before.

Was this evidence? I froze at the thought. I'd picked it up, touched it everywhere; my fingerprints were all over it. I'd love to think that Key had left it out for me to find, but deep down, I knew better. He'd never leave any camera out to get rained on or bake in the sun, especially not this one.

Yet it was here.

It was here. My hands tightened around it like Gollum with the ring.

Who else could have left it here, if not Key? There wasn't anyone else who would know, who would leave *this* camera out for me to find. My brain chugged, working a puzzle with no solution when I became aware of a new chill to the air, an unpleasant dampness I could almost smell, bringing to mind the man I'd seen. The Ragged Man, Maxine had called him. His clothes and hair had undulated like he was underwater. Like he'd sunk to the bottom of the pond a long time ago, but had never quite finished drowning.

My eyes slowly fixed on the shadowy corner of the yard behind the maple tree. I couldn't see anything, yet knew there was something there to be seen, if it wanted. If I wanted to walk over and meet it.

Introduce yourself.

It could explain everything, solve the riddle and lay the mystery to rest. Just twenty feet farther, and I could understand it all.

So close.

No more secrets.

The Ragged Man was there. The only one who knew where Key was, and how to get him back. I hugged the camera close to my chest and took a step.

Backward.

My feet slid around in the stretched-out lawn shoes, but each step was as careful and precise as a tightrope walker's. Five feet from the porch, I turned and ran to the door. I yanked it open and turned back to look.

The Ragged Man stepped out of the shadows, barely visible in the fading light. His long gray hair and coat still flowed unnaturally, but less translucent than before. He stood still, only hair and fabric waving around him in a breeze that wasn't there, his eyes black pits in an ashen face.

Come and see.

Fuck. That.

I slammed the door and locked it, but couldn't stop looking through the window. For a moment, my reflection was superimposed on the glass, and I was both here and there. The trees were nothing but a watery green blur.

The kitchen faucet sputtered and water shot out, sporadically at first, then gushing, scummy and dark, and smelling like rot.

I recoiled, pressing my back against the wall, clasping the camera to my chest, transfixed by the muck rapidly rising in the sink. And when it was full?

It would be free. It would flow over the counter and onto the floor. It would head straight for me. It would spread over my feet and up my legs, until I was submerged in a place I'd never thrash free of. I darted forward, turning the faucet shut.

Outside the window, the Ragged Man's face twisted, the closest to a smile he could get. He took a step back into the shadows and was gone.

I waited. Ten seconds and I'd move. I'd . . . do something.

One thousand one, one thousand two—

Squinting through the glass, I couldn't see him anymore, and couldn't feel him, either. I shivered and grimaced, a bitter taste in my mouth. I leaned against the wall, still holding the camera. The only fingerprints on it, I knew, would be mine and Key's. It was only evidence of something impossible, and I now knew the cops would just lock it up. They already thought they knew what had happened.

At the purr of mom's car outside, tears of relief welled up in my eyes. It wasn't that long ago that I'd believed my mom's presence would drive away the imagined monsters under my bed. Now I had a real monster after me but clung to the thin hope that having someone else there would keep him away. But if I told Mom, would he come after her, too?

I sprinted to my room and dug a nest in the pile of old clothes in the back of the closet. I wasn't going to hand over the camera to a bunch of cops who'd already decided Key had run off and gotten lost after a fight we'd never had. I would keep it safe. Key would want it when he came back.

I placed the camera in the middle and carefully covered it up, put a pile of shoes in front of that, and stepped back to gauge the effect. It looked good, like a natural part of the landscape of the room.

In the bathroom I caught my reflection in the mirror. I looked stunned. Or high. If I could push it a little more toward "tired," I'd be okay. I rubbed my face to bring some color back, rinsed my mouth out to get rid of that bitter taste, downed a full glass of water, flicked off the light, and made it to the kitchen as my mother walked through the front door.

Mom dropped her bag on the dining table and continued into the kitchen, complaining about the road work near the hospital. "Construction season." She shook her head, emptying her lunch bag, her voice just background noise, far away and soothing. While Mom talked, I thought about the camera, about what to do with it. At the very least, I should tell her about this impossible thing that had appeared, but I knew she'd brush it off as a coincidence. I should give it to the police; I'd watched enough *Law & Order* to know that. I also knew it wouldn't help. Key hadn't gone walking through a bad part of town late at night in the big city. He'd gone looking for a place that shouldn't exist. And it seemed like he'd found it.

"What is this?" Mom looked down, her hands braced on either side of the sink.

My stomach lurched as I sprang to my feet, not wanting her anywhere near that. "Don't touch it!" I shoved her away.

Mom stared at me, then slowly raised her hands in surrender. "No kidding. I'm not doing your dishes, missy."

That's all it was—my cereal bowl with bits of granola sitting in the sink. I pressed the heels of both hands over my eyes. I couldn't take much more of this.

"What do you want for dinner?" Mom waved her hand in front of my face, clearly not asking for the first time.

Dinner. Like dinner mattered anymore when anyone I loved could be next on the menu.

"I could grill some chicken and vegetables." She held the fridge door open and mulled the possibilities. "There's rice from Sunday," she said over her shoulder.

I wanted to talk about Key. I wanted to beg for help from the one person on earth I was supposed to be able to count on.

But I couldn't stand to see that blank look on her face that I'd seen on the cops and Key's parents. Were those my choices? Keep it all to myself or be one of the few cursed with knowing the truth? The past few decades must have been hell for Foster, I realized as my mom buzzed around the kitchen, chatting about work.

Why would the decades in front of me be any different?

"Does that sound okay?"

"Sure." I nodded mechanically, having absolutely no idea what I was agreeing to.

"After dinner we'll watch a movie. You'll feel better." Mom reached across the counter and patted my arm. "We can make spicy popcorn, like we used to."

She was trying, and I would let her. I'd sit on the sofa, eat spicy popcorn, and pretend to watch a movie while my mind buzzed with fragments of ideas, anything I could do to find Key. By the time morning came, I'd choose one and go with it. Something was better than nothing.

I let my mom's voice wash over me, willing it to sweep away the one complete thought that went round and round in my head: I was the only chance Key had. If he were coming back, it was up to me to find him.

FIFTEEN

THE PINES TOWERED ABOVE ME, SWAYING AND whispering in a breeze I couldn't feel. They sheltered and protected me. In the meadow, the sun shone bright, but I knew if I stepped out into the grass, the light would turn gray and dirty. There would be no birdsong and no stopping.

Maybe I'd stay in the pines forever, in the stillness and quiet. Or maybe I'd go out into the meadow, and see once and for all what was really in the black water.

I strained to see, but couldn't get a good look. One step into the meadow wouldn't hurt. Just one. There was a disruption in the stillness and I glanced behind. Someone was in the pines with me. Deep in the shadows, I saw the vague outline of someone watching.

"Shé:kon."

"Mreow." Buttons gazed into my eyes and then rested his chin on my chest, his big rumbly purrs vibrating through us both. My thumb stroked the space between his ears and then slid down the back of his neck and traced his spine. I gave his butt a little pat, making his purrs go crackly. I was fine to lie in bed like this, trapped under the cat; his weight and purrs soothing, grounding me in a way I was desperate for. But nothing could stop my mind from spinning off its axis, like a top about to fall.

The dream last night hadn't been terrifying like the other dreams of the black water, but I didn't like it any better. The others, scary as they were, faded after I woke. I could remember the feeling—the fear, the panic—but the content was cloudy and blurred. But this . . . If I closed my eyes now, I could see the figure of a woman standing deep in the pines. I could hear her voice and an answering stirring in my chest, something waking up that wanted to go explore. This dream was different and I wanted to know why.

Which is what had led to me putting on my shoes, downing an energy gel in lieu of breakfast, intending to talk to the only person left who might be able to help me. The purple tank with the cutout back didn't smell too bad, so I put it on and grabbed one of the seemingly hundred pairs of identical black shorts I owned. Dressed but for socks, I sank to my knees in front of the closet and dug through the pile of clothes until the camera sat naked on the floor like a recrimination. Who knew if my mom might get inspired to clean up—she considered my room off-limits, but things were already not going well for me. With my luck, I'd come home to find out she'd cleaned out everything, found the camera, and had questions. It would be safer with me.

I wrapped it in a T-shirt featuring a kaiju menacing a city that Key had given me and let it settle into my backpack, images from last night's dream fighting for brain space with the number of unanswered messages on my phone from Key's parents. They kept updating me on where the search team had been, what they had found, if anything, but I'd only responded to a few. What could I say? The idea that Key's parents would have any faith in small-town, very-pasty-faced law enforcement to find their son was in itself a sign that something very weird was going on in Crook's Falls. I had to act. With the camera safely zipped into my backpack, I shoved my feet into my shoes and pulled the front door open.

Maxine's story had rung true, but she'd been dead longer than I'd been alive, and so she wasn't a super-accessible source of information. I needed to talk to someone who knew about the black water, someone who believed. But what about someone whose mind was different, wasn't capable of being influenced? Minutes ago, I'd been drained of hope but now I was energized, on a mission to try out the only idea I had left. I would visit my ihstá Lily.

I strode down the sidewalk with the camera in my pack, bouncing gently against my back. I buckled the chest strap to keep it steady, not wanting to be reminded of the dark thing that had come calling steps from my back door. I'd waited until my mom was off to work just for some peace of mind that I wasn't leaving her defenseless and alone. Which . . . I myself currently was. The knowledge slowed my steps.

Chirpchirp!

A dropping heart rate meant it was time to move. Everything would be fine, I decided, as I picked up the pace. I would find Key and get him back. How, I wasn't super clear on that yet, but hopefully I'd get some help with that today.

My best thinking happened while running, so walking should be a close second. As long as my body was moving, my brain did its thing without me. I wound through the neighborhood, not really present, letting my eyes skate over the houses and lawns I'd seen a million times. Visualizing a blackboard in my mind, I ruthlessly erased any thought that dared to pop up there in an effort to let the other, smarter me figure out what to do. The sun was out, a breeze blew, but I didn't clock any of it. I was locked in a little room in my head, desperately seeking a way to set things right, to put the most important things in my life back where they belonged. Down the hill and around the bend, and I found myself back where it had all started—the park entrance to the forest. I skidded a little on gravel that had migrated out of the parking lot before stepping onto the grass and stopping completely.

It was full.

Not totally, but getting there. Half of the parking lot was blocked off for the base camp of searchers, filled with a white tent, a huge map of the forest, police cruisers, and people in uniforms of all kinds. The setup itself looked urgent, but the people were standing in groups, chatting like they were at a barbecue. The east side of the lot was packed with kids and adults exiting vehicles loaded with bikes, picnic baskets, and backpacks. Beside a red SUV, a little boy stood with his arms outstretched and his eyes screwed shut as his mother sprayed him with sunscreen. A group of three mountain bikers divided up the contents of a cooler between them. Two shepherds strained at their leashes, pulling their owners toward the trailhead. I stood still, watching it all, a sense of unreality settling over me.

A group of four searchers wearing hi-vis vests were shouldering backpacks and checking radios. At a table under the big white tent, getting himself a coffee—I recognized him even though his back was to me—was the slouching cop from the interview with Key's parents. My feet started moving before I knew it.

I would just—have a word. My jaw and fists clenched. Absolutely polite and totally in control. This was me. I crunched up the gravel to stand so close behind him, he almost spilled his coffee on us both when he turned, startled.

"What's going on?" Not the civil tone I'd planned on, but the sloucher didn't deserve it because obviously I knew the answer.

"Uh . . ." He squinted at me and jettisoned his stir stick, missing the trash can and not batting an eye. "We're continuing to search." He used his coffee to point in the direction of the hi-vis group heading down the path that led to the forest.

"But the park is open." I swept my arm to include every picnicker and hiker at the other end of the lot. "You're letting people in there." My voice was tight and angry and I didn't even care. The sloucher took a long, slow sip of his coffee; slow—that fit him and everything that was going on here.

"We interviewed you." Recognition dawned on his face. "You're the girlfriend."

I didn't need a mirror to know my face was flaming red, remembering the "interview" when *they* had told *me* how things had happened.

"Just stay on the trail and you'll be fine." He waved his hand dismissively. "It's just people that go looking for trouble that get into trouble."

I'd never hit anyone in my life, but oh my God . . . "Key did not go looking for trouble," I snapped.

He blinked like I'd just asked him to do mental math. "Key? Ah. The Rogers kid." He nodded. "Sure, sure. Just a little overly adventurous, maybe."

"So, entrance fees for the park are more important than finding him?" My voice was heading into the danger register.

The sloucher's face hardened, and I saw the real him. Lurking under the "miss" and small-town drawl, this is who he really was. This is who Key's parents were trusting. Had everyone lost their minds?

"This is an active investigation." His smile was tight, liable to snap at any moment. "Lots of professional experience here, because of the forest." He gestured behind us, as if its existence were news to me.

Lots of experience—yeah. Doing half-assed searches for show when you'd already decided what happened and then writing off scores of people who just vanished.

"You have yourself a nice day." Voice low and quiet, looking me dead in the eye and with more interest than I was comfortable with. I'd already woken a scary thing in Crook's Falls. I couldn't afford to provoke another one.

I made a sharp turn on my heel and headed back the way I'd come, into the parking lot without a word. If I turned around, I knew he'd be watching, probably already rehearsing how he'd tell the others that it was no wonder the Rogers kid fought with the girlfriend, bolstering the theory they were taking as fact. Would Key's parents believe that, too?

The idea brought me to a stop facing the wall of trees that rose up and seemed to go on forever. The thought of going there made me shiver. I didn't want to and none of the people streaming past me should be allowed to go in there, unaware and unprotected.

I stepped aside to let a couple with a dog and a stroller pass. None of these people knew who Key was or what was waiting out there in the trees, watching them. A group of Nordic walkers passed by, chattering, sticks clacking on the gravel path. There were so many people. If I had two brain cells left, I'd get back on the sidewalk right now and keep going; I had someplace else to be. I should just stick to the plan.

And I actually did. I turned but didn't go. I couldn't. Key was out there and the only people looking for him was a search team who didn't really believe they were actually going to find him. No one was truly looking for him; there was just me now, standing on the path and staring at the forest. It was a reflection of the dreams, everything backward. In my dreams, I desperately tried to stay away from the black water.

But.

Maybe the new dream was right. Key was in there somewhere. If nothing else—and this concept floated into my mind consciously for the first time—this was the last place he'd been. There were so many people in there walking the trails, all easier pickings for the black water than me. We were a herd, but I was the strongest member, not the weakest. Because I knew the black water's tricks. Some, anyway.

My heart beat a little faster, from excitement and not fear for once. I squinted at the ground, trying to hold on to the kernel of the new plan unfolding in my mind. There were so many people on the trails. If the black water wanted to take someone, let it try. Let it. I'd been going to talk to Lily, but maybe this was the way to find Key; my feet, already moving, agreed. Maybe Foster and his granny were way off course. Go in deeper, flood it with people and distract it. Do the exact opposite of what the black water was expecting. Flush the Ragged Man out of the forest and force him to show himself. Do the opposite of what I was best at—instead of running away from things, I would run *to* the black water.

Chchchirp!

My watch, now asking if I wanted to end my walk. I tapped it sharply. No, I did not. I bit my lip and started off at a trot down the main loop. The rational part of me hoped I wouldn't find anything weird or creepy. The part of me missing Key like I was missing part of myself hoped I would. If it happened, if something dark and dripping was waiting for me in the trees, well—that was a problem for future me.

For the number of cars in the lot, I'd expected to find more people on the trail. There were a lot of places to be in the park, though. The fish pond, the turtle pond, a picnic barbecue area—the trails through the forest were just part of it.

The lack of traffic on the main loop would have been good for a run but now made me feel uneasy, unprotected. It wasn't logical because I couldn't count on any of the hikers, dog walkers, or people pushing strollers to protect me; I knew that. It was just human nature to feel safe in the middle of the herd, especially when you were faster than the others. Even from a danger the herd would never see coming.

I was relieved to note that the forest itself didn't bother me. The breezy green quiet was still soothing and the trees still felt like friends. I'd been afraid that I would be afraid, that being in the forest would always be associated in my mind with the fear of the black water. I'd hate to have to give up the forest, once I had Key back and life was normal again.

I let out a long, slow breath, looking up. It would be. I was going to make sure of that. Sunlight filtered through the leaves. No darkness here. Just quiet green, a warm breeze, and the soft crunch of my shoes on the trail. It felt welcoming. Key was here somewhere, and even if I didn't know quite where, exactly, the fact that he was near was kind of comforting.

I tried to keep my pace up without mowing down any pedestrians or causing a bike wreck. I hadn't meant to run, but once I got going, it was hard to stop, even wearing the backpack. My body did its thing, and my mind clicked over to autopilot. Almost.

Keep track of the sun—the trail runner's commandment.

Watch out for monsters—my new personal amendment.

Because that's how this had all started.

The big hill came into view around the bend, signaling the farthest point of the loop. Everything after this would be in the direction of the parking lot. The hill wasn't generally my favorite part of the loop, but today I was glad to see it. While I wasn't afraid of the forest, there was definitely a new feeling—an expectant hush, a tension that hadn't been there before, and the camera was oddly heavy on my back.

Key was here somewhere.

I slowed and then stopped. Nothing seemed willing to show itself to me, so I would have to look.

Focus.

I closed my eyes and took in a deep breath, air so clean and fresh I could taste the green. I released it so gently I could barely feel the air pass over my lips.

Focus.

I shook out my hands, trying to relax. Another slow breath in. The sun came through the leaves, on the back of my neck, a kaleidoscope of warmth. A jumble of thoughts swirled through my mind—my mom, Stella, Key's parents worrying—and Key, smiling and warm, eyes crinkled at the corners. This is where I wanted to go. I willed the camera to find its owner.

Another breath, this one a little more tense than the last.

The meadow had been sunny, full of long, flowing grass surrounding a pond that absorbed the rays of the sun. I pictured it, barely aware of the fresh smell of the forest suddenly undercut by something damp and rotting. I had been on the main trail and seen—

My eyes snapped open, and I whirled around to my left. This way.

It was this way. I sped up, breaking into a trot because I knew it was just down here. Over the hill and around the bend, and I'd find the opening—no, wait.

I slowed and stopped. I turned a slow 360, suddenly recognizing nothing. It had been so clear just a moment ago. Over the hill . . . I scuffed my foot in the dirt, frustrated. Over the hill . . .

No. Not over the hill. Back the other way. Down, down into the dell. Down toward the grove of ferns that thrived in the lowest part of the trail system, where the moisture settled and the air was cool no matter the time of day.

Yes. Turning on my heel, certain now, I went back the way I'd come, letting gravity pull me out of a trot and into a run. The trail would open ahead, I'd slip through and find the black water again. Find Key. The breeze cooled the sweat along my hairline, reminding me that the sun wouldn't stay up forever. I had to find the black water before it got dark. No good could come out of traipsing through the forest at night.

Luckily, I didn't have far to go. At the bottom of the hill, I could feel it pull me on—the cord that bound Key and me together stretched and tightened, like a big fish on a line.

I slowed once again, resumed walking, afraid that each footstep might be one too far. It was like crossing a minefield and *wanting* an explosion. Another step on and I stopped. It was gone. I could no longer feel the pull, and I was standing on a part of the trail I didn't even usually run. So how . . . ?

Reality slammed in like a fist to the center of my chest.

It wasn't Key leading me; it was the black water yanking my chain. *This way! No, over here!* It was watching me run around in circles like an idiot and laughing. The black water was playing with me. I clenched my jaw and stared into the ferns huddled together on the forest floor.

You only find it if it wants you.

Not if you want it.

The silver turtle was warm against my skin, just under the notch in my collarbone. I held it between my fingers, rubbing absently, at a loss for where to go next. Deep steady breaths and I closed my eyes.

Where?

And when I opened my eyes, I knew, clear and certain this time: a memory, not a feeling. Back the way I came, off the main loop and onto the Headwaters trail, at a slow trot, then faster. I was floating, barely aware of the turns I was making, my vision only clear on the path right in front of me. The green on either side of me pressed in closer and tighter, like a crowd that wanted to get a good look at me as I passed.

And then I stopped.

There was no gradual transition. One minute I was thrashing my way through the brush, and then the pines rose up in front of me like a black-green wall, a fortress I should never have breached. I craned my head back and stood for a moment, looking up but unable to see the tops of the giant trees. On either side of me, saplings and bushes shivered in a breeze that I couldn't feel.

The first time, everything had been hazy, but this point, I remembered. I remembered the pines and I knew what would lie beyond, which made me hesitate—did I really want to go in there after all? The leaves in the brush stilled, and the whole forest went quiet, watchful, waiting to see what I would do.

This wasn't like the first time I'd found this place—the little voice had clouded my mind and steered me here—but this time, I'd found my way myself, a different force pushing me on; my own motivation. I wiped my damp hands down the sides of my shorts, eyes fixed on the shadowy pine interior. This might be a massive mistake; I might be about to make things immeasurably worse. But there was no little voice calling to me this time, blurring my thoughts; the black water didn't want me here now.

Good.

One step into the pines and the air instantly wrapped around me like a blanket, heavy but cool, every breath leaving sweetness on my tongue, like this was a protected area. There was no breeze here, no unseen creatures scurrying, but I felt safe. Running here seemed wrong, disrespectful, so I walked, winding my way between tree trunks too big to wrap my arms around. Each footstep sounded oddly muffled, like the ground under the pine needles was hollow. I imagined a mirror version of the pine cathedral, a cavern of roots where the air smelled of damp and earth; where something massive had been hunched in the dark, guarding this place for a very long time.

The pine needles gave way to scrubby grass, each sleek green blade lengthening until I was in the meadow proper. The heat of the sun pressed down on me, sending a trickle of sweat down my neck and along my spine. This, too, I remembered: the ring of tiny grass-covered mounds and beyond that, the pond, perfectly black and perfectly still, giving the impression that I'd stumbled onto something sleeping, like I'd crept up to a wild animal napping but liable to wake at any moment.

Using my foot, I lifted the long strands of grass, revealing a hard mound of earth the size of a baseball—natural or created? I'd never seen anything like it. There were hundreds of the little mounds that I couldn't help but think of as tiny graves, uniform, encircling the pond like a moat. Or a trap.

I couldn't think about this now, not the tiny graves or the unnatural stillness around me. I picked my way through the mounds with exquisite care, right up to the edge of the water, where I'd been the first time, where I'd crouched and seen my reflection that wasn't me.

So, what would be a really bad idea? I crouched down again and, ignoring the tremor in my fingers, peered over the edge and down into the black water.

It was definitely me—my ponytail hanging to one side of my neck, the silver turtle dangling like bait, the sun in the sky and the wide-eyed look of apprehension on my face. I stared into my own eyes until I had to blink, but my reflection blinked with me; it didn't change. I watched the same bead of sweat that I felt tracing down my cheek slip down my reflection's, the water impossibly still, like a mirror. But beyond that, the water gave up very little. Even this close to the edge, if I were foolish enough to step in, I couldn't tell if

I would wade slowly into deeper water, or plunge in over my head immediately. The pond was murky and opaque, offering only the vaguest impressions, barely perceptible shapes, but there was . . . something moving. My breath caught and I leaned forward, my face closer to the water than I was comfortable with, but there was something down there and I had to see. The meadow around me disappeared; tunnel vision took me down, let me see a shadow gliding in the water. Down deep, something huge but indistinct soared like a dark whale. I frowned, because something that big couldn't possibly fit. I was looking into an ocean, not a pond. The leviathan moved past the reflected sun behind me, and a sudden chill, a darkening of the sky, made me turn my head to check over my shoulder, making sure the darkness was on that side, not this. The sky on my side was still bright blue—it hadn't dimmed and there was no shadowy giant here. Which should have reassured me and should have slowed my pulse. I raised my hand to my throat, feeling the thump of my heart, each beat traveling through the silver turtle and into my fingertips.

And then I wasn't alone.

Still grasping the turtle, I froze, suddenly convinced that I wasn't the only sentient thing in the meadow.

I slowly rose to my feet, then stood like I was made of marble, eyes locked on the water, unwilling to look away. When I had first started running the trails, Mom warned me about bears—don't run, move slowly and quietly. It's faster and bigger than you. I swallowed hard, my throat gone tight and narrow. What I wouldn't give to be facing a bear right now. I sent one cautious foot back, transferring my weight carefully, far slower than my pounding pulse wanted to go. Another step back and the mound under my foot moved ever so slightly, shifting like something getting ready to spring. I bit my lip, imagining what could be under those mounds, buried but not dead.

Stay.

I shouldn't have gotten so close to it, leaning over with my face inches away. I'd wanted to look, strained my eyes to see. The thought hadn't occurred to me that I wasn't the only one watching.

On my left, something whooshed by, a dark, filmy wisp. My heart was racing, skin cold. Another on my right. Another step back, my ankle threatening to turn. I reined in the urge to just *go*, but only barely.

Wouldn't want to break an ankle here, a voice in my head whispered.

No, I wouldn't. Another achingly cautious step back and then I froze, wide-eyed as a big bubble burst on the surface of the water, heralding the arrival of something huge.

I was getting out of there, no matter what. Coming here was my latest terrible mistake. Each step and rebalance was costing me time—but wasn't that the point of the moat? Another step back and I almost went down. I kept my eyes on the *pop!* from the center of the pond. A soft touch against my ankle, a whisker brushing skin.

Popppp! Bubbles came faster now, bigger and closer to the surface.

I held my arms out from my sides to balance, but I had to take my eyes off the pond to be sure of my footing. I had to look down and when I did, my mind seared white and went blank.

The long grass on the mounds was moving, slithering like a million needle-thin snakes, waving and swaying as if they were moving with a current. Long green strands lifted and rose, sending out tendrils in search of something to wind around and hold fast.

The caution I'd held onto shattered; I turned my back on the pond and dug in with my right foot, pushing off against the mounds that were now squirming to life beneath me.

I let the overwhelming urge to get back to the pines pull me, reel me in until I scrambled onto the needles, grabbed on to the nearest tree, and swung around to hide behind it, peeking out to see if anything had followed. Each breath was a ragged burn in my chest, loud and unnatural in the shady silence. From here, the mounds weren't moving; the pond looked placid and still with nothing emerging. But what I saw didn't comfort me; it didn't mean I was safe. The black water was everywhere, all through town and in people's heads.

In mine.

I sank to the ground, panting, feeling the tree against my back press against me with every breath, like a mother comforting a crying child.

There, there.

The cool air that had been refreshing now chilled the sweat on my skin, making me shiver. I would never forgive myself, as long as the black water had Key. It would eat away at me until there was nothing left. I looked into the future and saw a lonely life ahead of me, sleepless nights wracked with nightmares and guilt that would only end when the black water tired of me and found a new toy.

Foster may have accepted that life, but I wouldn't. It wasn't over. I needed to stop the black water from taking anyone else *and* get Key back. Just because no one had returned before didn't mean it couldn't be done. There had to be a way, and I was going to find it.

I set off the way I'd come, through the pines hoping I'd be able to find my way back to the main trail. The sun was high in the sky—I had plenty of time, and at some point, my GPS would wake up. But how to return to the trail wasn't the question that rolled over and over in my mind as I ran through the brush on the narrow deer trail.

You only find it if it wants you.

But I had found the black water on my own. I didn't know why I was different, but I knew I needed to get back to my original plan and talk to someone else, someone wiser, who was different, too.

SIXTEEN

ONCE I WAS SAFELY ON THE MAIN LOOP, I RAN flat out, into the parking lot, past the big white tent, skidding a little on the gravel, and down to the sidewalk. I didn't think, barely breathed, totally forgot about the camera snug in my pack. I shouldn't have let myself get sidetracked, and what if the black water had sucked me in, too? Lily's retirement home was an easy jog from the park; halfway there and I had mentally rehearsed exactly how I'd broach the subject, necessary preparation because I didn't want to upset Lily. Talking about the forest at dinner last week had obviously disturbed her. But, bottom line—I needed help. Key needed help, the Ragged Man was taking people who would never see him coming, and I was certain that Lily knew something about the black water. It might be locked away in the tangled labyrinth of her mind, but I had to tease it out. There really wasn't any other choice. As I waited for the light to change on Cross Avenue, a red Mini pulled up smoothly beside me.

"Get in," Stella called through the window, like she'd been waiting for me.

I hesitated, but only for an instant. It had been hard enough leaving my mom alone with that thing roaming town, and my mom was tough. Besides, I'd tried to do things on my own. And look where it had gotten me so far.

I leaned down to the open window. "Where're you headed?" Because right now, Stella should be at pottery class or drum lessons— she was always learning how to do something new.

"I'm going wherever you're going," Stella said with a satisfied nod, checking the rearview mirror.

"Stell—"

"Ave." Stella's long pale fingers tapped on the steering wheel, nails always short and unpolished. "I know you and Key are . . . whatever. I'm happy to be a third wheel."

"Stell! You're not."

Stella waved away my words like they were so much fluff and not bearing the truth we both knew they did. "My point is"—she turned to fix me with dark blue eyes—"I'm pretty invested in this, too." The barest frown drew her eyebrows together. "Have you noticed that people aren't really worried?"

I waited, my body taut as a wire.

"Like, everybody's saying that Jackie ran off, that lady with the dog had a boyfriend somewhere—nobody's *worried*. They're not going to find anyone if they think they already know what happened."

I nodded, unable to tell her that even Key's parents believed the rumors and that I was unspeakably relieved that for whatever reason, she didn't.

"So." Stella threw the car in gear. "It's up to us to actually do something. He's not gone." The last few words came out unsteadily. "He can't be."

I bit my lip, hesitant to drag Stella any further into this than she already was. But like she said, I wasn't the only one worried about Key. And sticking together had to be better than being alone. How many times had the three of us yelled at the screen when the group split up to explore the haunted house?

"Come on, let's go." Stella lowered her window the rest of the way, impatient even though she didn't know where we were going.

I opened the door and folded myself into the passenger seat with a sigh, like *I* was doing *her* a favor.

"So where are we going?" Stella patted my hand and left hers there, cool and slight, a paler version of mine.

We. One minute I was fine—tense, worried out of my freaking mind, but fine—and the next, at that one syllable, my throat tightened and tears welled up.

I folded my other hand over hers, pressing my lips together to stop whatever sounds wanted to spill out, remembering the last time I'd held hands with someone, and how that had worked out. Knowing me as she did, Stella turned to look at the traffic passing us, giving me a moment. I cleared my throat and pulled myself together.

"I was on my way to my ihstá." I extracted my hands from hers, like I could infect Stella.

One more check over her shoulder and Stella put the Mini into gear and pulled out onto the street. "I love her. She's such a lady."

I slouched in the passenger seat, pressing my hands between my knees. If Stella was with me, that was something. I'd run plenty of races that initially seemed hopeless. Rain, cold, muddy trails—none of it had stopped me. Races are long and if you give up too soon, failure is guaranteed, but I'd never been a quitter—I'd endured a lot of self-doubt and discomfort, and that was when I was competing for a medal or ribbon. The prize was much bigger now.

"Turn right up here." I pointed at the next intersection and turned back to the window. Running had made me stubborn, and that's what was going to get Key back.

We took Lewis Drive, which wound through a nice older residential part of town. Mostly young families that somehow still had money for renovations lived here. Stella drove with one hand on the wheel, her left arm resting on the open window, hot air rushing in and freeing more and more strands of her already unruly hair. Key was a careful, responsible driver, always checking the blind spots before making turns. Stella drove with the faith she lived by—other drivers would stop in time, her tires would grip the road in any weather, and traffic would part to let her merge. It was a superpower she'd been born with—the ability to move through the world like it was made for her—that she never even noticed.

People like me noticed; people like me who overthought every word, every moment—we weren't born with the advantages Stella had.

Stella hadn't been corrupted by her superpower because she didn't know it existed. I wasn't sure how she'd actually *use* her power, except that she'd use it for good, but Key would give her a superhero name.

My throat tightened. I missed him so much, and now I had to deal with the fact that he might not be the only person the black water was going to take from me. The stress sometimes felt like it was going to rip me open, but I held my lip between my teeth and kept my face turned to the window.

The Mini was passing Falls Park, a playground generally full of parents on benches sipping coffee while their kids threw sand at each other or chased each other up, down, and around the play structure endlessly.

Stella slowed for a speed bump, and I clocked the scene. The people in the park looked happy. It was just another day for them—walking, drinking, talking, playing. They were living, like everything was normal. At the edge of the sandpit, one little girl stood alone, watching the others.

I straightened up, squinting out the window. As if she could feel the weight of my gaze, the little girl slowly turned toward the road and my blood went cold. It was her. The girl I'd seen downtown. Everything about her was the same tepid color, like weak tea, stained. The eyelet trim of her dress hung free from the hem in the back, the edges of the collar were frayed. She walked like something being remotely operated, something hastily constructed to resemble a child. A lure. Not perfect, just close enough to get the fish to bite. A vague suggestion of a face.

Unfinished.

Icy cold flooded my body. It was the girl I'd seen, but she had changed. There was nothing gauzy or transparent about her now. She looked just as solid, just as real, as anyone else in the park. The girl tracked the movement of the car with her head and bent her crude mouth into a smile. A white woman passed right by her, offering a hat to her child, somehow not seeing the girl with no eyes. As she drew near, the woman's face went slack, her eyes skipping over the monster two feet away, seeing only what the black water wanted her to see. As Stella's Mini cleared the park, I stuck my head out the window and looked back. The girl was sedately making her way toward a lone boy twisting on a swing.

"Did you see that?"

Stella turned to me.

"See what?"

Clearly, she hadn't. A girl with no eyes, that's kind of something you remember. I, however, was leaning forward, fingers gripping the dashboard, breathing like I'd been sprinting. "There! In the park. The girl . . ." The girl who shouldn't be here. The thing that looks like a girl. Was I the only one who could see her?

Stella frowned.

I tapped her arm. "Faster."

By the time we got to Lily's retirement home and into the elevator with Stella solid and loyal beside me, I knew what I would say to Lily. I just didn't know if she'd be able to respond.

After my signature *knock, knock, knockknock*, I opened the door to find Lily in her favorite chair as usual, sitting by the big window with a view of the willow trees beside a spotless round glass-topped table, just big enough for two people to eat. Lily's tiny apartment—one room opening to a kitchenette tucked in the corner—was decorated in soft greens and yellows, framed pictures on the walls with a large, ornate mirror in the center.

"Avery! Shé:kon!" Lily threw up her hands, dropping the blanket she was knitting and the needles attached to it as she half rose from her chair to greet me. "And . . ."

"Stella!" Stella beamed.

I quickly put down my backpack of secrets, under the wall mirror by the door, stepped out of my shoes, and crossed the little room to spare Lily the trouble of getting up.

"Hi, Ihstá." Bending down, I wrapped my arms around her,

careful not to crush this woman made of bones and spirit. I wished I could hold on tight, burying my face in her lilac-scented hair the way I had as a child. I wished she could be the person she used to be because I really needed her now. Tears rose in my eyes, twice in the last ten minutes—who was I? In a rare moment of tact, Stella sat down on the sofa against the wall next to us and picked up a gardening magazine from the glass-topped coffee table, pretending to be interested.

As I straightened up, Lily brushed her finger against the silver turtle dangling between us, the softest of smiles telling me that today at least, she still recognized it and remembered what it meant to us.

I moved the other chair closer to her, sat down, and took her weightless hand in mine, took one deep breath and said the words I'd rehearsed in the car, before I lost my nerve. "I wanted to ask you about the pond I found. In the forest."

Lily gently drew her hand out of mine, picked up the blanket and needles, and drew a length of yarn from the skein beside her. She held up the blanket, recognized the pattern, and started knitting. "Pond?"

The only sounds in the apartment were the soft clack of the needles, Stella flipping pages, and my heart playing counterpoint. "The black water," I prompted softly, unsure of the effect the words would have.

The steady rhythm of the needles faltered for an instant, then Lily shook her head, frowning at an errant stitch. "Well, that's just . . ." The needles picked up speed. "You shouldn't think about that." Lily kept knitting faster and faster, dropping stitches and not noticing.

"Ihstá, what is it? What's out there?"

"Nothing that can hurt you." She nodded firmly and the needles finally stilled.

I sat back in the chair like I'd been pushed. Nothing that could hurt *me*? But what about everyone else?

Lily picked up the blanket, squinting at the holes that had appeared like she'd never seen them before. "Tsk," she clucked. "Look at that." She pulled the yarn, ripping stitches back far enough to correct her mistakes. "Tea?" She looked up, smiling brightly.

"Sure. I can make us some tea." I filled the kettle in the kitchenette and turned it on, aware of everything I was doing but feeling slightly out of sync with my own body.

"I'd always bring tea fishing with Daddy." Lily smiled down at the yarn passing through her fingers, the mention of tea an off-ramp to another thought.

"One day we were out on the water, fishing for trout, and something took my line."

I placed a tea bag in each cup and put the box back in the cupboard. Stella started at the front of the magazine again.

"I couldn't see what had bitten," Lily continued, telling her story like a prayer. "The water was deep and muddy. But it was strong, jerking at the bait so hard our little boat rocked. I asked Daddy to take the rod, but he said it was mine, so I held on." She frowned, staring at nothing, back in the moment. "That's what it's like. Something from the deep rising and wrapping around your ankle, holding you fast and yanking you under." She snatched a fistful of air, knuckles gone white.

I froze, a chill creeping over me. Lily had fallen silent, but I needed to hear the rest before she forgot the story she was telling.

"What happened?" I whispered, turning to her.

Lily pulled more yarn before continuing. "Daddy cut the line and let it go. Whatever it was swam off, and our boat settled."

Let it go. The advice Foster had given me.

Lily had told me tons of stories throughout my life, but I never thought of them as anything other than stories. Now I had the feeling that it wasn't just a random memory that had popped into her head. Lily—the real Lily—was trying to tell me something in the only way she could. I hadn't thought I needed her stories, and now they were all I had.

"What if you don't want to cut the line?" I breathed. "What if you can't?" Because I didn't think I could let that thing take Key and just swim away. The soft gurgle of the kettle sharpened and turned shrill.

Lily's needles stilled and she turned her watery eyes on me, expressionless. "You'll fall," she said flatly. "You'll fall down into the water."

Like my dreams. Like Sky Woman.

"He should have known that," she said, pursing her lips and frowning down at her hands. "Maxine told him a hundred times."

Maxine.

What? Stella mouthed from the sofa.

Lily's head snapped up at the whistle of the kettle.

"Are you making tea? How about a biscuit?" Her eyes lit up at the thought and she was the Lily I knew again. Whatever she'd been about to say sank down and out of sight.

I gave her my best "everything's fine" smile and turned back to the kettle, suddenly forgetting how to make tea. "Sure."

Stella silently appeared beside me. "I've got this," she murmured, a small, sympathetic smile revealing the dimple in her right cheek.

Maybe I'd been wrong about Lily's mind being immune to the black water. But where else did I have to turn? I watched her resume her knitting, a beam of sunlight illuminating her hair like an angel's. It had been a long shot—whatever she did know might still be in her mind somewhere but she was resistant to letting it out. Who could I turn to now? Stella didn't seem to have fallen under the black water's spell, but she had no actual information. Anxiety thrummed in my chest. How much time did I have to figure this out? Clinks of cups and the sound of water flowing behind me as Stella poured the tea were punctuated by the ticking clock and the clack of Lily's needles. I gripped the edge of the counter and closed my eyes. It was all so quiet, so hypnotic; I was so turned in toward myself, pondering my next move, that I jumped at the knock on the door.

SEVENTEEN

FOR A MOMENT, NEITHER OF US COULD THINK of anything to say.

"Uh . . . shé:kon." Foster rubbed at the back of his neck.

What. My hand on the door was the only reason I was still standing. My mind didn't know what to do with what my eyes were seeing, like I was looking at a horse wearing pants.

"I just came to . . ." He raised a small bouquet of white daisies and gestured toward Lily in explanation.

Foster knew my ihstá.

While my mind was still spinning its wheels, Stella popped her head around the edge of the kitchen cupboard.

"Oh! I'll grab another cup." As if Foster turning up was totally expected.

"Uncle." Still looking for words and feeling numb, I moved aside and Foster stepped awkwardly around me, waving to Lily.

"Shé:kon."

"Foster!" Lily put her knitting in the basket on the floor beside her. "So many visitors today. I'm so happy!"

And she did look it. Foster sat down in the chair I'd vacated; Lily reached over and took his hand, which sent my eyebrows up just as far as they could go.

Foster knew my ihstá pretty well. Would the surprises never stop?

"Oh, aren't these pretty!" She raised the daisies to her face and turned them toward the sunlight streaming in the window.

"Daisies for a Lily?" Stella set down a tray with four teacups on the coffee table, scrunching her nose at the obvious missed opportunity.

"You know how much lilies cost?" Foster groused.

Lily smiled at him, a small, secret smile I hadn't seen in a long time. "It's an old joke," she told Stella demurely.

What? Jaw-dropping implication right there.

With my brain threatening to go offline for good, I dropped onto the sofa, accepting the tea Stella put in my hands. I didn't even like tea, and here I was, a cup of tea in my hands for the second time this week.

With people who were hiding things.

Lily was my ihstá, but it was Stella who'd made the tea and brought out the plate of cookies like Lily was hers, enviably comfortable everywhere she went. Foster looked up at Stella as she passed to set the cookies on the table and smiled fondly. Another fan for Stella. Everybody loved Stella. Not everybody loved me—just a few and none I could afford to lose. The silence that ensued was excruciatingly awkward, but I let the tea burn my hands through the cup, biting the inside of my lip and feeling Stella's gaze beside me. If he didn't say anything, I would. This was my day of Saying Things.

In four.

Three.

Two.

"I didn't realize you already had company." Foster's chuckle was more uncomfortable than amused.

"Oh yes. My Avery." Lily's eyes shone with a dreamy quality whenever she looked at me; that much had never changed. "You'll help my Avery, won't you?"

Foster's head snapped up, and our eyes met.

Lily had always been my champion, always stood up for me and helped in any way she could. And even now that she wasn't able, she still found a way.

"Oh." Foster tried to set his cup down on the table. "Lil—"

"I would." Lily crunched a biscuit. "But, you know." She smiled sweetly at him, but there was something else underneath, something harder.

"She already found me." Foster sipped his tea, clearly stalling.

"She's in trouble," Lily murmured to her cup, barely audible. This was not the drifting, dreamy Lily I'd known for the last few years. This version of my ihstá was a throwback to a fiercer, more focused Lily. It was comforting, really, to know she was still in there somewhere.

Foster closed his eyes for a long moment, and I waited.

"It always goes the same. First"—Foster held up one finger—"one of us wakes it."

"Me." This much I knew. But did I really count as "one of us"?

"Then"—another finger—"he shows up."

"The Ragged Man." Stella nodded.

"Next"—a trio of fingers—"he takes people."

"Key," I breathed. He'd been taken—but where?

Foster clasped his hands together between his knees. Lily turned her face to the sunlight streaming in the window and stared into it. Wherever the black water wanted to send us, Key was already there.

Foster shifted in his chair and cleared his throat. "The last time he was here, we cornered him and burned him till there was nothing but bones."

"Um." Stella spoke around shortbread. "How can you burn a ghost? Ghosts don't have bones."

"He's not a ghost. And he will have bones if he stays long enough." Foster shuddered. "He's new every time. It all repeats—including him. At first, they're like ghosts, not quite real." Foster nodded to Stella, wiping one hand across his brow like the room was suddenly hot. "The—" Foster's voice dropped, as if he were loath to speak the last word. "Unfinished. The more that come through, the stronger, the more solid they all get."

Everyone went silent, even Stella.

I jumped up to retrieve my backpack. "He brought me this," I pointed out, pulling the camera from my bag. "He's solid enough to pick it up. Look." I opened the viewfinder, but when I turned it on, it just showed me the floor.

"Here." Stella gestured for the camera, brushing crumbs from her hands. I handed it over, with just an instant of hesitation. It would be covered with prints now, but I was fine with that. As evidence, it had been worthless from the beginning.

"The card's almost empty," Stella mused, clicking through the menu I hadn't been able to access. "Three images." She leaned forward, holding the camera out so that Foster and I could see it at once.

One. A single cloud against the backdrop of a brilliant blue sky. It billowed up like a tower, but it was . . . a cloud. Key must have seen some shape in it, but it was just a cloud to me and he wasn't here to help me see it as anything else. I bit my lip and Stella clicked again.

Two. Hands—one resting on a tabletop, one palm up, caught mid-gesture. My hands. The beige-and-white-flecked coffee shop table. What had I been saying? I didn't remember Key taking this photo, but he was always snapping away; over time it had just become background noise to me. It wasn't a spectacular image, not to me, but he'd seen a reason to save it.

Three. A fist clenched around my heart at the same moment Foster gave a quiet gasp. This image I knew, and apparently, so did Foster. I reached out, hands gone cold and clammy, to take the camera from Stella, Foster and I transfixed, the only ones who knew what the image meant.

Taken from the ground with the camera pointed straight up. Pine trees, green-black and massive, spiraling up to a tiny point of light breaking through the treetops.

Over the camera trembling in my hands, Foster met my eyes. The pine cathedral. I'd been there, and from the tight look on his face, so had Foster.

And Key.

Lily's needles clacked away again, faster than before. Stella glanced from me to Foster, trying to parse what was going on. "So this . . ."

"Ragged Man." Foster and I quietly supplied in unison.

"He brought this to you."

I shut the camera off, half wishing I'd never turned it on. My fears weren't fears anymore; they were fact.

"But why would he bring it?" Stella nodded at the camera. I cradled it on my lap and waited for Foster to say something, because I sure didn't know the answer.

Foster's hands twisted in his lap. "He has a sense of humor," he muttered finally.

I wasn't the only one who didn't know what to say; the only sound in the room was Lily's needles working like she'd forgotten about us or was intentionally not listening. So the Ragged Man would take others. My next breath in was long and unsteady.

"Hmm. But why burn them? The bones?" Stella parked her chin in her hands.

Foster shrugged like it was obvious. "Fire, it's transformative. We send prayers up to Creator in the smoke. This is just a little different. Like return to sender."

I had only the vaguest idea of what he meant, but wanted to get to the important part: what I needed to do.

I narrowed my eyes. "How did you do that—get him to sit still long enough to burn?" Because it seemed unlikely for a demon-thing like the Ragged Man to just oblige while somebody torched him.

Foster glanced at Lily, then turned his face to the floor. "We had bait." A barely audible whisper loaded with regret.

Bait. My heart clenched into a tight, hard fist.

Lily placidly pulled more yarn like we were discussing the weather.

Foster's hands twisted in his lap. "We didn't quite finish. If my granny had been here, maybe it would've turned out better," he murmured. "We were just so frantic." He looked up at Lily, who stopped knitting to draw a single daisy from the bouquet and twirled it slowly between her fingers as if she were alone in the room. "We got distracted. It was hard and we thought it was enough, that it would keep the black water asleep. I always thought someone else would come along someday, braver, better than me, and do things properly," Foster said, an apology, his words tumbling over each other. "Things were okay for a long time, so we thought it was enough."

"You knew it would happen again eventually, though, Uncle." I clenched my fists but kept my voice even. "So why not tell people? Warn them?"

Foster snorted. "And say what? Everyone knows the story. You." He jabbbed an accusing finger at me. "You talked to the cops—never, ever talk to cops, by the way—and did they believe what you had to say? What do your friend's parents believe?"

He had a point.

"It's not stupid." Foster tapped his temple. "It pulls the wool over their eyes to keep them placid and passive. Doesn't like the food getting riled up." He stopped short, lost in thought.

"But we're riled up," I reminded him.

"We woke it," he whispered, leaning forward, tapping his chest like I was failing to understand something painfully obvious.

Stella raised her hand. "Uh, I didn't. So . . ."

"You're in the circle." Foster dismissed that technicality with a flap of his hand. "You're connected to her." He waved at me. "There's always a circle of the same generation."

Every word from Foster's mouth just added to the swirling storm of impossible information in my head. None of it made any sense, and the urge to curl up in a ball and cry was strong. Foster was finally coming clean, telling me everything. So why was one little detail itching in my mind?

"Uncle, you keep saying 'we.'"

The flower in Lily's hand stopped turning.

Eyes scanning the rug as if help lay there, Foster licked his lips and nodded slowly. "Me. And Frank."

"Frank?" Which explained his weirdness, but it hurt, to know that Frank had chosen not to tell me anything even when Key was missing.

"Don't hold it against him," Foster soothed. "He's just worried about you. Doesn't want you to end up like me."

"Okay." I let out a long breath, shoving my new feelings about Frank into the growing pile of stuff I'd have to deal with later. "So you and Frank—"

Foster's eyes found mine, his voice barely audible. "And your ihstá."

Lily.

Bait.

I wasn't sure my heart would beat again. My sweet ihstá. I'd been worried about the black water taking the people I loved.

Maybe it already had.

Lily looked up and caught my eye, her smile a secret code for all the love her heart had ever held, mine forever.

"There's always a circle," Foster said numbly. "Last time it was me and Frank and . . ." He gestured weakly to Lily.

"So I'm . . . Frank?" Stella asked. "Is that why I know Jackie didn't run off?"

"Akhsótha warned us." Foster drew one hand down over his face, ignoring the question, lost in regret. "So many times."

"Sorry." Stella raised her hand "Akhsótha?"

"His granny," I supplied. "Maxine, right?"

Foster smiled at the name, but it was thin. "How do you know about her?"

"We found a video clip online." Stella pulled out her phone. "I can show—"

But Foster was way ahead of us, nodding and rubbing his chin. "I remember when they made that. Be nice to hear her voice again."

"You can sit here, Ihstá." I patted the sofa. "I'll sit on the floor." I stood just as Foster dropped onto the sofa where I'd been.

"Oh, my knees are mouthy today, dear." Lily smiled gently, inspecting her knitting. "I'm fine here. You watch your program."

I didn't know that Lily ever turned on the TV my mom had gotten her for Christmas, but I was truly glad for it now, grabbing the remote and turning it on. Stella cast the clip to the TV, and I tried to ignore the thumping ache behind my eyes. The video started with a tumbling view of the floor, the view steadying just as Maxine appeared, seated on the blue easy chair like a throne, adjusting the pin on her shawl. On my side of the screen, I sat in front of the sofa, with Stella and Foster behind me. Maxine's grainy image seemed out of place on the big screen, like two timelines colliding.

"My family, my people, have been here a lot longer than yours," Maxine said once more. In her chair, Lily let her head drop back and closed her eyes.

I put down the remote and wrapped my arms around my knees. On this screen, Maxine looked big enough to step through the TV into the living room.

"A white man who wasn't white."

Maxine swung her head, eyes closed, a slow and heavy rhythm. My eyes followed her.

Back and forth.

"Half of my family. Gone."

Back and forth.

Back and forth.

"It's buried safe. Karhá:kon. Deep."

I sucked in my breath. Karhá:kon. In the woods? This was new. She hadn't said any of this before.

"We tried to stop him." Head moving again.

I shifted closer to the TV, because this was impossible. Video didn't just change on its own, but what I was seeing now was different from what Stella and I had seen. The screen showed my reflection, my face hovering just above Maxine's shoulder.

"He's buried deep, behind the blue box, where the trees don't watch."

The blue box. The house that had once belonged to Maxine.

Back and forth.

I turned up the volume and knelt on the floor, face inches from the screen.

Maxine stilled and looked up, eyes blazing. Looked at me.

"Ragged Man." An urgent whisper, all vowels, trailing off into silence.

My skin prickled. I knew exactly who Maxine was talking about. I knew the uneven slope of his shoulders that left the hem of his ratty coat longer on one side. I knew the measured steps, as if he weren't sure of the surface he was walking on. A damaged statue, patched up by someone who had never seen the original. His eyes just suggestions, two vague pools in his ruined face. Maxine held my gaze through the screen and across time.

This was a dream, a hallucination. Had to be.

"The door opens," Maxine said to me tonelessly. "One in. One out. To the other side, the nothing."

None of this, none of this, none of this was real. There was no dead lady talking to me through the TV. She was not watching me as I scuttled over the rug until my back hit the sofa. This wasn't happening because it couldn't. The other side, the nothing, were things I didn't want to hear. Didn't have to—

"Into dust so fine the wind can carry it," Maxine whispered, leaning toward the camera.

Because it wasn't real.

"The Ragged Man."

My foot hit the remote and clicked it off without meaning to. I released the handful of the rug I'd gripped, dropped my forehead to my knees, and wrapped my arms around every bit of myself that I could reach. What was happening?

This wasn't the video I'd watched with Stella. Something was coming apart—either my mind or the world.

Who would understand? Key.

Who would help? Key.

But Key wasn't here.

Key wouldn't be here ever again.

I raised my head.

Unless I did something.

I closed my eyes against the floaty feeling that threatened to drop me all the way to the floor. My fear was turning to anger, purifying and hardening like a diamond.

Key had always teased that I ran really fast but never went anywhere, since all my routes were loops. But I'd always had a destination. Whether Maxine was real or my mind was splintering, it didn't matter. There was one thing I'd wanted, longed for so badly, that I had resisted speaking it even to myself.

"I'm getting him back," I whispered. Whether it was possible or not, it didn't matter. I knew what I'd been running to all this time; I knew what I wanted. I wasn't going to give it up now.

The nothing. The black water. The Ragged Man.

They had no idea.

"Ave?" Stella pressed her hand onto my shoulder. "You okay?"

"She didn't say that the first time," I breathed, still unable to take my eyes off the blank screen.

She frowned and pursed her lips. "It's the same clip, Ave."

For her, maybe. But I turned to face the sofa and settled back on my knees. Foster was looking at me carefully, and I had to wonder what he'd seen, what Maxine had told him.

I pressed both palms against my knees. If anybody, dead or living, thought that I would leave Key there, they were wrong. Dead wrong. Key was coming back. I would do anything to make that happen. "Uncle, the people it takes," I said, "how can they get back?"

Foster held my eyes for a long moment, breaking away to glance at Lily and then down. He had something to say, I was sure of that. But for some reason, not in front of my ihstá.

Foster's watch buzzed. He pushed his sleeve back and held his arm out almost straight to read the reminder and nodded, clearing his throat loudly. "Doctor's appointment. Maybe we can—" He tilted his head toward the door before laboriously rising to his feet, reaching out, and patting Lily's hand tenderly. She sat up with a jolt, as if she'd been asleep. "I'll come back soon, Lil," he said softly.

I sprang to my feet and a startled Stella followed, collecting cups.

"We should go, too. We can give you a ride, Uncle."

"Oh." Lily surrendered her cup to Stella. "It was so nice to see you, Avery."

I bent to place a kiss on her cheek. "Ó:nen ki' wáhi," I whispered.

Lily beamed, always entranced by hearing the language in my mouth. "Ó:nen."

At the door, I glanced back, now knowing that of all the hurts in my ihstá's life, there was one more she'd kept to herself. I let the door click shut quietly behind me, leaving Lily intent on her knitting as she had been when we'd arrived, as if nothing had been said, as if we'd never been there.

One extremely quiet and awkward elevator ride later, I was crammed in the back of the Mini, more than ready for Foster to say whatever he hadn't wanted to say in front of Lily.

"It's Dr. Liu, just off the square. You know him?"

Stella nodded and turned out of the parking lot. "The medical building? I know that."

"Just picking up a requisition for bloodwork," Foster added.

"We can wait for you." It wasn't an offer; Stella had decided and Foster didn't argue.

The cramped back seat of any vehicle was usually Stella's territory and now I understood why. I shifted, my knees jammed against Foster's seat, literally biting my tongue and waiting for him to speak. In the sideview mirror, his fluffy hair fluttered in the breeze, the sun casting half of his wrinkled face in shadow.

"How could you two not have known each other?" Stella asked, ever tactless, turning east to head downtown.

"Why should we?" I snapped before Foster could even draw a

breath, almost like she'd hit a nerve, almost like it was a seething, barely perceptible wound. "You know all the other . . . Viking families in town?"

Stella raised her eyebrows but kept her mouth shut. Yeah, maybe I was being bitchy; okay, for sure I was. But it was hard waiting for Foster to speak. I was also trying to process all the new information that had just been dumped on me.

Foster, Frank, and Lily.

Avery, Stella, and Key.

I didn't like the pattern I was seeing there but didn't know how to change it.

Yet.

The cops, my mom, even Key's parents would never look for him in the right places, in the right ways. I couldn't go to them for help. If I let those thoughts circle in my head too long, I might just start screaming, so instead, I sat in the back seat with my fingers twisted into a knot in my lap and my eyes fixed on the window beside me. In the front seat, Foster's head was turned to the window like mine.

"So . . . ," Stella tried again. "Lily went missing like Key?" She kept her eyes on the road, asking the question I'd been afraid to. "Is that why . . ."

"We got her back." Foster spoke quietly. "Just not all the way. At first, she seemed fine, but over time . . . it's like she got stretched too thin."

So even if I got Key back . . .

"While we were dicking around, Frank and me, trying to find a way, the Ragged Man took so many others." Bitterness crept into his voice; he shook his head, heavy and slow with regret.

Let it go.

Was this why he'd told me that back at his house? Because even if I got Key back, it wouldn't be all of him? I tried to imagine living as long as Foster had, weighed down by all the lives he could've saved but didn't, all because of his focus on that one. No wonder his house was a shrine to the past—he'd made his choice then and had never been able to move on from it.

But were there only two choices—save Key or save others? And if so, how many? Who? I bit the inside of my lip, because that was a pretty cold thought—who would I sacrifice Key for? If it were three strangers, would I do it? What if it were my mom and Stella? What then? Panic stirred, tiny flutters against the insides of my ribs, threatening to spiral out of control. I focused on what I could see out the window, counting the houses that we passed, hot air blasting against one side of my face.

When Foster finally looked up at me in the mirror, there was absolutely no hope in his eyes. The sight sent a jolt of adrenaline through me. "Once it takes them, it doesn't give them up. Not really," he said. "We lost so many others and only got part of Lily back. I'm sorry." His voice trailed off like flecks of dust being carried on the wind.

I pressed my back against the seat, flexing my fingers against my thighs, needing to ground myself somehow. Foster no longer believed he'd made the right choice, sacrificing others to save Lily. The only living person with any experience thought it was over. My fingers curled into tight fists. Foster and Frank had made one mistake—who was to say they hadn't made more? Just because it hadn't been done before didn't mean it couldn't be. Other people's mistakes in the past had no hold on me.

Stella pulled over to the curb and for an instant, I feared that Foster would bolt rather than tell me. He fumbled with his seat belt and my heart sped up. What was I going to do—tackle an old man on the sidewalk?

"How did you get my ihstá back?" I clutched the headrest; whether it had worked or not, I had to know.

Foster opened the door, planted both feet on the sidewalk, and turned to look me in the eye. "I should have told you everything from the beginning, but we were trying to protect you, keep you safe."

I glanced across the square at the façade of Frank's Books. "Safe? What about her?" Jerking my thumb at Stella. "Or my mom? What about Key?"

Foster nodded, acknowledging his mistake. "Your ihstá called to me that day," he said simply, opening his palms to the sky. "I followed the sound of her voice but how she actually came back— that part of my memory is gone."

My stomach dropped so fast, I had to close my eyes and rest my forehead against the door. Because of course. Why would the black water leave the one piece of information I needed free in the wind?

Foster levered himself up and out of the car and tugged at his cardigan. "The last thing I remember is stepping out of the pines, into that meadow. It isn't like in the movies, you know." A hint of heat in his voice. "Not everything gets neatly explained. This is life. Sometimes you never know why. And you have to live with that." He steadied himself on the roof to pop back into view in the window. "Shouldn't be more than fifteen minutes." But he was talking to Stella now; he was done talking to me.

EIGHTEEN

AFTER CIRCLING THE SQUARE FOR A BIT AND finding the perfect parking spot for her baby, Stella took my hand and dragged me to the Pink Unicorn, our favorite ice cream place for miles around, originally started by two tweens and open only during the summer. It was just a garage, the big roll-up door painted pink, matching the bubblegum-pink interior, which was lit by mismatched cast-off chandeliers. In front was a small roped-off patio with picnic tables where you could people-watch for hours. The Pink Unicorn was popular in town more for the fact that it represented the start of summer than anything else. We'd been coming here for years, all of us.

"I think we need this," the queen of self-care told the queen of self-denial.

While Stella continued to mull the frozen possibilities up at the counter, I stuck the little plastic spoon in my cup of mint chip and looked down at the table. Pink, of course. Underneath the thick coat of pink there were hints of the table's former life in a park some-where. Partially legible initials carved into the wood collected the melted leavings of the Unicorn's patrons. *AS hearts.* Who AS hearted at one point in time was a mystery, although I personally felt the clues were incomplete. I suspected there was another *S* missing.

I'd sat at this same table before. The last time was with Key.

We'd both been in a good mood that night, a little moment that I would put in my pocket, something I found myself doing these days—squirrelling away memories to save for later. How did that work, though? Should I visit the memory often, to keep it sharp and fresh, or would that eventually wear it out, like looking at a photo so many times that it started to fray and fall apart? Over time, I might unintentionally add little details, like what color shirt he'd been wearing. I didn't know; I just remembered his smile and the crinkles at the corner of his eyes. But over time, the shirt might become blue or cherry red. It would make the memory more vibrant, but it wouldn't be true. Eventually, the memory would become its own thing, separate from me and Key. It would become warped. I didn't want that. I wanted that moment, exactly as it had been.

I ran one finger under the chain around my neck until the turtle popped free of my collar. This, at least, never changed. My fingers slipped over the shell, tapping in turn the suggestions of four feet and the head. I rubbed it between my fingers, mulling over what Foster had said. I'd found my way back to the pond once; maybe I could do it again. But what to do when I got there?

Stella sat opposite me with a cone in her hand, and the turtle went back under my shirt.

"Strawberry?"

"Yup." Stella licked the already-melting ice cream.

Unbelievable. All that considering and reconsidering, and nine times out of ten, she ended up with the same thing. A single scoop of strawberry.

Stella shrugged. "I like what I like."

We sat in silence, the breeze lifting strands of Stella's hair and making individual curls float around her head as if they had a life of their own. I'd always been a bit jealous of that hair, framing her pale angular face like a flame; it was pretty much the opposite of mine—dark and incapable of holding a curl for more than an hour. My hair was limp and heavy, but Stella's moved. It was kind of hypnotic, and as I ate my mint chip and watched her hair sway like she was underwater, I felt my pulse slow and settle for the first time in forever. Across the square there were beeps and clanks and shouted instructions of workers, the beginning of FallsFest rising in a cordoned-off section beside town hall.

"So . . ." Even Stella, who could talk to anyone about anything, was at a loss for words for once. "I saw his parents," she said like a confession. "They're . . . pretty desperate for answers. Ready to believe anything."

I nodded. I could understand that, given the things I'd recently accepted as fact. I couldn't blame Jeannie and Michael. I'd sat in their kitchen with my mom, her still-warm banana bread wrapped in foil on their counter. We'd sat around the table, a map of the forest covering the whole thing and dripping over the sides like it was growing too slowly for us to notice, until it took over the entire house. I kept my hands in my lap but traced all the trails I knew with my eyes, skipping over the red Xs that denoted areas the search teams had cleared, Jeannie's way of coping.

"They're getting closer." Key's dad had rubbed his mouth, nodding. "They have to be." An admission that his optimism was based on nothing but the misdirection the black water was putting in his mind.

I'd sat quietly, letting my mom talk. She knew far better than I what to say to parents missing their child, and I couldn't bring myself to encourage their delusions of a twisted ankle or the fight Key and I had never had. Key had gone somewhere a search team couldn't follow, even if they wanted to.

"I've been thinking . . . ," Stella said softly, jolting me back to the present. "I just hope he never took the things I said seriously. I thought we were just playing, you know, but maybe sometimes I went too far." If there was more, Stella swallowed it down and proceeded to methodically tear the paper around her cone into strips, making fringe that draped down over her hand.

My eyes snapped to Stella's face; I was jolted by the words. So selfish. I'd been moping through Avery Land, ignoring the fact that there were actually other people who loved Key. I reached out and wrapped my fingers around Stella's wrist.

"No." I shook my head firmly. "He never thought that. It's just how you guys are."

Stella nodded, but I knew that there was only one person who could reassure her, and he wasn't there. And after what Foster had told me, my faith that he would be ever again was wavering.

I followed the long, stretched-out shadows cast by the sun from the sidewalk onto the street—including the tip of my own elongated form that didn't end until it was almost touching the sidewalk around the town square. People walked by, carefree in the bright sunlight, thinking they were safe. They didn't know. Things that used to go bump in the night had branched out—there was a day shift now. Which was why my head was on a swivel, always wary.

My mouth was full of mint chip when I saw him. A man, standing at the fountain. He was looking into the basin, as though the lack of water offended him. Tall and lean, in a suit that, while formal, had seen better days, the hem ripped loose on one leg and a long seam up his back popped open. The fedora cast a shadow onto his face, but if he looked up, I knew what I would see there.

The mint chip slid down my throat, but the chill that spread through my body wasn't from the ice cream. The man turned, settled on me among all the other people, touched the brim of his hat, and leaned back against the fountain basin, like there was nowhere else he wanted to be. The sun behind him obscured his face, but I knew. A sudden flood of icy cold rushed through me, raising goose bumps on my skin. I tried to move and found I couldn't.

"Stell," I said evenly. "You see that guy?"

Stella followed my gaze behind her. "Creepy."

Stella could see him. He was one of them, the Unfinished, I was sure, and Stella could see him. She hadn't seen the girl in the park an hour ago, but she could see the man now. He was solid enough to *be* seen. What had changed between then and now so quickly? I didn't know what it meant, but it couldn't be good.

"Should I be worried?" Stella reached up and wound a strand of hair around her finger.

"Probably." I didn't know what else to say.

And then probably became definitely.

I stuck my plastic spoon in the mint chip and set it down on the table.

"You're not finishing that?" Stella frowned. "You're hardly eating these days."

Stella's voice faded into the background as my attention focused farther down the street. Popping in and out of view among the other pedestrians, a woman with a tattered parasol strolled down the sidewalk. The parasol spun erratically, and the woman's head tilted and turned, the choppy movements of a bird.

"You're a very tightly wound person, you know." Stella pointed her cone at me to punctuate the understatement of the year.

A quick glance confirmed the man at the fountain hadn't left his post. We'd have to go south, then. We had to get out of there, and that was the only way free.

Except it wasn't.

Making her way from the south side was a woman I didn't know but somehow recognized. Head down, she shuffled along the sidewalk like she was fighting gravity or moving underwater.

"Look at all of them," I breathed, my head snapping one way and then the other.

Stella squinted down the street, misunderstanding. "Tourists? In town for FallsFest, maybe. It's a pretty big draw for a small-town thing." Her voice rose in uncertainty.

"We have to go." My knees bounced under the table, and the mint chip roiled in my stomach. The two women were still on the move, and the man at the fountain was still . . . waiting. In a flash, it hit me. The women were moving slowly, but they were moving. Toward us. A net was closing, and we were the fish. Foster had said they don't take the ones who wake it. . . . I slowly turned to look at Stella.

Stella.

Mom.

"Let's go." I pushed back from the table and grabbed Stella's wrist, pulling her up.

"I'm not done," she protested. "And also— Ow!"

"We have to go." I pushed Stella ahead of me, speed-walking out onto the sidewalk, heading straight for the town square.

"Okay, okay." Stella followed my eyes and finally got it. "Oh! Okay." She ditched her cone in the trash and followed close behind.

The man seemed to be tracking us as we crossed the street. I reached back blindly for Stella's hand and he took a leisurely step onto the gravel path, moving to intercept us.

Crruunch.

But I wasn't planning on getting up close and personal with the Unfinished today. Tightening my grip on Stella's hand, I veered left, cutting through the roped-off area where town crews were setting up festival lights. We were going to sail right by him, through the square, and out the other side.

Crruunch, crruunch, crunch.

I couldn't afford to check on the two women, but Stella's rapid breathing behind me was enough to push me forward. Under the other side of the roped-off area, over a knee-high hedge fence and out of the square. Onto the street—*BEEEEEEPP!*

"Sorry, sorry." I waved at the driver who'd almost hit us and pulled Stella up onto the sidewalk on Elm where the Mini waited, spinning to look back the way we'd come. Nothing. The net had closed and come up empty. This time. I pressed my back against the car and kept scanning the streets. "Stell, let's go."

"Ave." Stella leaned forward, hands on her knees and panting. "What was that?"

"I think it was the black water."

"Here?" Stella's eyes widened. She fumbled the key fob, finally unlocking the car with a blessed beep. We both slid in, slammed the doors, and locked the Mini up tight. Inside, the sounds of the street were muffled, our breathing and the pounding of my heart the only clear sounds.

"I think . . . everywhere." In my head, on the bus, in the bookstore, and now in town. "There are people who . . . don't look right." Understatement, but hopefully Stella wouldn't have to see one of the Unfinished up close. "You couldn't see them at first, but you saw that man." I took a long pause and swallowed hard, ready to say it out loud. "They took Key."

"And now they're after us." I could practically hear Stella's mind racing, clicking into gear, reframing everything Foster had said. "Who else? What about my parents? Jackie!" She gripped my arm hard. "Oh my God, is that what happened to Jackie? What do we *do*." She held my arm tightly with both hands, like she could squeeze a solution out of me. Now she knew what we were up against, she was scared, and it was like a fist around my heart that I couldn't make it better for her.

The fragile fibers of a plan that had been floating around in my mind were knitting together now, out of necessity more than anything else. Things were speeding up for some reason, like the black water had been eavesdropping on us at Lily's.

"It—it'll be okay." I'd always been a terrible liar.

Stella nodded, looking down and then producing the worst fake-smile I'd ever seen on her. "Well, at least I know I was right—to be worried about you."

"Be worried about *you*, Stell." I gripped her arms and looked into her eyes. "Let's get Foster."

It would have made more sense for me to run screaming through the streets. But it wouldn't do any good. The Unfinished were everywhere, but not everyone could see them yet, which I chose to take as a positive sign. I hadn't known how good I had it at the beginning when it was just me. Now it was threatening everyone. Things were getting worse, and I couldn't see the end of it. It would keep taking people—until what? I realized I hadn't asked Foster that. Was there a magic number? Was there a scenario in which it wouldn't stop at all, just keep taking us until only the ones who woke it were left to live in a town full of the Unfinished? Would it spread beyond Crook's Falls? I turned the little silver turtle between my fingers, agitated because I was thinking of all these questions way too late. Time was running out, and I still had no plan. This had all started when I just had to look at the pond, and now it was spreading. I'd knocked something loose in the forest and set it free, allowing it to spill out into town much faster and farther than I could hope to stop.

"We need Foster."

The Mini roared to life, and Stella pulled into traffic without looking, took the corner at the square so sharply I grabbed on to the dashboard, and screeched up to the curb in front of the medical building where Foster stood, astonished, clutching a folded piece of paper in one hand and his cane in the other.

"Uh, maybe I'll call a cab." Foster took a step back.

"Get in!" I waved him over.

"Is everything . . . uh, okay?" Foster asked, still not moving.

"Nope." I hopped out and hustled Foster toward the car, my head on a swivel. To anyone watching, it would definitely look like an abduction, but better by me than *them*.

"Oh, right." Foster sounded resigned rather than surprised. He knew what I meant.

"We're going to Foster's?" Stella shifted into gear and peeled away, the second I squeezed into the back, driving only somewhat more responsibly.

"Behind the blue box," I said firmly. "Karhá:kon. In the woods. We're going to do what your granny said."

I didn't hear the sigh, but I saw Foster's shoulders sag. He nodded slowly and raised his hand, pointing one finger at the corner. "Then turn here. I can't walk from the house," he said slowly. "We'll take a shortcut."

NINETEEN

"NOT TOO FAST, STELL," I CAUTIONED FROM the back seat. The last thing I needed right now was to see flashing lights behind us and the sloucher's smirk at the window.

The official plan, such as it was, involved getting the bones as close to the black water as possible and burning them into nothingness—fine enough bone ash and dust for the wind to carry. Assuming Maxine was right, that should get rid of the Unfinished wandering around Crook's Falls, snap the Ragged Man out of existence, and close the black water, hopefully forever.

But.

Maybe I'd seen too many horror movies, but it seemed too easy. Even if it was the right thing to do, exactly why hadn't Foster finished it before? But the alternative was doing nothing and watching the missing posters in Crook's Falls multiply until there wasn't anyone left to put them up.

Yeah.

Warm air rushed over my face, sweet like clover come calling from my childhood. If I closed my eyes, I could pretend I was somewhere else, maybe in the back of Dad's car when I was little, him and Mom murmuring together up front, before things got so complicated in so many ways.

Mom.

I pressed my fingertips against the reassuring solid bump of the turtle pendant and pulled out my phone. Mom was at work and wouldn't be looking for faceless monsters intent on dragging her off to hell. I had to know she was safe, at least for now. Two rings and she answered.

"Hey, Mom. Everything . . . okay?" I picked at a loose thread peeking out under the hem of my T-shirt as the neighborhood became a green blur beside me. "No weird people?"

On the other end, I could hear the sounds of the radiology department—voices, beeps, and footsteps that thankfully seemed the same as every other time I'd called her at work. Mom sighed, and I could picture her shaking her head with a smile. "Sweetie, you're the only weird person in my life." As alike as we were, I knew that I mystified her sometimes. "What's this about? Are you upset about Key? They're still searching for him."

I nodded, lips pressed tight to stop myself from pointing out the fact that everyone kept talking about *searching*, but the word *finding* had so far never been uttered.

The background noises disappeared with the click of a door; she'd stepped into the quiet of the staff room. "He probably left the trail and got lost," she said gently. "He's smart, though. He'll sit tight until help comes."

For three heartbeats, I considered for the thousandth time begging her to come home and fix this the way I'd believed she could fix any problem when I was little. But I knew she couldn't help me; the black water wouldn't let her.

"He's going to turn up," she tried to soothe me.

Yes, he was. But it wasn't the police who would find him. My head bumped the roof as Stella turned onto a dirt road that was more of a worn track. "I gotta go, Mom. Lots to do."

Stella turned the car off, and for a moment, we just sat in a rough turnaround carved out of the edge of the brush, just deep enough to hold the Mini. I followed Stella out, unfolding myself gratefully from the back seat. Stella's face was tight, and she hadn't said a word since we'd picked up Foster, not something that came naturally to her. She was worried about . . . everything—I could see that much in her face. I put on the calmest face I could, opened Foster's door for him, and surveyed the trees.

Stella pulled out her phone behind me—"Mom?"—and turned away, murmuring.

So many thoughts swirling around were making me lightheaded. Burning the bones might close the door of the black water; it might get rid of the Ragged Man and stop him from taking more people. But what if Key needed the door open to come back? If Foster and Frank had finished burning the bones, would they have still been able to get Lily back?

So really, I had two plans. I would follow Maxine's advice and burn the bones; finish what Foster had started. But when I found a way to get Key back, I was abandoning everything else and doing that.

Which is exactly what Foster had done, the little voice whispered. Look how that turned out.

At the Mini's nose, I came to a stop, needing Foster to guide me. "Which way, Uncle?"

He shuffled up and by me without a word, the tortoise overtaking the hare.

"Okay." I glanced back at Stella, still on her phone, and followed him.

As we entered the woods, the sun was hitting only the very tops of the trees; I was always running out of time these days.

"Aren't we going to need a shovel?" Unless I was supposed to dig with my hands.

"You are, but there should be one there." Foster huffed, eyes on the ground, picking out each step.

Okay. He kept shovels in the middle of the forest? From the mild hoarding in his house, it wouldn't surprise me, and from the state of my own room, I couldn't judge. I kept going, two steps behind him, close enough to catch him if he went down.

"We should have brought flashlights, just in case," I said over my shoulder to Stella, who was bringing up the rear. "Remember? The time I got lost?"

Stella didn't bite, which made me stop and turn. Stella and Key loved that story; their go-to making-fun-of-Avery story. But Stella's face was set as she walked right past me.

"We should keep going," she muttered.

I looked after her before setting my feet in motion again. This was . . . a different Stella.

"You don't have to come all the way. You could take Foster back to his house." I caught up, falling into step beside her. "I just needed the ride out here."

"You don't know where you're going," Foster called back.

True.

"Luci's gone," Stella said, her voice flat, still not looking at me. "Her mom called mine, frantic."

Luci. The kindergartner Stella babysat and perfected her grilled cheese skills with, who'd made her a painting Stella treasured. Gone. I tried to picture the chubby little cherub transformed into one of the mindless Unfinished and then shoved the image away. The black water was taking little kids, and it was my fault. What would be the story there? That a five-year-old ran away? Would the black water's powers hold against a story that ridiculous, or would people finally wake up? I swallowed around the lump in my throat.

"I'm sorry, Stell." A stupid thing to say, but what else was there?

"We can fix it." Focused on Foster ahead, Stella walked a little faster. "We can fix it all. Right?" We walked on in silence until Stella suddenly shook herself, cleared her throat loudly, and became my Stella again. "Right," Stella whispered, keeping her eyes down. "So, we need a shovel," she recapped to herself. "To dig up . . . ?"

"The bones Foster buried."

"And then . . ."

Foster walked ahead like we weren't there, trundling along like an old-man tank.

Well, yes. I wasn't super sure about that part just yet. Burning, I guessed, like Foster had done, but this time I'd finish the job. Where and how—that's why I needed him.

I'd wasted enough time already, time that Key didn't have. The Ragged Man may be a demon from hell or whatever, but I was going to find Maxine's spot, dig up the bones, and use them to get Key back and shut down the black water for good. Whatever mistakes Foster had made, I wouldn't repeat. I'd get Key back whole without sacrificing anyone else. Nothing could derail me now. I shoved a branch out of the way like it was personally trying to hold me back.

Ahead of me, Foster shuffled along the trail although I had the feeling that he was still reluctant about what I was going to do. The trees here were dense but smaller than the old giants of the big forest and the air had a different scent—it was stronger, like freshly turned earth. Unseen birds twittered around and above us, outraged at our arrival. I'd never realized it, but by comparison the trails I ran through the big forest were muted. No matter the season, things smelled and sounded pretty much the same. Maybe because there were always people on the trails and here, we were strangers. Or that Granny's woods were free and the big forest was being held hostage by something as old as itself.

"There." Foster stopped and lifted his chin, too tired to raise his arm. He coughed, wheezing a little, but waved me on when I hesitated. "I'm coming."

A few more steps and I stopped. I couldn't have said what I was expecting, exactly, only that this wasn't it.

I frowned. "Are you sure?"

"That's Granny's house." Foster pointed through the trees to the hint of blue in the distance. "Granny's fields. Granny's woods." He swept his arm around us. "Granny's boy." Tapping his own chest.

I had never been a good reader of people—that was Key's thing—but I was adept at reading situations. I would have been sitting in a *Titanic* lifeboat while everyone else was still at dinner. I could tell when things were going to go bad, and this—this was not good.

In the middle of Granny's woods, a peeling, sagging structure stood in a small clearing ringed by aspen trees. It was either a small shed or a large outhouse—one seemed as likely as the other at this point. In fact, if I walked in to find it was indeed a really inconveniently located outhouse, I wouldn't even blink.

"Looks like an outhouse," Stella observed at my shoulder.

"It's not an outhouse," Foster snapped, pushing past us.

"I'm just saying." Stella raised her hands in surrender.

Foster shook his head and scuffed the toe of his shoe in the fallen leaves. "I don't know what you think you know." His voice was low and tight. "But if you're going to do something, you need to know more than you know, which is a lot less than you think you know."

Beside me, Stella raised a timid hand. "Sorry, could you repeat that last part—"

Foster planted both hands on the cane and wavered for an instant. I stepped forward to help him, suddenly conscious of his fragility and my need for him, but also feeling a flicker of fondness. I gripped his left arm and had the impression that he was nothing but clothes and bone, that he'd been waiting for so long that this was all that was left of him. Once securely vertical again, Foster just stood, breathing hard.

"You'll need this." He pulled the biggest key I'd ever seen from his pocket and held it up, dangling from a length of twine. "Didn't think of that, did you, miss smarty-pants?" He laughed, a raspy, disused sound.

"You carry that with you?"

He shook his head, lifted his cane, and pointed. "Let's go if we're going."

Foster fumbled with the lock long enough that I felt justified in stepping up and politely taking it out of his hands. He took a step back, rubbing his fingers, allowing me to grasp the lock in my left hand and turn the key with the right. The key clicked, and I stood, the lock a cold heavy weight on my palm. It . . . shivered? Was that possible? Or, not the lock but the door itself, the whole building letting out a sigh of relief that I was here to deliver it from the secret it had kept for so long.

I felt it again, slight but definite movement, like a window shutter shaking in the wind. The lock was free. All I had to do was pull to release it. To release . . . what might be waiting for me on the other side?

"Go on," Foster murmured, waving his hand at the door.

But I didn't want to open it. My hand was clammy on the lock, yet I didn't let go. I wasn't convinced opening the door was a good idea, suddenly wasn't so sure about any of my plan, my stomach a tight, hard pit. But I pictured Key as clearly as if he was standing there next to me. He needed me to open the door. He needed me to go inside.

So I did.

TWENTY

NOT AN OUTHOUSE, THEN.

We crowded inside the shed, smaller than it looked from the outside, like a reverse TARDIS. Or maybe just cramped with shelves on all sides. Tools, camping gear, Foster's house 2.0. So here we were, the three of us, crammed in a toolshed. Which was fine; it was totally fine.

Except I was supposed to be digging up something that would get Key back, and so far, all I'd accomplished was going on a long walk and standing in a shed.

"Are we here for a shovel?" I eyed the piles of tools, camping equipment, and rakes, spades, and axes crowding the shed.

"You'll need one, yup." Foster nodded, looking around with an affectionate air, like he was greeting friends he hadn't visited in a long while. "Grab that lamp, too." He pointed to a barely visible camping lamp on the floor, wedged under a worktable that I feared might be load-bearing.

"What's this?" Stella picked up a metal can with a net attached to the top.

"Stell, seriously." My chest was beginning to feel like it wasn't big enough for my heart. There'd been so much talking, and I wanted to *do*.

Reaching the shovel against the wall meant stretching out and over the worktable, extracting it carefully and lifting up, up, and over like a real-life claw machine. Everything in the shed sported a layer of grayish grit; the air was dry and odorless, neutral but expectant. I'd come here ready to dig, yet Foster had led me into a shed with a wood-plank floor.

"So, what now?" I brandished my shovel.

"Okay. You have to back off." Foster shooed us away.

"Back off?" My back hit the table behind me.

"Off what?" Stella had nowhere to go.

"Off! Off! I can't open it if you're standing on it!" Foster grumbled and flapped his hands at us.

I stepped back as far as I could to the perimeter of the room, while Stella hopped up onto the edge of the worktable behind her while I held onto the shelf behind me, partly for balance and partly to prevent one of the avalanches that seemed to follow Foster like ducklings.

"You might consider a garage sale at some point," Stella offered politely, looking up at the mountain of random objects that could come down on her, each too small to cause real harm but cumulatively enough to bury her forever.

Abandoning his cane in the doorway, Foster leaned over and pulled on a dark metal ring set in the floor. Another pull and a rectangle appeared.

"Oof!"

Heart racing, I bent forward and hooked my fingers under the edge. "Don't let go," I warned Foster.

Together we managed to haul it up, and Foster slid in a length of metal to prop it open.

Trapdoor.

"Cool," I breathed.

"I'm glad you think so." Foster smiled thinly, hooking a rope ladder into two screws in the edge of the trapdoor, sending the whole thing unraveling into the void gaping below us and hitting the wall with a clunk.

"What is it?" I peered over the edge and into absolute blackness. Stella was silent beside me.

"It's a . . . storm cellar," Foster said unconvincingly. I'd never met a worse liar.

A storm cellar? So far from the house? I had no idea what kind of storm Granny could have planned to hide from here. The crawling skin on the back of my neck said different. I did know—the kind I was running from, hoping to get to safety before it obliterated everything.

"I go down there." Just to clarify. The cellar was so totally dark; like outer space, where there was just . . . nothing. "On that ladder." That had been moldering out here for who knew how long.

"Yup." Foster was still breathing hard, which was kind of alarming, but no more than what he was telling me to do.

"It's buried? Down there?" I pointed with the shovel, desperately hoping I'd misunderstood. Stella held on to the counter behind her, staring at the hole in the floor with wide eyes.

"What do you think?" Foster flapped his hand in impatience, but he was also maybe nervous about what we were doing. "I gotta . . ." He huffed. "I gotta go sit down." He braced himself on the shed door and hobbled out, making a hard landing on a nearby log.

As I kneeled at the edge, every cell in my body was telling me no. It wasn't just that it was dark down there. The more I looked, the more it seemed to be not a regular kind of dark where the light has its turn and darkness shows up for its shift. This felt different, like a place the light had never been. My throat went dry. There could be anything down there, and I now knew just what *anything*s were possible.

Under my knees the wooden planks were hard and gritty. My fingers gripped the edge of the hatchway all on their own. I did not want to go down there.

But Key would do it for me.

"I'll go first," I said, tying one end of the twine to the lamp.

"First?" Stella squeaked. "I . . ." She backed away and shook her head. "I can't go down there."

"Are you afraid of heights?"

"Yeah." She nodded, eyes locked on the yawning opening in the floor.

I shrugged and tested the knot. "I'm not a fan, either, but it can't be that big of a—"

"The dark."

"Sorry?" I turned to her.

Stella's hands were clasped together like they were trying to murder each other. "Tight spaces."

"You have these phobias?" None of these were unreasonable fears, but I was a little surprised to hear Stella confess to them. The way the world just seemed to open up for her, it had never really occurred to me that Stella was afraid of anything.

"Spiders."

"A lot of people are afraid of spiders, Stell," I said in my softest, scaredy-cat-coaxing voice.

"Insects in general," Stella admitted quietly to the floor.

How could I not have known all this? "You don't have to go down," I soothed, patting Stella's arm. There was only one shovel anyway.

"Bats."

"You think there are bats down there?" I said sharply, peering over the edge again. Heights and darkness were one thing, but I was not cool with bats.

"My therapist is working really hard." Stella's voice wavered. "I'm sorry. It's my krypton."

"Kryptonite," I corrected for the only person who cared about the distinction but wasn't present. "It's okay, Stell." It had never occurred to me that Stella actually needed therapy; it just seemed like a given in her family and for half of my class, just something you did, like a dental checkup. We'd known each other a long time, but looking at Stella just then, I realized I didn't know her as well as I thought; she wasn't the open book she seemed to be. Maybe no one was. I tried on Key's compassionate face and found that it actually fit pretty well. "One of us should really stay up here anyway. With him." I jerked my chin to Foster, slumped on the log outside. "Who knows how strong this ladder is? You might have to pull me up." Shuddering at the thought, I tugged the ladder, testing, letting it thump back against the cellar wall, like pounding for help from the inside of a coffin.

The door frame seemed a likely suspect as an anchor for the lamp, so I busied myself feeding the twine through the gap between the wall and the handle of the lamp, hooking it back onto itself and absolutely not thinking of the dark waiting for me. I inhaled and let a slow, controlled breath seep out between my lips as casually as I could, but Stella knew me better than that. She patted my back twice and left her hand there.

Old Stella would have been hyping me up, chattering about something silly and pleasantly distracting. New Stella was grim and silent, eyes cast down to where I was headed, apparently unconcerned and uninvested, like she didn't give a shit what happened next. I knew that wasn't true, that it must be anxiety, but was this how I always looked to her?

"Okay." I sat on the edge, legs dangling. It was kind of like sitting on a dock, swinging my legs in the water. Except it wasn't water—it was a menacing dark. And if I fell, there'd be no splash, just a long drop. The air that wafted up was cool but not in a refreshing way; it was clammy and close—like something that had been confined for a long time. With a firm grip on the top of the ladder, I turned and sent one foot down, feeling for the next rung. Or for something to bite it off.

"I'll lower the lamp with you." Stella looped the twine around her hand.

I turned a little, my left foot seeking a rung. Once both feet were stable, I could grip the first rung with my hands and start moving down, one step at a time, like a toddler learning stairs, taking more coordination and focus than I would have thought.

"Just get it and come back," New Stella reminded me.

I cast a look up, just to be sure that this stranger actually was Stella. My Stella. Key's Starla. She looked back at me, absolutely blank and unrecognizable. There was nothing to do but keep descending, but with a terrible premonition that when I emerged back into the light, it would be Unfinished Stella standing there waiting for me. The image was so clear, so strong, that I had to stop again for a moment and squeeze my eyes shut, afraid my fingers would go numb and lose their grip.

"You're okay," Stella said quietly.

I'd thought having the light would make it easier, but it didn't. Instead of total darkness, the light threw shadows on the wall— wild swooping shapes that didn't seem to have a source. I focused on the ladder in front of me, on each step.

Left.

Right.

I descended slowly, searching and testing for each rung before trusting it with my weight. I thought of Sky Woman, who'd fallen much faster and farther, who fell and couldn't get back to her home.

Next rung.

Sky Woman had gotten stuck and had to make herself a new home. What if I couldn't get back up, either?

Next rung.

With nothing but darkness and shadows to see, my brain supplied images—me, in the dark forever, my home here in the damp earth, seeing nothing but feeling everything crawl, creep, and slither around me. The image made my fingers go tight on the ladder, threatening to seize up and strand me there forever. My heart thumped like it wanted out.

After what felt like way too long, my foot touched the dirt floor. I grabbed at the lamp dangling beside me and looked up. Stella's head was up there, way up there, silhouetted against the opening, watching. I clenched my jaw, driving away images of

Stella withdrawing and dropping the trapdoor shut. She wouldn't. Stella wouldn't, but my chest tightened. I held the lamp as high as I could, trying to cast light on her face. I just needed to know for sure, needed to see. But it was too far; the light didn't reach.

"Stell?" I called.

The figure above didn't move.

"Yeah." The only answer I got.

"Just—just checking." My voice cracked.

I detached the lamp from the twine and slowly spun around. The wavering shadows cast by the lamp almost made the dark preferable. Almost. The cellar was the opposite of the shed above— bigger than I'd expected. It was obviously hand-dug, the walls just uneven chunks of limestone; some of the tools used to do the job still leaned, abandoned and rusting. It may as well have been a cave, with the same cool, moist air and a breeze with no obvious source. I turned slowly in all directions, including up. Because—bats. There were places that looked like someone had started to dig farther and just given up, leaving the whole thing a shaky L to accommodate the outcroppings of rock that the digger had been too lazy to deal with or unable to cut out. To my relief, no bats.

There were, however, many spiderwebs.

"Here comes the shovel!"

I looked up in time to dodge the garden spade descending directly over my head like a missile, the movement of the air sending the spiderwebs fluttering like tattered wings. I put the lamp on the ground, trading it for the shovel, intent on just doing this and getting out.

"Got it." I looked around at the inky soil, trying not to imagine pale hands emerging, clawing their way out.

The trapdoor was far overhead, the light it allowed struggling to reach me. I turned slowly in place, eyes continuously catching on shadows, like I was looking a fraction of a second too late to see movement around me. The rugged stone walls were wider at the base, giving the impression that they were slowly closing over my head. By the time I realized it was happening, the light from the door would get cut off and I'd be down here alone, under solid rock. I squeezed my eyes shut and bit my lip. *Focus.*

"Where do I dig?" The echo accentuated the wobble in my voice.

"All right." Footsteps clomping above, and Foster was back. "See the far end there?"

I sighed, resigned to what was coming. "The darkest, creepiest part? Yeah, I see it."

"Okay. Walk straight toward the wall. A few steps."

"How many?"

"Five."

Okay. I counted the steps toward the wall carefully, suddenly overcome by the fear of a sudden drop to another, even darker level. There were boxes and trunks lining the walls—how had they gotten this stuff down here, and why? A tilted shelf of dusty jars watched me go by. I tried not to look, already a breath away from freaking out entirely.

I made my way deeper into the cellar, staying as far from the raw rock walls as I could. If I touched them, they would be cold and hard. But I was afraid that instead they'd be warm, like something that hadn't been dead long. The very thought shuddered down my arm, making the lamp shadows dance wildly. With every step, my shoes sank into black soil, down here for years but somehow freshly turned. A soft, pillowy layer that would gladly pull me down much farther than I thought possible, sliding up my legs and over my body, filling my mouth and holding me there forever.

Something was beating frantically in my chest, something other than my heart, like part of me trying to escape before it was too late. I stopped moving and closed my eyes for as long as I dared. It was just dirt. Just rock. There was nothing down here but me. I pressed my fingers against the silver turtle, reassuring myself it was still there.

I was happy to stop on the fifth step.

"What now, Uncle?" I called over my shoulder, wary eyes scanning my surroundings.

"Now . . ." Foster sounded much farther away than he had a minute ago. "Do a half-turn to the left. Or maybe, no. Like a quarter-turn."

"Are you kidding me?"

"It was a long time ago!" Foster snapped.

"Okay." I stopped. "Quarter-turn to the left."

"Start digging."

The shovel bit into the earth, easy digging. If this had all been done properly decades ago, I mused, none of this would be happening now. I'd be in the coffee shop with Key. I'd be on a training run. Instead, I was here in a dark pit, digging in what felt like a fresh grave.

"It's not buried that deep." There was a tightness to Foster's voice that hadn't been there before. I tried to dismiss it, but it nagged at me. Could someone else have been down here already? Was the Ragged Man solid enough to dig? Suddenly all I could think of was Key, debating the consequences to the timeline of digging up your own bones.

"You said a quarter-turn, right?" I called over my shoulder. The echo I'd heard before was suddenly gone, despite the fact that I was essentially in a cave. In this part of the cellar, the walls swallowed our voices; greedy, like something that had been alone for too long and desperate for company.

"It was a long time ago." But there was no heat in his words this time, only resignation. Was if it wasn't here at all? What would I do? What would happen to Key? My pulse thumped in my ears.

The cellar that had been cool now felt stifling, and my position at the end of the L meant I couldn't even see the trapdoor. There was a little quiet rustling from above, a distant *thunk*, then nothing.

I stuck the shovel in the ground and surveyed my work. Four holes and I still hadn't found anything. Either I wasn't digging deep enough or I wasn't digging in the right spot. Or there wasn't anything down here to find.

"Anything?" Stella called.

"Yeah," I answered over my shoulder. "I found it ages ago. I'm just hanging out down here for fun."

Murmurs from above.

"Maybe a little more to the left?"

I was done taking audience suggestions. I stepped back to the mouth of the little alcove I was in, to the toe of the L, surveying the ground. If it were me, if I were burying something I might need later, I'd make it easy. There was, of course, the possibility that at the time, Foster hadn't been thinking clearly. Or that he hadn't conceived of a day when he'd want to dig the thing up.

I stepped to the dead center of the little room and drove the shovel into the dirt. Two scoopfuls of soil in, the spade met resistance.

"I think I found it!" I forced the words out through my throat, which had suddenly gone tight, and wiped my forehead with the back of my hand, sweating despite the cool air.

Above, there was a flurry of movement. I used the shovel to scrape away more soil, revealing dull silver.

I scraped the grainy black dirt away with the tip of the spade, revealing a tackle box, a little bigger than the lunch box I'd carried as a kid, and that Stella had carried last year. There were two dents in the lid that I may have made with the shovel, but I didn't think so. They'd come from something else.

The box looked familiar somehow, sitting there in the dirt and the dark, as if we'd already met a long time ago. I knelt down, the damp coolness of the earth seeping into my skin. If I opened the box, I knew there would be a tray that rose with the lid. It would be sectioned off to hold hooks and weights and lures designed to attract all kinds of fish. Some of the lures would look silly, like cartoon fish. Others would have feathers, like tiny exotic birds. All of them would have sharp hooks.

The box glowed dully in the dim light. I leaned forward and blew on it, clearing a few remaining dark clumps.

Come.

Considering how long it had been down here, buried in the dark, the box was brighter than it should be, and it wasn't just the lamplight. I tilted my head, staring. It was mesmerizing. A button you're told not to push, but then you can't think of anything else. I wouldn't touch it; of course I wouldn't. But maybe . . .

Come.

I watched a hand drift toward the box, vaguely aware that it was my own. How interesting.

"Don't touch it!" Foster called, as if he knew. "Avery." Voices from above again, but I really wasn't listening to them now. "Are you okay?"

Come.

It was just a box. There couldn't be any harm.

"Avery!"

Just a little peek.

Come.

My head snapped up at movement in the corner. Spiderwebs fluttering in the liberated air. Maybe.

A split second. A wavering image. A new voice in my head, reedy and thin.

Don't. That was *Maxine.*

And then nothing.

Just me, kneeling in the black dirt, startled to find my fingers about to brush metal.

"Avery Ray, get up here right now!" Stella sounded close to tears. "Or—or I'm coming down!"

I stood. "I'm coming." I said, backing away from the box with measured steps, keeping my eyes on it the whole way. "I'm coming." Louder, for Stella.

At the base of the ladder, I put down the lamp and waited, wanting to be sure nothing else was going to try to hitch a ride out with me. The box was here. But I didn't know what to do with it yet. I flexed my hands, tingling with adrenaline, and stared, not able to see it from here, but the image of the gleam of the box nestled like a piece of silver in black velvet, clear in my mind.

Don't.

I bit my lip, really wishing Key were here to talk this through. "How am I supposed to get it?" I called up to the little square of light. "If I can't touch it?"

"You need— Give me that," Foster directed Stella above. "Here, use this."

I looked up in time to see something big and fluttering blot out the light above and head straight for me. Sheer panic sent me diving away from the ladder, scuttling backward in the soil until my back was pressed against the jagged rock wall.

A blanket—a quilt stitched in what once must have been vibrant colors, now faded and flat.

Jumping to my feet, brushing my hands on my shorts, adrenaline still thrumming, I reached out and picked it up between two fingers, holding it at arm's length. "It's really scary down here," I scolded.

"Yeah, sorry," Foster said. "It's just a blanket. Same one I used last time."

Last time.

This time had to be different. If I had only one chance at it, I had to get it right. But the question was—if I burned the bones now, would Key be gone forever? Would the pond sleep, and would Key disappear with it? I couldn't let that happen.

I nodded to myself, and my shadow looming on the wall agreed. I would take the box, figure out how to save Key *and* close the black water. Back to the far end of the cellar, armed with an ancient blanket like it was an oven mitt for evil. The silver tackle box would be right where I'd left it—I just had to pick it up safely and get out. Foster would tell me what to do next. Away from the ladder and back to the toe of the L, I smelled stagnant water on a breeze that shouldn't have been there. My nose wrinkled but I kept going. At the heel of the L, I turned to my left and raised the lamp. Just get the box and go.

The shadows on the wall lurched as I stopped short with the lamp.

"Ave." Stella's voice was very far away. "Do you have it?"

No.

No, I didn't have it. I froze, blood pounding in my ears, heart stuttering in my chest.

"Avery?" Stella, sounding more like herself. "What's going on?"

I couldn't get to the box, couldn't move, couldn't imagine ever moving again. The lamp threw shadows that rose and flickered on the walls like flame.

"Foster! Come back in here!" I heard Stella scrambling to her feet.

It didn't matter, none of it. Not anymore. I had come for the box, but it was impossible. The box was there, at the very end of the cellar, sitting in a little nest of dirt, just as I'd left it. But it may as well have been at the bottom of the ocean. I couldn't get to it, not now. The way was blocked, and I was as still and cold as the rock surrounding me.

I stared into the shadows.

And Key stared back.

TWENTY-ONE

IT WAS EXACTLY WHAT I'D WANTED AND EVERY-
thing I'd feared all wrapped up into one terrible moment that seemed
to stretch on forever.

"Key?" A question, but also a plea. It wasn't him; it couldn't be.
I was hallucinating this, just like Frank in the store or the water
on the bus. If I squeezed my eyes shut hard enough and willed it, I
could wake up; I could make this go away. It wasn't real.

But deep down, I knew it was.

Standing between me and the box was something that looked
like Key if someone had tried to make a washed-out replica of him
but hadn't gotten it quite right. His eyes were flat and fixed and
reflected nothing back to me, not even the light of the lamp. There
was no brightness, no recognition—no life. Everything Key about
him, everything magical, everything I'd loved, was gone. I'd had
so many chances and wasted them all. I hadn't ever said the words
because I was afraid to lose him. But it didn't matter. I had lost him
anyway, and the reality of it was a rock—an actual physical weight
I could feel in my stomach. Looking at him felt like my heart was
slowly being shredded, long, leisurely strips ripped off in dark and
dripping fingers. Seeing him like this made it a thousand times
worse, but I couldn't stop.

"Key, I'm so sorry." I bit my lip, blinking. "This is all my fault." My throat was closing; my chest was collapsing in and exploding out all at once. Let it. Let the hungry black earth pull me down and swallow me up. The tether that joined us had been cut, leaving me to drift in the cold and dark alone.

A tear welled and slipped down my face, leaving a trail the damp air kissed. He didn't change, didn't move. I was crying and he didn't care. That would never happen. My Key wouldn't just stand there and watch. He was really gone.

The other Unfinished I'd seen felt like something was inside them. They radiated hostility or need. But the Key in front of me was different. He was just . . . nothing. I'd never seen his face so blank, so empty. The black water had the part of him that made him Key. All that was in front of me was his body. He was still wearing the blue T-shirt and green cargo shorts he'd worn at the bookstore. The bookstore. When he'd taken my hand and held it, a million promises tucked safe between our palms. Now his arms hung slack at his sides, and I knew if I touched him, his hands would not be warm.

"The Ragged Man, he's taking people," I tried to explain to the thing that looked like Key. "I have to stop him. I need the bones." But it seemed like the black water already knew that. Just as Maxine had said—it was smart. It had snatched Key and dumped him here for me to find. Key wasn't like the other Unfinished; the Ragged Man had drained him, but Key was not disfigured like the others. Why—to be sure I'd recognize him? To make sure it hurt? It wasn't chance that it was Key here staring at me and not Jackie or one of the others; it was an intentional choice. The black water thought

Key was the one weapon it had that I wouldn't fight.

And it was right. My mind was blank, and with Key between me and the box, standing here forever was the only outcome I could see.

"What should I do?" Every bit of me was crumbling. "How can I help you? Key, what should I do?"

My question echoed in the cellar, but no answer came back.

I shivered uncontrollably—cold and hot, numb and burning at the same time, my mind skipping wildly from one thought to another like a train jumping the tracks. Only in my very core was there stillness and quiet. If the Ragged Man knew I'd come for the bones, why hadn't he gotten them first?

He couldn't.

Foster and my own instincts had warned me not to touch the box—maybe the Ragged Man couldn't, either. All he could do was leave Key here to stop me, which was probably the worst mistake the Ragged Man had ever made. Key, who'd learned about long-distance running for no reason other than it was important to me, who'd seen all of my flaws and still cared. If the black water thought it could use Key as a weapon against me, it was very, very wrong.

And then he proved me right. Nothing about Key changed, but he moved. One step to the right—slow, like it was difficult to accomplish, like he was moving against a force holding him in place. One agonizingly slow step to the right, overriding whatever the black water had done to him and opening a path to the box.

The part of Key that survived in this husk wanted me to have the bones. The little ember of him was still strong enough to fight the black water, to disobey.

"Will it help you? To burn it?" I searched his face for a response of any kind, but got the same blank stare. "How do I get you back? Can you come up with me?" But I knew he couldn't—the black water didn't want him to.

I had to do something. I had to try, so I carefully inched past him. I dropped the blanket over the box and picked it up, feeling a thrum of energy underneath the old blanket. I stood there, holding the box against my chest that was about to burst, watching him watch me. There was a dimension in the universe where we stood like this forever.

I stood opposite him and studied his face as the spiderwebs fluttered around us. It was him. Every bit of this face was his, right down to the tiny scar on the point of his chin that only the two of us would ever be able to spot. He was at once beautiful and the worst thing I'd ever seen. I had a fierce desire to reach out and touch him, but the dullness of his eyes told me I'd regret it. I had waited too long. Although I desperately wanted to believe I could help him, that I could do something, I was afraid that time had passed. My throat closed up like it would never allow another breath. Pressure built in my chest, my ears, my eyes, and then I burst.

A sob rolled up from deep inside me and rang off the stone walls. The person I would have been turned to dust and fell. Without Key, that girl was gone. We would never grow up, never grow apart. I'd never see him smile again or hear his voice. Key and Avery crystallized as a thing in the past.

I dragged in a breath that burned my throat. "I'm so sorry," I whispered. "Key."

He was not going to speak to me, and I had nothing for him but apologies. All I could do now was carry out the plan that I didn't even care about anymore. I forced my body to turn and move, not feeling the soft earth now, not afraid of the cold walls. At the base of the ladder, I tucked the box under my arm, then turned out the lamp and set it down on the ground. If he wanted me to burn the bones, that's what I'd do. Maybe it would help him somehow.

I could feel him behind me, still watching. If there was anything left of him in there, I wanted him to know. For sure. It might be too late, but it was all we had.

"I love you." I tried to keep my voice steady as I looked into his dark, bottomless eyes, trying to send the words to wherever he was now. "I love you, Key." I always had and would never stop.

He didn't answer, but it didn't matter. I didn't need the words. He'd tried to help me, even when he wasn't himself anymore. The black water didn't want me to have the box and thought Key would stop me.

It didn't know.

Key would do anything for me.

I grabbed hold of the ladder and started climbing, barely able to feel my hands on the rungs, vaguely unbelieving that I was really leaving him down there.

Near the top, I stopped and looked down. The light from above was enough to see him, standing by the ladder, empty face turned up like a tired swimmer treading water in the middle of the ocean. If I could save him I would, but he was actually drowning some-where else. I kept climbing, watching him watch me, until at last his face was consumed by the darkness.

I was out of the cellar and scrambling to my feet on the gritty plank floor; I almost knocked Stella and Foster over in the doorway as I lurched out of the shed, cradling my terrible bundle.

"Ave!" Stella grabbed my shoulders and peered into my face. "What happened? Are you okay?"

Foster reached out and leaned against the door. "What . . ." He panted.

Stella's fingers dug into me. I searched her face, but she was just normal Stella.

"Key was down there," I whispered, crumbling inside.

Stella's eyes widened in shock, and she turned back, suddenly willing to brave the dark. "Then let's get him! Why'd you turn the lamp out? Is he . . ." She trailed off, realizing what I meant.

Foster's face was grim. "What do you mean?"

"He was there." But I knew if I had the guts to turn around and go back down that ladder, he'd be gone. Impossible, but true. What I'd seen was his shade, only a projection of what the black water was holding hostage.

Foster's gaze drifted, a frown appearing. "That didn't happen last time," he whispered.

The words gave me an unreasonable hope, one I was afraid to acknowledge.

Foster's arm slipping around my shoulder surprised me, bringing me back into this world a little. He had skinny old-man arms, but he was stronger than I would've expected. He smelled like bar soap and fresh grass.

"Sakatathré:wa't," he said softly, looking me in the eye, as much in sympathy as apology.

If I'd known what Foster knew, if I'd listened to the stories, maybe I would have seen the black water for what it was sooner, before it took anyone. My culture wasn't extra—it was a blanket I could draw around myself, woven by my ancestors and passed down to keep me warm and safe. Was it too late to pick it up and wrap myself in it? Having ignored Lily and Maxine and all my ancestors for so long, would they listen to me now?

At powwows with Lily, I'd always felt the music, *felt* it pull at my chest. I would have liked to lose myself in it, to dance, but I'd never been taught how, a skill my mom deemed unnecessary and dangerous to have but was actually essential to part of me. Maybe it wasn't too late to learn. I'd always stomped on my feelings, shoving things I didn't want to say or acknowledge down into a hard little ball that sat in the pit of my stomach—my losses, my love, my insecurities, and my dreams—all mixed together in a heavy lump that I hid away just to avoid the pain of dealing with things. Just like my mom and the hurt she carried.

But I'd hidden so many good things in that ball of feelings, too. I'd hurt myself more than I realized. Avoiding discomfort in the moment led to long-term regret, like never telling Key exactly how I felt. If I'd been more honest, we could have had more time together. Like, together-together. And if I'd let the powwow music pull me to my feet, I could have learned to dance.

I could have been dancing this whole time.

I searched Foster's face for a clue, really seeing him for the first time. He'd done the same thing—stopped dancing long ago. His fluffy white hair, and the way he pursed his lips, made him look like Maxine. His eyes were brown but a little milky. Key would never have skinny old-man arms or failing vision. I would never know old-man Key, and it was my own fault. Tears started falling, and I was just too tired to even try to stop them.

"Here. Why don't you put that—" Stella grabbed her backpack from the floor and held it open. "Put that in here."

I sniffled. Turning my head felt like shifting a boulder. I was so tired in every conceivable way. Stella and Foster both had eyes on the box I still clutched, as if it might spring forward to bite them, and I couldn't be certain it wouldn't. Stella stood back, arms outstretched, holding her pink, sequined backpack open, looking like she'd scream if the blanket-wrapped box even brushed her fingers. I felt like screaming, too, for different reasons.

But I slipped the box and blanket inside and took the straps out of Stella's hands. The last time I'd seen this bag, I'd been with Key, upset and scared because the dreams had gotten so bad. I hadn't imagined things could get worse. I could tell Past Avery a thing or two about being scared. I could tell Past Avery what happens when you go beyond scared, when the fear swallows you up, pulling your nerves tighter and tighter until the world goes silent and you feel nothing at all. I could tell Past Avery that keeping secrets didn't stop them from being real and running didn't get you anywhere; in the end, it kept you from moving forward. Key would be so impressed with that analysis. Something like a laugh huffed out of me, making Stella and Foster glance at each other.

"Let's go." I nodded in the direction of the house and slipped the straps over my arms, wearing the pack in front like something I wanted to protect. I didn't, but I didn't want the black water to get hold of it, either. I was not going to make the same mistake as Past Avery—things could always get worse.

Stella closed the shed door, and Foster straightened up, sighing at the prospect of walking all the way back so soon. Stella hurried to walk beside him, and I brought up the rear, walking mindlessly.

I put one foot in front of the other, following the soft murmur of voices up ahead, carefully keeping my mind as blank and empty as his eyes had been.

Left. Right.

Left. Right.

My arms were wrapped tight around the pack on my chest, even though it was like hugging a block of ice. I let my fingers trail through the sequins and draw a heart. Just left of center. Where mine used to be.

That didn't happen last time.

From the beginning, my experience with the black water had moved in lockstep with Foster's. Until now. He'd never encountered Lily outside of the black water, which meant that maybe the narrative had been forced off the repeating loop. The black water and I could already be hurtling toward a new ending; maybe the story didn't always have to be the same.

I put one foot in front of the other and tried to focus on what I knew.

Something was different this time.

Which meant we had a chance.

TWENTY-TWO

AFTER THE CELLAR, THE AIR ON MY FACE, WARM and fresh, was a revelation. Foster limped toward the porch, one hand low on his back like he was trying to hold himself together, the other holding onto the railing to haul himself up the steps.

"I shouldn't have let you go down there alone." Stella's face was tinged golden by the sunlight.

"It's okay, Stell." I shrugged like what I'd experienced down there was no big deal, like it hadn't shattered my heart into shards like stars in the sky.

I didn't blame Stella for being afraid. It felt like my default setting these days. But I also had a sense that Stella's fears were for the best, that it was better that she hadn't gone down into the cellar. I suspected that I wouldn't have found the box at all if Stella had been with me. The more I thought about it, the more I was willing to bet it was true. The tight fist in my stomach agreed.

You only find it if it wants you.

"I'll go get the Mini." Stella pulled an elastic off her wrist to tie her hair back.

"I'll come, too."

"It's not far." She shook her head, her curls half a beat behind. "You stay here." Stella nodded toward Foster's slow progress up the porch steps. "You just . . . settle." Stella patted my arm and looked into my eyes with more feeling than I could handle right then. So I nodded and moved toward the little blue house, turning after only four steps to watch her go.

Stella headed down the driveway, off to retrieve the car. I shouldn't have let her go alone, knowing what we all knew. I shouldn't have let her go alone. But I did.

I got up the creaking steps just in time to help Foster ease down into the porch swing with a puff. I'd wait with him until Stella returned and then I'd burn the bones and end this. It didn't even scare me now, the thought of it. Somewhere between the shed and here, an empty numbness had settled over me. I dropped onto the swing beside Foster.

"I come out here to talk to her—akhsótha," he said.

I didn't reply, just pushed off with my feet, setting the swing in motion, a quiet *squeeaak* that was more companionable than annoying. The metal was cold against my bare arm, and my finger had found a rusty patch on the edge of the armrest that I tried to resist flaking off with my fingernail, but it was an oddly satisfying occupation. I stared out toward the road thinking that this wasn't Foster's first time doing this. He'd been here before—he'd been me, and if I wasn't careful, I'd end up in the same spot. I'd be him, trapped in the past for the rest of my life.

"My granny," Foster began again. "She's been gone a long time. She was special to me. And I was her favorite," Foster said in a low voice, still keeping Maxine's secret. "Last time I saw her." He leaned back, stretching with a grimace. "Oh, before your parents were born."

I raised my eyebrows and favored him with a hint of a smile. That was a long time.

"The rumors are true." Foster nodded. "I'm old. It's been a long time, but she's never left me."

I kept my eyes on the driveway, waiting for the Mini to appear and letting the sound of Foster's voice wash over me, warm and comforting.

"We had a connection between us, like an elastic. Right here." Foster tapped the center of his chest. "Right here."

I went still, because I knew exactly what he was talking about. I'd felt the pull a million times, but when I raised my hand, it was the silver turtle my fingers found.

"It's strong. Even though she's as far away as she can get, it stretches. It can do that." He looked up at the sky, and I followed his gaze but didn't see whatever he did. "It'll stretch, but it will not break." Foster's voice was quiet and firm. He'd lived with these things, all of it, for far longer than me. I wanted to believe what he was saying, wanted to think Key wasn't lost to me forever. My mind was fixed on that and stuck in a loop. How to stop it always led to how it had started—with me.

"I started this," I muttered. "Because I couldn't resist. Like her." I jerked my head over my shoulder, to the living room window.

"Sky Woman?" Foster frowned.

"What I had wasn't enough." I grimaced, disgusted with myself. "I had to go looking for more, off the trail. And this is what I found." I looked down at the pack on my lap, the nightmare it contained. "This is what I did."

"First . . ." Foster raised one finger. "It's always someone. It wasn't just you. Second . . ." He scratched his temple. "Yeah, she made a mistake to start, maybe. But she gave us Turtle Island." He swept his hand out. "We wouldn't be here without her. So it actually turned out okay for us."

Us. I'd started this, but so had he. Foster had been where I was. He was the only one who could understand me right then, more than my mom, more than Key or my ihstá. Foster and I were members of a very select club, and the knowledge made tenderness for him bloom in my heart. I didn't want to be telling my own version of this sad story years from now to someone else.

He leaned forward, looking at me carefully. I wasn't sure what he saw. "You don't know how the story's going to turn out until you get to the end."

The end.

I nodded. The end of my story would be different from his. I'd make sure of it.

I turned my gaze out toward the grass, to the empty driveway. "You got Lily back."

Every second that he didn't answer, my heart skipped another beat.

"Not without making things worse," he whispered, looking down.

The flood.

Foster looked me in the eye. "The Ragged Man—he's not the scariest thing in the black water."

The thought made me numb, because I couldn't imagine anything scarier than the Ragged Man. Except losing Key.

"You got her back," I murmured. That was the important part. Foster himself had said this time was different. I had to try.

"I knew it was a gamble to even try." Foster shook his head, reading my mind. "Akhsótha warned me. You can't see; you don't know what you're pulling to the surface." His voice tightened and thinned, rose and cracked. "You don't know what else you can lose."

One tear too many for Foster to contain shivered for an instant and then fell. "I was so focused on her, distracted." He slid both hands slowly down over his face. "I thought it would be okay."

"What else did you lose? What did getting Lily back cost you?" I leaned forward, eyes locked on him. But as soon as the words were out of my mouth, I knew.

Maxine.

I understood now why Foster had failed to burn the bones last time. He'd tried to land a fish too big for his boat and whatever he'd brought out of the water had taken most of his family.

Cut the line.

But I didn't think I could. I sagged back on the swing, empty.

Foster had withheld the truth so I wouldn't repeat his mistakes, wanting me to do what he hadn't, to go right where he'd gone left. He looked at me through the shimmer of tears, hands clasped tightly in his lap, and part of my heart broke for him. We stared at each other, his eyes begging me to understand.

"This time is already different," I pointed out.

He nodded, collecting himself. "I wish I could tell you what I did to get Lily back," he whispered. "But all I remember is hearing her call to me, and finding myself at the pond. After that is a blank. Maybe the black water took that, too."

I patted the brown hand resting on his knee and let my hand stay there.

"One of us always wakes it." Foster breathed the words out into the evening air, the end of daylight making his profile glow like a bronze statue. "But I wish it hadn't been you."

Whether I'd believed it or not, I was one of "us." And so were Foster, Maxine, and everyone who had come before. I felt something then, sitting on the porch swing and holding Foster's hand. It was, I don't know, like a lifeline had been thrown to me and after flailing in the water for a long time, I'd finally managed to grab hold. I didn't have a firm grip, but it was in my hand. What happened next would be up to me, but I wasn't alone.

I turned to find Foster looking at me intently, like he'd made a decision.

"It's not good," Foster said evenly. "But it isn't over."

The words made my breath catch in my throat. This. This is what I had wanted to hear. I knew things were bad. Only an idiot would deny that. Key gone, people from town disappearing, dark things emerging from the black water. Hard to put a positive spin on any of it.

But.

In a 5K, if you had a bad start, it was pretty much over. It was a fact. But in longer races, in the distances that I ran, there was time to fix your mistakes. A bad start didn't have to mean a bad finish. You had to remember that things might get worse before they got better. After you hit bottom, there was still an opportunity to pull yourself back up. You had to keep that possibility in your mind, though, repeat it until it was true.

It isn't over. It isn't over.

You had to hold on to that belief. You had to be stubborn. And although I had no patience—something Key had lamented many times—I did stubborn very well. Stubbornness, refusing to know when I was beat—those were some of my best qualities. If Foster believed there was another leg of the race ahead, that the worst outcome wasn't a foregone conclusion, then there was time. Time to figure out how to save Key without losing anyone else. Foster's face got a little blurry then, but the tears that rose in my eyes were from relief.

A beep as the Mini came down the driveway and rolled to a stop. I rose, blinking away tears and adjusting the backpack over my chest. In my place, Key would never give up, never stop like the superheroes he loved. I heard his voice in my head, a little admonition in his tone. "Heroes keep going when the rest of us would quit."

Foster may have made mistakes, but I wouldn't. This time things would end differently. I steadied the swing while Foster stood, wishing he could tell me exactly how he'd gotten Lily back. But that was just one more thing the black water was keeping from me.

"Stell, we're leaving." Stella was exiting the Mini even as I waved her back. I just wanted to get out of here. Who knew what the black water had been up to while I was in the cellar?

"Well, I think we should . . ." Stella discreetly pointed to the porch where Foster was heading to the front door, one hand gripping the swing armrest, the other on top of his cane, which was shaking precariously.

"Right," I whispered, trying to remember that I was not, in fact, the center of the universe. "Two minutes." I held up two fingers to be sure Stella understood.

"Fine."

Stella bounded up the steps ahead of me and put her arm around him while I gripped his other elbow. Together, we supported him as I burned with shame. I was supposed to save the whole town when I'd been about to leave without helping one old man get into his house? Foster's face was a little flushed, too.

"That walk did me in." He chuckled, but there was no laughter in it, no lightness. "Just need a proper sit-down."

Holding the door open while all three of us shuffled through was no small feat, but by then I was genuinely afraid to let go of Foster's arm. I hadn't known him very long, but he'd grown on me—one prickly pear recognizing another—and losing him was a prospect I didn't even want to consider. In some ways, Foster knew more about me than anyone else, even Key. I'd always fought to keep my secrets, but being with someone who already knew them was comforting.

"In your chair?" Stella asked, pointing to the easy chair in the living room.

"Kitchen." Foster straightened up a little and pulled his arm out of mine. "Tea will do me good. I'm fine." He waved me off and made his way slowly into the kitchen, with Stella's help, hand hovering over his back but not touching, the way she did with Luci when the little girl was feeling independent.

I moved to follow, but a prickle on the back of my neck stopped me in my tracks. The air inside the little house was cool and still, but something felt off. I toured the living room cautiously, because the vibe of the house had changed. Stella murmured in the kitchen as I peered at the faces in frames that lined the walls and inspected the spines of the books stacked on the floor beside the easy chair. The painting of Sky Woman on the wall opposite the front window was my last stop. Up close, I could see her expression—her eyes wide with fear staring out from a numb mask. My blood thrummed in my veins, my pulse a single beat shooting a circuit through my whole body. Sky Woman had had no idea what she had fallen into, no idea that her life would never be the same.

A movement caught the corner of my eye, and I spun to the window with a quiet gasp. There was nothing in the yard except the Mini and the tree, but as I looked, something dark and fluid shot across the wall beside me, constantly just out of my sight. I tracked a beat too slowly, my eyes coming to rest on the big mirror hanging over the smoke-blackened fireplace.

"Milk?" Stella asked in the kitchen.

"Black, please," Foster murmured, barely audible.

Everything else fell away as I focused on the mirror, suddenly wary. Reflections had not been what they seemed lately. The mirror showed me the room and the painting behind me, but something was not quite right. I moved a step closer to the mirror, frowning, struggling to put my finger on it. The quality of light in the reflected living room was darker, as if the glass were smoked. Another step, and my heart sped up, knowing something I didn't. The painting, the sofa, the window, the chair—all the same.

And yet. I had seen this before, a reflection not quite true to the original.

At the pond.

One step away from the mirror, I stopped. There I was, the painting behind me, the sofa to my left, all of it as it should be. I stared into my own face—looking tired but otherwise the same. There was no mark on me announcing Key's loss, which seemed wrong, but as I watched, the mirror shivered once and settled, still water disturbed by a single drop. I swallowed around the pulse pounding in my throat and clenched my fists at my sides, wanting nothing more than to run but unable to look away. Another step closer, face inches from the glass, which was fogging slightly from my breath, I saw it: in the mirror, my neck was bare; there was no silver chain, no turtle pendant. I gasped so hard it burned, raised my hand to touch the tiny turtle resting against my skin. My reflection broke into a slow smile, knowing and sly; her hands did not follow mine.

One step back, two, three. Heart pounding, I stumbled on the edge of the rug, spun, and burst into the kitchen.

"We should go," I said hoarsely, unable to articulate anything more. My reflection in the pond that first day—this was how it all started. "Stella."

Stella turned from the back door, where she and Foster were standing. "Foster was just telling me how he used to play on the hill."

"The green sea." Foster pointed at the hill that rose like a wave about to break over the little house.

It did look like a sea. The hill was covered with long, slender blades of grass swaying in the breeze, a beautiful sight that shouldn't have made my stomach clench with fear. It looked like the meadow, soft and gentle from a distance, but I bet that lurking in this grass was something with teeth.

"We need to go," I breathed, staring out at the hill. Bad things were happening, and a little house in the middle of nowhere was not a great place to be. "Stell."

"What is that?" Stella squinted through the window.

At the top of the hill, something small and dark bobbed just

above the green waves of grass. Into sight and out, each time popping up closer and closer to the crest of the hill. *We have to go* was
the message in each beat of my heart.

"Stell. Keys?"

Still looking out the window, she raised her hand in response,
where the fob dangled. "It's a hat!" she exclaimed.

A hat.

Attached to a man.

Stella stepped back from the door, suddenly serious. "Is that the
guy we saw downtown?"

The man by the fountain who'd tried to ambush us, cresting the
hill with more Unfinished at his back. Foster's jaw dropped. The
man started down the hill, each step careful but full of purpose,
heading straight for the back door, straight for us. I shoved Stella
aside and flipped the lock.

"We need to go." Each word ground out.

This time Stella nodded.

We moved as a group into the living room, fear making Foster
suddenly agile. I kept my eye on the corner of the house through
the front window, but no shadows appeared. The wind shushing
through the grass and my own heart were the only things I could
hear.

"Do we make a run for it?" Stella whispered behind me, clutching my arm.

The Mini wasn't far, but it wasn't close, either. I'd never seen
the Unfinished run, but that didn't mean they couldn't. And was
running an option for Foster? I shot a glance his way, trying to gauge
his thoughts. He was staring out the window, too, breath rapid, his

skin pale, probably feeling like he'd been sent back in time to relive his nightmare. We huddled together in the center of the room waiting for the Unfinished to show their hand—but nothing. The back door rattled gently in its frame. Maybe it was the wind sweeping over the grassy hill, looking for a way in. Maybe something else.

Had they given up? If I went back into the kitchen, would I see them standing motionless, waiting? The Ragged Man had brought the camera, but even he had never opened a door. I glanced at the painting in the mirror. Sky Woman had fallen down into nothing. She was the reason the nothing had changed. A minute passed that felt like forever, and the Unfinished hadn't appeared around the front. Was it that easy? Locking the door? Stella and I exchanged a look and turned to Foster, who shrugged as casually as he could.

"Maybe—"

Something scuttled across the roof. My head snapped up and our little knot tightened. I felt a heart racing somewhere, but we were crowded so close, I wasn't sure if it was mine or Stella's. Foster's fingers dug into my shoulder, his face raised to the ceiling just like mine.

Ssskkrriiiittch . . . ssskkkrriiiitttchh.

My heart. It was definitely my heart pounding high in my throat like it was trying to escape.

"Ave," Stella whispered into my ear.

"Shh." Foster raised an unsteady finger to his lips, never taking his eyes off the ceiling, where something rasped and slid, rasped and stopped. It wasn't fair that Key wasn't here; he was the one who would know what might make that kind of sound, because all I could conjure up was a dripping dark figure, all angles and joints, crab-walking across the roof wanting to drag us off. To the nothing. An endless nightmare, Maxine had said. The black water.

I was frozen, listening to a few quiet scratches above the fireplace. Stella's hair caught in my mouth as she whipped around to face me, eyes wide.

At the sound of something scuttling across the roof again, we drew closer together, eyes raised as something slid, scratched, then stopped. I held my breath, scanning the ceiling. There were a few exploratory scratches against the roof, like a claw testing the surface to gauge the depth needed to break through. Another *sccrriiitch*, then silence except for the three of us breathing unevenly and the tick of the clock on the mantel.

I let my eyes drift down from the ceiling to survey the room and the doorway to the kitchen and the hall where the bedroom and bathroom doors stood ajar. I continued turning on the spot, Stella's fingers gripping my sleeve, until I was once again facing the kitchen and gasped, yanking Stella back.

The man in the hat stood on the other side of the back door, glowering through the glass.

"What?" Foster twisted around in our little knot to see. "Oh boy."

Even without a face, the man was seething, furious. He raised both hands and placed them on the window, each fingertip pressing into the glass.

"Ave!" Stella whimpered.

"Go." Foster pulled away and then pushed me toward the front door.

At the back door, the man still stood, his ruined face unchanged.

Under the pressure of his fingers, a crack in the glass appeared, a splinter that grew by the second.

"Go. I'll hold them off." Foster gave my shoulder a shove, hard enough to knock me off-balance.

"No." I shook my head. Foster had suffered enough, given enough of himself. I couldn't let him do this. The black water hadn't taken him before, but Foster wasn't the first anymore. Which might mean he was fair game this time around.

Sccrriiitch . . .

Dark flakes of soot fluttered down into the fireplace.

"Go." Foster was staring into the kitchen, but I couldn't bring myself to look that way.

"We can run," I reasoned, but even as I said it, I knew not all of us could. Foster couldn't get to the Mini fast enough, and if Stella and I stayed with him, we'd get to meet the Unfinished man at the door personally. But the determined set to Foster's jaw told me he had no intention of even trying to get away.

"Come on." I crowded both of them to the front door, ready to push it open and bolt.

"What?" Stella's eyes darted back and forth between me and Foster. "Out there?"

Heavy-footed scuttling on the roof overlapped with something large and solid toppling in the bedroom down the hall.

"Go," Foster said urgently, nodding at me, eyes still focused on the back door. "Save them. Don't make the same mistake I did."

But that was exactly was I was planning on doing, except I didn't think trying to get Key back would ever qualify as a mistake. "Stop it." I scowled, adjusting the backpack. "Get ready to run."

I grabbed Stella's wrist and opened the lock on the front door, peering through the glass. There were shadows moving around the corner of the house and ten long strides for us to get to the Mini.

"Ready?"

Stella nodded sharply. I reached back for Foster's arm, my fingers finding only air. "Uncle?"

One glance back showed me Foster in the kitchen doorway, drawing himself up and out, back to the size and solidity he must have had years ago, the first time he'd done this. My heart was tight and hard, knowing deep down there was no convincing him.

"Go," Foster said quietly, standing straight, fists clenched by his sides and staring through the kitchen to the back door. "Go."

The window in the back door shattered, and I wrenched the front door open, tears clouding my vision, leaving Foster to the last stand he felt he should've made the first time. Maybe this was what he'd been waiting for all those years—a second chance. If Key were here, I knew he'd make the same choice. With Stella's arm in my grasp, I bolted off the porch and sprinted across the grass with tunnel vision for the Mini, hearing something land with a thump on the ground behind us. At the car, I tore open the passenger door and slammed it shut so fast it caught the edge of my shoe.

"Stell. Go."

Stella jammed her foot on the gas, sobbing, and for one horrifying moment, the Mini's wheels just spun. I gripped Stella's arm with one hand, and the door handle with the other, fiercely looking anywhere but back at the house and willing the car to move. After what felt like an eternity, the tires bit into gravel, and the acceleration pressed me back into the seat.

I couldn't let myself think about Foster in the house. The time for thinking, considering, and planning was over. There were no more decisions to make. I was going to find the black water and close it, kill it, make it suffer.

This cycle may have been repeating since the beginning of time, but this was the last leg of the black water's race, and it was going to lose. I would make sure of it.

TWENTY-THREE

THE PARKING LOT WAS ALMOST EMPTY, SEARCHers and picnickers clocking out for the day in the face of the ominous clouds billowing overhead. A few people hurriedly secured bikes to car racks, and a family of four threw their towels and cooler into the trunk before buckling the kids in. Stella prowled the lot until she found a spot at the far end where we wouldn't be visible from the road. The last thing I needed now was some cop in my face about park fire regulations when I was trying to stop evil from crossing into the world. I sat in the passenger seat, hands in my lap and staring at the sky where the light illuminated the incoming clouds, lighter on top but bellies of deep purple. The stormfront was moving in from the southwest, where I'd left Foster alone to face the Unfinished. I ran my hands over my face and let them drop back into my lap, a puppet with the strings cut, useless without direction.

"What now, Ave?" Stella mirrored me.

"Don't know, Stell," I murmured.

Key was the designated zombie-apocalypse leader. I knew about training and protein and fartleks. Stella knew about research, citing sources, and archiving documents. Neither of us was prepared to face off with craggy-faced demons from another dimension. Not even a little.

278

But if Key *were* here, if I *were* taking orders, what would they be—look for him or burn the bones? Follow Maxine's advice, or strike out on my own? I closed my eyes and tried to picture him, tried to conjure up my Key, the one who could tell me exactly why my house would be indefensible from the brain-eating hordes, the one who would know which creatures to run from and when to stay absolutely still. But the only Key that came into my mind was the one I'd seen in the cellar—the empty, dead-eyed version. And that Key had already given what help he could. And now Foster . . .

Those thoughts hurt too much. I opened my eyes and found Stella hadn't moved, so I waved my hand in front of her face.

"We don't have stuff for a fire," Stella said without blinking.

I winced. The lack of supplies was a problem, but looking out at the rapidly darkening sky and gathering clouds, it wasn't the only one. Even if we could get a fire going, how would we *keep* it going? Unless it got really big, really fast. It seemed unlikely that I would be the first person to try to get rid of the black water by just burning the entire forest. That must have occurred to some desperate person over the years. But accidentally starting a massive fire that would only bring more grief and pain into the world was out of the question for me. We'd have to be careful.

"What are we going to do?" Stella asked dully.

The one thing that we absolutely needed was tucked on the floor between my feet. Even starting a fire, I could do somehow. But where? And what about Key? A ball of heat in my chest grew and spread, but my skin was papery and dry. I stared down at the box, hating it.

It was stifling inside the car. We'd rolled up the windows for fear of something getting in, but I rolled mine down now and stuck my head out like a dog to get a taste of the rain-scented wind that was picking up, sending tiny cyclones of dust swirling and skittering across the ground. Beside the parking lot was a sign welcoming visitors and reminding them of the "pack out what you pack in" rule and arrows pointing to the different trailheads, the restrooms, and the grill area.

I sat up and elbowed Stella. "Look."

Stella followed my gaze and then nodded. "Let's go."

We got out of the Mini cautiously, sticking close together and surveying the parking lot to make sure whatever had been on Foster's roof hadn't followed.

The designated grill area was the size of a football field, and apparently BYO. At the height of summer, this place would have been teeming with picnickers; the air would have been thick with the smells of charcoal and sunscreen, but the clouds had driven everyone away. It was eerily quiet. As we stepped off the gravel path and onto the scrubby grass, we were the only people in sight. Picnic tables, some brand new, some about to fall down, sat beside circular cement pits, but as we crossed the field picking up twigs and sticks, we peeked into each pit, and they were all empty. There were no actual grills, except one, partially disintegrated with rust. No wonder it had been left behind.

"I guess this is us," Stella muttered. She dropped her bundle of kindling and began rooting around in the nearby trash can like a particularly desperate racoon.

"How are we going to start a fire?" I set the backpack on the initial-scarred picnic table next to the grill.

"Somebody left tongs!" Stella hooked a plastic bag on one finger and gingerly drew it out of the trash. "Here, take this." She tossed a section of newspaper at me.

"What am I supposed to do with this?" The wind swirled around us, and panic fluttered in my stomach. The bones had to burn—but how? All I'd needed was a few more minutes with Foster to ask him the particulars, but once again, the black water had made sure that I'd run out of time. My eyes snapped skyward at the distant rumble of thunder. "You have got to be kidding me."

"We can use the paper to fan the fire." Stella set her plastic bag of treasure trash on the table. "That's good, right?"

Anything that got me one bit closer to my old life was good. If I could have boring, crappy runs and steal Key's fries again, if the only posters around town were for garage sales, that would . . . My eyes filled with the crushing longing for it.

"Okay." I sniffed. "But—"

Stella reached into her pocket and casually placed a lighter on the table.

"Stell." Surprise and disapproval colored my voice. What else did I not know about?

"What?" She shrugged, not meeting my eyes. "Sometimes I just— Look, it doesn't matter."

She sifted through the ash in the pit, tapped off a few pieces of leftover charcoal, and placed them carefully on the grill, which was nestled in the crumpled sheets of newspaper I had placed. Stella bent over the grill with the lighter, and I moved closer, using the rest of the paper and my body to shield the tiny flame from the breeze that was on the verge of becoming wind. The paper caught, and at the sight of the flames, I started breathing again, not even realizing I'd stopped.

Okay. Fire.

"So, let's . . ." Stella waved me over, squinting up at a dark purple cloud directly above us that boded nothing but trouble.

Now that we were going to do it, I was suddenly unsure. I would get only one shot at this. I swallowed my uncertainty, unzipped the backpack on the table, and unwrapped the tackle box so it sat naked in the light, covered with a fine grit. Had it leaked in the backpack? I couldn't worry about that now, as dots appeared on the table with the first fine drops of rain.

"Seriously." I gazed warily at the sky overhead, thick with looming black monsters.

"Well, open it," Stella said impatiently.

"You want to open it?" I dared her.

Stella pursed her lips and continued fanning.

"Didn't think so." I flipped the latch on the box open with the end of a stick and took a breath. Key had allowed me to get the box. Maxine thought burning the bones was the right thing to do, and Foster, too. But no one *knew*. The black water really seemed against the idea, though, and that's what pushed me on.

Stella stretched to watch over my shoulder.

"Coward," I muttered to myself, because that's all it was. Key wouldn't stop now; Foster hadn't. I bit my lip, lifted the lid, and forced myself to look at the contents.

"What. The hell. Is that?" Stella said.

I looked up at her, frowning. "It's bones. Just like Foster said."

Because it was. Inside the tackle box was a jumble of pale bones, fragments and chunks, but no more than I could hold in my two cupped hands. Not that I had any intention of actually touching any of them.

"No." Stella pointed over my shoulder, still fanning. "That."

I turned, and Stella leaned around me to look.

A girl in a neon-pink bikini, long red hair hanging tangled in her face, was lurching across the field, jerking like a marionette with the strings knotted up. Behind, a woman in shorts and a T-shirt, all the same color as the ash in the grill pit, stepped out of the trees, dragging her feet through the grass, an empty leash dangling from her hand.

"Ave?" Stella's fanning slowed as the women advanced toward us. "Hey, that's—" Stella squinted through the fine drizzle falling. "That's Jackie! Jackie!" She waved letting the newspaper flutter to the ground. Stella might not know the other woman, but I did. I'd seen Cara's face before, her photo next to her dog on one of the posters in town, and when the black water sent her to ambush us at the Pink Unicorn. She and Jackie were both shuffling forward slowly but steadily, like a tide coming in.

I picked up the paper and shoved it back into Stella's hand, keeping my eyes on the two figures. It was Jackie. Or it had been.

"What do we do?"

"What do you mean?"

Stella gestured at Jackie. "Can we save her? Like Key?"

My heart twinged. Stella, the eternal optimist. We hadn't saved Key, not yet, and I had no idea what would happen when the bones burned. Would it just wink the Ragged Man out of existence, returning everyone else? Or would he take everyone with him?

"You never know," Stella said, reading my mind. But deep down,

I did know. Jackie was gone, and unless I figured out how to find him, Key would be, too.

"I . . . don't feel good about this." I didn't like the blank way the two women were staring and coming straight toward us, leisurely, like they had all the time in the world. It shouldn't have been menacing, but it was. We'd known Jackie—been friends—but I didn't think she knew that now.

"There are only two," I said, half to myself. "We can handle this." I caught Stella's eye. "Are we cool?"

Stella picked up the newspaper and nodded. "There are only two."

A third figure stepped out of the trees without disturbing anything around her, like she'd materialized right there.

"Shit!" Stella jumped.

The little girl.

Stella resumed fanning, maybe too fast.

"Oh." I took a step back. The girl with no eyes.

I squinted as more shadows in the forest approached the tree line through the falling rain. The black water was going to defend itself. It knew about heroes, too.

"Stell, watch it!" I snatched the flaming newspaper out of Stella's hand and shoved it away. "Let's do it!"

"It's not hot enough." Stella plucked the remainder of the singed paper out of my hand and kept fanning.

How hot did it need to be to burn bones? They were old, so they should burn faster. Should. But how hot was hot enough? I cast a doubtful look at the grill. Just one of a thousand of otherwise-useless facts Key would know. I grabbed a couple more twigs from the ground.

The twigs I threw on the grill flamed up immediately, but the flames died off just as fast.

"More. Keep it going," Stella ordered.

I hesitated. There wasn't any other way. This had to go faster. I picked up a chunk of bone between my fingers and dropped it on the grill. It caught the flame almost as quickly as the kindling but burned steadily. Rubbing my fingers on my shirt didn't stop the tingling where I'd touched the bones; it seemed to drive it deeper, through my skin with my own bones answering.

"Yeah!" Stella nodded, fanning the flames carefully now, leaning down to blow gently on the grill and still trying to keep an eye on the progress of the black water's army.

I dropped more kindling on the grill and added another piece of bone. I'd already touched one. What would it matter now? Not too much at once—fine enough for the wind to carry away—that was what Maxine had said. How long would this take? How long before Key ran out of time?

Stella held the plastic bag with one hand, trying to shield the fire from the intensifying rain. "Keep an eye on them, Ave."

Way ahead of you. Jackie was closest to us, and still coming, but something was happening. With every step, she seemed to become less solid, and as I added a third piece of bone, Jackie's fingers glowed around the edges like paper catching the heat of an ember. The deep orange intensified in her fingertips until they disintegrated into dust that the breeze caught and carried off. Jackie glanced down, her terrible focus finally diverted. She raised her hand, and we watched together as the glow continued, up her arms and into her shoulders.

"I'm sorry, Jackie." Another few seconds, and Jackie was gone entirely. One person I'd failed to save. I could only hope that there was something different about Key, that burning the bones wasn't having the same effect on him.

I shoved the three large bone fragments around with the tongs, making room for more and panting like I was sprinting. I couldn't think about Jackie now, I had to *do*.

"What's going on?" Stella asked around the end of the bag held between her teeth to form a canopy over the grill.

"They're burning," I said quietly, watching the same thing happen to Cara. She looked at me quizzically, opened her mouth as if to speak, and burst into flakes of ash. "They're burning with the bones."

"These things are lighting up really well," Stella muttered to herself, then looked up to find the little girl less than ten feet away. Still fanning, she reached down, picked up a rock at her foot, and hurled it in the girl's direction, but, one-handed and distracted, her aim was way off. The girl stopped and looked down at the rock for a moment before resuming her course. Stella's eyes went wide, and she abandoned the plastic bag.

"Do something, Ave!" she called. "We need more time!"

Or bigger flames. There weren't many of us left, Foster had said. It was hard. I understood now. The black water had an army, and all I had was Stella and no more kindling nearby.

I tensed at the sound of footsteps behind us, because whoever this was wasn't shuffling. They were sprinting. Which was so great. The Unfinished could run now?

"Avery!" I spun around because the Unfinished didn't speak, and I knew that voice.

"Frank!" The hurt I'd felt when Foster had named him flared up like one of the embers Stella was fanning frantically, but it died down just as fast with the knowledge that he was here now.

Frank was panting, and I reached out to take his arm because although he was in much better shape, he wasn't much younger than Foster.

"I'm so sorry. I—I wanted to protect you," Frank wheezed.

"How did you know?"

"Foster called me," Frank said, bent over with both hands on his knees.

Hope surged in my chest—Foster was alive. Frank showing up now wasn't going to make up for everything, but it was definitely a good start.

"He was in trouble but—" Frank elbowed Stella aside and twisted the cap off a small tin of lighter fluid he carried, spraying it on the grill. The flames shot up over my head, driving us all back one step.

"Where were you all this time?" I snapped.

"I'm so sorry," Frank said over his shoulder, smoothly grabbing an orphaned flip-flop from the bag of trash and launching it at the Unfinished like he'd done this before, which he had.

"Avery!"

My head popped up. *Mom?*

"Ave, honey!"

Dad. I squinted into the dim light, toward the parking lot, but couldn't see them. *My parents. Here?*

"Ave, we've come to take you home! Let's go!"

"Sweetie!" my mom's voice called, closer but still out of sight. "Everything is going to be fine. Just like before!"

Frank darted back from the edge of the field with a stick some dog had cast off. "Don't listen, Avery." He panted, poking the stick at an Unfinished man in jogging shorts who was drawing far too close to the grill. "It's not real."

No kidding. My parents couldn't even talk to each other on the phone, let alone be in the same physical space. I turned back to the fire, having no interest in seeing the black water's version of my parents, making my dream of reunion the ultimate nightmare. But a sudden surge of hope bloomed, warm in my chest. Thinking I would fall for my parents being anywhere together? That was a desperate move.

Five feet away, the jogging shorts man wrestled with Frank for the stick, ripping it out of Frank's hands and flinging it to the ground, where it stuck in the soft earth like a spear.

"Ave!" Stella fanned frantically, eyes locked on the other side of the field. I followed her gaze to see the woman with the parasol shielding her ruined face and marching steadily across the grass through the drizzle. "Ave!" Stella pointed, her eyes wide.

"Yes! I know, I know!"

I dropped the last piece of bone onto the grill and then shook the box upside down over it for good measure. Some of the first pieces were in flames and had fallen down to rest directly on the coals. Would they smother the heat?

"Keep going." I gave Stella the tongs and took over fanning. Stella used the tongs to shift the other pieces as if she were browning sausages, keeping them moving.

Frank was now chucking everything he could reach in the trash at the Unfinished. A half-full water bottle. Three beer bottles. An empty pickle jar.

"We've got a problem." Stella shifted bones with one hand and pointed with the other.

"I know," I muttered. A clap of thunder startled me. This was only going to get worse.

The little girl had stopped less than twenty feet away. I'd beaned her in the head with a couple of chunks of concrete someone had used to weight a towel, to no real effect. I'd felt bad about the first one, but this wasn't a kid, not really. The second rock really had some force, knocking her back a step, but none of it was slowing her down enough to suit me. Then the girl suddenly stopped on her own. I hesitated, the rock in my hand a cold possibility. The girl held out her hands in front of her, as if inspecting a manicure. I didn't know what had her attention, but it wasn't the grill, so I was all for it.

When the little girl's fingers started to glow, I couldn't help but feel satisfaction, a tiny release of the tension in my chest. She probably hadn't always been what she was now. Maybe it wasn't her fault. But if little Luci was gone forever, that would break Stella. So I wished whatever this little girl was would go ahead and burn already.

The girl held her hands up now as if to show me, or to ask.

"Yeah, I know," I said softly, fanning the flames roasting the bones, never taking my eyes off the black water's little minion.

She didn't go piecemeal like the others. The glow ran up her arms, down her legs, and around her head like a halo. Her sightless face looked different just then, something shifting, sliding underneath.

"Sorry, kid." My fanning slowed a little. Was the same thing happening to Key? Lily hadn't appeared to Foster the way Key had to me in the cellar, which made me hope there was something different about him from all the others. If I had a chance to protect everyone else in town, I had to take it, even if it broke me. The little girl took a step, and then she was gone. I sagged with relief, but too soon.

The woman with the parasol stepped forward, where the little girl had just been, bits of her ash settling like snowflakes on the woman's hair, sending my heart right back into my throat.

I scanned the ground for something else to throw, mind racing in desperation. If we could just hold off the Unfinished, the fire would take care of them. I hooked my foot into the handle of the bag of trash and dragged it closer. Plastic cups, juice boxes, an empty squeeze bottle of mustard, they all became ammunition against the black water's army marching across the grass.

"It's not enough," I whispered.

Stella pulled a flattened pizza box and held it over the grill in an attempt to protect it from the rain now swept sideways by the wind. The bones were burning, but to let them burn into ash would take more time than the Unfinished were going to allow.

"Frank, we need more." More time, more fire, more help. Just more. "Frank!" I turned over my shoulder to see what Frank was doing.

Frank was not doing anything. He was absolutely still, the wind lifting the edge of his shirt, staring at the horde advancing toward us. A new figure in a tattered dress was making its way across the scrubby grass.

"Margot," Frank whispered.

"Frank! Help me!" Panic rose in my chest. I wanted to shake him out of it, but I'd have to abandon the fire, which was exactly what the black water had in mind. The Unfinished were moving in, but

Frank was hypnotized, slowly walking toward the sister who was finally coming home.

"Ave." Stella's voice was low and shaky. "We're in trouble here."

My skin prickled. *It was happening again.* Maybe it really was fated to go the same every time. Maybe every decision I'd made was an illusion, another inevitable part of the loop.

Thunder rumbled close enough that I could feel it, and lightning lit up the field for an instant, showing me many more figures still emerging from the trees. How many Unfinished had the black water collected over the decades? I stood for a moment, letting the rain soak me, not feeling the cold, not hearing Stella call. This was all going wrong. I understood now why Foster hadn't finished it the last time. I understood why he'd cut and run. The black water was fighting back. But it had underestimated me.

I was scared, but I was also stubborn. I would do anything to stop the black water. I would bite and claw, kick and thrash. I would scream myself hoarse and burn everything to stop it. The familiar pre-race tingle of adrenaline flooded my body. I set my jaw, took four steps forward, and snatched the woman's parasol out of her hands, whacking her in the head with it as hard as I could. She didn't back off, but she fell back a few steps and was definitely pissed.

This had to go faster. I raised the parasol to hit the woman again, then froze. Maxine hadn't said they had to *burn* completely. *Until the wind carries them away.* Thanks to Frank's fuel lighter, the bones were a lot closer than they had been minutes ago.

"Frank!" I called, but Frank was motionless, staring across the field, as his sister advanced.

"Hold on." I handed the parasol to Stella and darted away from the grill.

"Hey!" Stella jabbed the woman in the chest with it. The woman yanked her parasol back out of Stella's hands and cast it aside furiously. "Oh boy." Stella's eyes went wide.

Come.

The faceless woman lunged forward and gripped Stella's wrist. "Ave!"

I scanned the ground closer to the parking lot, grabbing the two biggest chunks of concrete I could see.

"Yeah! Throw!" Stella ducked down to give me clear aim.

Ignoring her, I put one rock on the ground next to the grill and plucked a piece of bone out of the flames. I placed it on the rock on the ground as carefully as my burning fingers would allow, gripped the second rock in both hands and lifted it over my head.

Behind me, Stella twisted away from the woman. One more moment and Stella would either panic and break away or the woman would succeed in pulling her away from the grill.

I brought down the rock on top of the bone with all the strength I had left. The half-charred bone exploded into a puff of white dust, and I looked up to see the parasol woman starting to go orange around the edges.

"Oh, yes," I breathed. "Please."

"Keep going!" Stella tried to back away, but the woman gripped her T-shirt in both hands, seeming to blame her for the strange thing that was happening.

I grabbed another chunk of bone and smashed it like the first.

"Holy crap!" Stella waved her hand through the dust where the woman had been.

"Help me." I held out the rock in blistering fingers I couldn't fully feel. "I can't, Stell."

"I'll do it. Look at your hands," Stella chided.

"Just these?" I arranged the last of the bones onto the slab and then looked up.

Across the grass, the Unfinished were winking out, candles that should have burned down a long time ago. The black water hadn't counted on the current home team getting help from their predecessors.

Now that Margot was close enough, Frank began backing away, finally understanding that his sister was long gone.

"Avery?" he called over his shoulder.

"How will we know it worked?" Stella lifted the rock to smash one of the last bones. "I mean, it's getting rid of *them*, but . . ."

"I don't know." I shook my head, breathing heavily as the air around me suddenly grew dense and heavy. "Are you sure there are no more bones?" Across the field, more of the Unfinished were coming out of the trees. Stella grabbed the backpack, looked inside, and paled.

Stella may have answered, but I didn't hear. Every sound—Stella's voice, rain pattering on leaves, the crackle of flames and peals of thunder—merged, crescendoed to a *pop*, and went silent. I was left alone with the sound of my own breathing.

Here.

I spun, expecting to see him, the Ragged Man.

Here.

Nothing.

But there was movement, one figure, deep in the trees. I squinted into the green and, without thinking, raised my hand to touch the turtle, ever warm against me, even in the cold rain.

Here.

I tilted my head. The black water had spoken to me before, but this was a different voice. This was not like the fake voices of my parents; I wasn't hearing this voice with my ears.

Ave.

I stilled, staring. The movement in the trees receded; was it a trick? My eyes burned with tears.

"Ave!" Stella called, shaking the backpack over the fire, dust and small chunks of bone raining down. "We have a problem!"

"Avery!" Frank ran toward us, hands pressed to his temples, a once-delicate woman wearing a tattered full-skirted dress looming steps behind. "It's happening again!"

Here.

No.

The world fell away.

This wasn't the black water calling.

Here.

Into the trees, I ran.

TWENTY-FOUR

WHERE? WHERE WAS IT?

It all looked the same. Dense brush in every direction, with no path visible. I stopped and did a slow spin. Tall weeds, low bushes—a seemingly impenetrable wall closing ranks in a perfect circle. How could I possibly get through here? How could anyone? I didn't know where I was, and I had no idea which way to go. Time was running out.

I closed my eyes and tried not to panic. The brush was not impassable. There was a trail. The black water didn't want me to see it, but it was there.

"It's there," I said out loud.

And then I knew.

Here.

The bushes were dense and weaving themselves together, a crowd locking arms to stop me from moving forward. This had to be the way.

Here.

The brush, the weeds, knitted together, trying and failing to stop me. I barreled ahead, pelted by rain, feeling nothing. An ocean of green, waves breaking against my chest, one after another. The grass and ivy, creeping vines down around my feet were even thicker, as if the roots of the forest itself were reaching up to grab hold of me. I pushed on, barely seeing, just listening. The tingle in my fingers crept up to my elbows.

Come.

It was easy now, to hear.

It wasn't the black water calling, pulling me on. The door was still open.

It was Key.

Avery.

The one voice I could hear from the depths of any ocean, across any distance, and through total darkness.

Avery.

The one voice that could rouse me from any sleep. The one voice I would answer forever.

Branches and brambles rose to tear at my clothes and skin, attempting to stop me, to slow me down. If anything, I sped up. I plowed right through, letting them rip away and hang from me like streamers.

Here.

Here.

Here.

This way.

My lungs burned. Branches grabbed at my face as I flew past, forcing me to close my eyes and turn away, but it didn't matter. I didn't need to see. It was this way, through the brush, through the trees, through anything. It didn't matter. If Lily had had the strength to call to Foster, to lead him back to the water, so did Key. It was the only way.

"Key!" I yelled, but my voice bounced back to me, absorbed by the foliage. "Key!"

Avery.

Faster.

This way.

Here.

I broke through the bushes into an opening. The pines—sheltering and cool. This, I remembered. After the dense brush tried to slow me down, the pines opened up, heavy branches pulling back to either side so that I could pass. It wasn't just a trail now—it may as well have been a lighted runway. I sped up, feeling the little silver turtle knock against my collarbone with every step, urging me on.

"Avery!"

Not just in my head anymore. It was Key. A sob pushed its way up my throat, bursting out with my next breath. It was *Key.* I could hear him calling up ahead, each syllable increasingly desperate.

"Avery!"

"Key!"

There was nothing stopping me now—no obstacles to jump, no branches clinging. I ran with tunnel vision, aware of nothing but the point the pines were guiding me to, where they opened out onto the meadow. I ran with a speed and purpose I'd never had before.

Then it was there.

At the center of the meadow.

Waiting for me. I was done running away from things. I left the pines and ran straight toward it, feeling my ankles turn on the grassy mounds and not slowing a bit.

Through the moat, I dropped to my knees, ignoring the mud

squelching and sucking at my skin, to edge as close to the pond as I dared. The surface of the water was unnaturally still, unaffected by the rain, but I eyed it warily, knowing that there was plenty going on underneath, with things far bigger than myself swimming around.

Bracing myself on my hands that sank to the wrists in cold muck, I leaned forward and peered at my reflection, lightning flashing in the sky behind me. My reflection could change at any moment, the features sliding and twisting into some dark, cruel version of me. But it wasn't the reflected version of me that held my gaze. It was Key, kneeling next to her, staring through the black water like I was the only thing in the world to see.

"Key!"

A little farther forward, looking only at him, my hand touched the barest edge of the water, and I saw the black water's trick. The water was icy cold and dense; it reached out for me, sending sharp sparks through my hand and up my arm. I jerked back but almost immediately shifted forward again to see.

The shores in the reflection teemed with Unfinished, shoulder to shoulder, seething and roiling, jostling at the water's edge, each impatiently waiting to be brought through to my side. Behind them, a darker, deader version of the forest rose and swayed, something with unimaginable bulk making the canopy tremble.

The flood.

I started at the sight and sank low. I gave a quick look back to confirm there were no blank, ruined faces hovering over my shoulder, because for a second I wavered, unsure of which side of the black water I was on.

"I'm here." A whispered assurance to myself. "I'm here."

But Key was on the other side.

Could I do it? My stomach was a tight knot.

I had no choice. I rose to a crouch, steeling myself to take the first step into the water, then tried, but found I couldn't. There was something holding me back. I whipped around to see.

The Ragged Man, towering over me, a crack opening and spreading across his face. A smile? Ice flooded my veins. My mind shuddered, stopped, and went dead silent.

Until the hand, hard and cold as stone, clamped around my wrist.

Clarity came in screaming, too bright, too loud.

I was back in the meadow. The Ragged Man was dragging me across the meadow away from the black water. Away. Why?

It doesn't take the first.

The black water didn't want me. I dug in my heels, but just as in my dream, it did no good. The grip on my wrist was a vise; the force pulling me was unstoppable.

"Key." It came out as a whimper. Wherever he was, he'd know. And he'd blame himself.

Chirrrp!

"Key." One shivering syllable. I'd made a mistake. I should never have let him go that night at the bookstore. I'd been too scared, too weak to apologize. Mom—would she think that I'd run away? That I'd left her? Would Lily remember me at all? Something in my heart twisted. I was sorry, so sorry, and now it was too late.

I tried to hold on to hope, but the necklace was all I had.

"Key!" I squeezed my eyes shut and tried to visualize him, the real Key, sending the image out like a beacon and hoping he would see it.

We were heading through the moat, the long grass whisper-gripping at my ankles. I couldn't take my eyes off the water, the thing that had haunted me for what felt like forever. The water was inky black and undulating slowly, like it had all the time in the world. How had I ever mistaken it for water? It was dense and sluggish, like a beast waking. I didn't want to know what it felt like, what Key had felt when it closed over his head.

"Key!"

I just wished I'd had more time. I should've . . . I should've done things differently. I should've said things, asked more questions, been more open. With everyone. To everything.

Chirrrp! Chirrrp! Chirrrp!

The watch thought I was having a heart attack. Maybe that would be best.

Tears burned my throat, and I threw my weight back as hard as I could. The Ragged Man didn't even notice, just kept on his course for whatever was waiting for us. Underneath the hum of sheer panic, I wondered where he was taking me, what he had in mind. The unseen giant plowing through the reflected forest—was its shadow-self waiting for me here? Was there something even worse than the Unfinished waiting in the forest?

I swung my free arm backward and grabbed a handful of grass, trying to slow us down, but the grass came up in my hand as easily as if it was planted in sand. I dug my fingers in the wet earth anyway, raking a trail. I wasn't going to make this easy.

If Key was watching, if he knew, he'd see me fight. He'd know I tried.

Key.

If the Ragged Man was still here, it meant the door was still open, and as long as that was true, there was a chance for Key.

I thrashed like a fish on a hook, flinging my arms and legs out, trying to get a grip on something to slow our progress away from the black water. My fingers grabbed onto grass, dirt, and mud but all of it came away in my hands. In my mind's eye, I imagined myself a stone, a rock, a boulder too dense and solid to be moved.

And then the Ragged Man's steps became slow and labored, each one taking all the energy he had. With every step, the Ragged Man's boot sank deeper into the grassy mounds of the meadow. But it wasn't the meadow giving way—it was him. A crackling, sizzling snap and the icy hand on my wrist warmed and then went hot, setting off a spark of hope blooming in my chest; Stella and Frank must still be tending the fire.

The Ragged Man's legs dissolved up to the knees, pitching him forward and down. He wasn't smiling now—he looked surprised and confused, like the little girl before she burned. His gaze lowered to where his boots had been. This was my chance and I took it.

Wrenching my arm hard enough to hear a crack, I broke free of his failing grip and scrambled to my feet, ready to run.

The Ragged Man lunged at me, sending me flying back onto the grass. Up close, the jagged contours of his ruined face shifted and slid, trying to be many faces and succeeding in being none. Every soul the black water had ever taken was pulsing, pressing from the inside against the Ragged Man's skin. Different faces flashed into view and disappeared. Every face contracted in pain, desperate to get out.

The Ragged Man's hand shot out toward me, his fingers brushing my arm, melting against my skin like wet sand unable to grasp or grip. Finally, just like the other Unfinished, the Ragged Man was winking out.

I scuttled backward toward the pond, and the Ragged Man followed, dragging what was left of him, reaching out for me again, his touch barely registering against my leg. His face was almost formless, but I hoped he could still see—I was going to be the one left standing at the end of this fight. I moved into a crouch, heart pounding in my throat, watching as the Ragged Man tried and failed, this thing that had stalked me and stolen the ones I loved.

"Fuck you," I whispered. A flash of lightning so bright, I shut my eyes against it.

Unable to get a grip on anything, the Ragged Man flung his arm out one more time, but not to me. The remains of his arm outstretched was answered by the pond, sending out a slender stream, merging with the Ragged Man's arm and pooling around him, like the ocean eating away at a sculpture of sand. The Ragged Man struggled and flailed before he finally sank down, dissolving back into the black water. I swiped at the cold rain streaming down my face and watched blankly, all feeling gone, maybe forever.

Key.

The surface of the pond was undulating slowly, alive and watching me. I straightened up and took a step closer, still afraid, but encouraged by the fact that the Ragged Man had tried to keep me away. My senses were in overdrive, every brush of my fingers against my shorts electric; I heard each drop of rain pelting down, everywhere except the pond. The meadow was a riot of noise, but my head was the quietest and calmest it had ever been. Foster had failed, but I would do things differently. It always repeats, Foster had said, but maybe that's because we had always played the same part, made the same moves. What if I did something different?

Sky Woman had fallen, but what if I jumped?

It doesn't take the first.

But what if *I* took *it*?

I rose to my feet, turned my back to the pines, faced the black water, and did what I did best. I ran.

One, two, three strides, my foot slid a little on the now-slick grass. Two more long strides, picking up speed, and I hit water, the splash of my feet hitting the ground indistinguishable from the rain pelting down.

One, two, three strides more, knee-deep water trying and failing to slow me down. As much as the water pushed against me, there was something stronger at my back. In the center of my chest, Lily's turtle shone, warm and suddenly heavy against my skin like it had tripled in size. I'd never been alone in this; I'd never been adrift. I hadn't understood that I was connected to all the ones who'd come before me—I'd never known them, but they knew me. Together, we ran.

My heart knew running—it beat steady and strong, my eyes locked on the center of the water. My mind went quiet, and the noise of the storm raging around me faded. Maybe it was this simple—the world requires balance—a night for every day, a win for every loss. One in, one out. If that was the price to keep Key in the world, I was willing to pay it.

Two more sloshing strides and the water became too deep to run in. The others who ran with me drew close, and I gathered them around me like a shawl, protection from the storm. Without missing a beat, without a second thought, I took one last breath and dove.

There was no resistance to the water, sliding against my skin like cold silk, caressing gently but with the promise of a bite. It was dark and hazy. I could see shapes moving below, down in the depths, but they were indistinct and shifting. I closed my eyes against the sentient water slipping over my face, looking for a way in. I ignored my pulse pounding in my throat, the fear of knowing where I was, and pictured him.

I stretched out my hand and someone took it.

You don't know what you'll bring back.

But I did. I gripped his wrist tightly and knew it was Key. I'd know him anywhere, anytime, in any form. I pulled him toward me, but the black water gave very little. The black water could pull all it wanted—I wasn't letting go, even after my lungs emptied. I would stay here forever if I had to, locked in this tug-of-war. I would never quit.

I clung to Key as we continued to fall through the water, pulling his limp form in close to me, my lungs burning and fingers going numb. We fell, deeper and deeper with every passing second. We might fall forever, I thought calmly, until something huge and hard rose up to meet me. This close, I could make out a giant dark shape, wider than I was tall, bumpy and ridged.

A shell.

One arm wrapped around Key, the other hand gripping the edge of the giant shell that lifted me, slowly, carefully at first, then rocketing toward the surface, back the way we'd come.

Up, up, up. The force of our ascent flattened me against Turtle's back, my ears ringing and my lungs burning to take a breath. Up above, a small patch of light, soft and shimmering like dawn, was opening. It grew bigger, brighter, and sharper; too strong for closing my eyes to bring any relief—the burst of white light became a spike in my head. I closed my eyes against the pressure that struck and bloomed, intensified and blazed until I couldn't feel, couldn't think, couldn't be.

And then everything went dark.

My head surfaced out of the black water, and I dragged in a ragged breath of crisp air, so relieved to see Key still wrapped in my numb arm, terrified to lose him again. I struck out with the last of my strength for the edge of the pond, heart hammering against my ribs even after my feet touched muddy bottom. I scrambled on hands and knees, every muscle shrieking as I hauled Key clear of the black water.

One in, one out.

The words were a vise around my heart. But it was Key, and I didn't care about whatever rules the black water might have.

Chirrrp! Chirrrp! My watch was singing a different song.

The sound roused me into rising, dragging Key away from the water much like the Ragged Man had tried to drag me. By the time I laid Key in the meadow, the black water was still, looking like it had never been disturbed. Yet I kept my eye on it, because this was definitely the part of the movie where the dead monster came back to life.

A bubble rose to the surface and popped. Then another.

Chirrrp! Chirrrp!

"Key, we have to get—" I grabbed him under his arms, my feet sloshing through the water.

Had I been standing in water a second ago? Because I was now.

Water bubbled and rose around us, rising through the mounds of slender grass where the Ragged Man had dissolved. The black water overflowed its banks with no sign of stopping, over the muddy shore and up into the grass, flooding the whole meadow.

A whole new level of panic set me to floundering and splashing back toward the pines, Key a deadweight in my burning arms. Every step was controlled panic, because if I fell now, the water would close over us both for good.

Breathe in, breathe out. I kept my eyes on the edge of the meadow, managing to stay one step ahead of the floodwater nipping at my heels.

Finally, out of the meadow and into the pines, the cathedral branches arched protectively over us. The air here was fresh and green; the rain pattered softly far above but failed to reach us. I gently laid Key's head down on the soft carpet of the pine needles and stroked his face.

"Key." He was soaking wet and pale, and his lips were a little bit gray. I had never seen anything more beautiful.

Chirrrp! Chirrrp! The Ragged Man was gone, the black water was overflowing the meadow, and my GPS had come back to life.

I sat at the edge of the pines, tiny waves lapping toward the toes of my shoes, as the water in what had been the meadow rose, my chest so tight, I couldn't tell if I was breathing or not. Key was still and cold, but breathing and gloriously alive. Lightning flashed in the sky over the meadow, but the rain was already subsiding. I let my hand rest on Key's chest, comforted by the rise and fall.

Clear water inched along through the grass, but farther out, in the center of the pond, big bubbles rose to the surface and broke.

I kept my hand on Key's shoulder, afraid to let go but equally unwilling to take my eyes off the expanding pond. The Ragged Man was gone—I'd seen it. I'd watched the Unfinished wink out in the park. So why was I still humming with adrenaline? Why did I still want to run?

"We burned the bones," I said to no one. I'd done what Maxine wanted, so what was this?

One in, one out.

I turned to look at Key, pressing my palm to the side of his face as the water bubbled and gurgled behind me, the rumble of thunder still loud enough to feel. In stealing Key back, I'd tipped the scales; I'd put everything out of balance, and maybe the black water had some things to say about that.

The pond was now bubbling chaos, more water spreading farther out into the meadow. I stared out at it with a cold certainty that I'd always been coming here, to this moment. All the people the black water had stolen, none of it was my fault. The black water had been playing this game for centuries—someone would always start the cycle; it didn't matter who.

In a brilliant flash of lightning, what was left of the meadow lit up like day, and a crack of thunder left my ears ringing. My spine stiffened and my hand curled protectively around Key's shoulder. I went still as a stone, my breath shallow. Behind me, in the pines, the *crack!* of a single branch. My head snapped up. "Stella?" I scanned the pines but saw nothing. "Frank?"

It was over. We were safe.

Still, my heart pounded like a drum.

TWENTY-FIVE

KEY'S DAD SMELLED LIKE CITRUS, A FACT I USED to distract myself from the awkwardness of my face pressing into his shirt.

"Anything you ever need, Avery." Key's dad held me in a bone-grindingly tight hug that his son was still too frail to receive. "Forget need—anything you want. I can't believe that water was in the forest all this time. What a menace to public safety." His voice rang in the hospital hallway, raising heads at the nurses' station. He shook his head and pulled back to look me in the eye and lowered his voice. "We can never repay you." By his shoulder, Jeannie wiped her eyes and stroked my arm for the millionth time since Key had been admitted. My stomach turned, roiling with guilt. It was hard to be around his parents now; they treated me like I'd saved their son, when really I was the reason they almost lost him.

"You'll call us if anything changes." A promise Key's dad had extracted from me every time we changed shifts.

I waited until they got into the elevator, their hands clasped tightly, before I turned and slipped into the room.

I'd grown to love the beeping.

At first, it had grated on me, the constant beeping of the machines, but it was comforting now. I could lay my head on the edge of the bed so that the top of my forehead was touching his arm and close my eyes, letting the beep keep watch for me, letting it quietly reassure me that he was still here.

I put my palm flat on his chest, just to check. Machines break down, after all. But there it was, the soft thump under my hand and then the beep after a delay, almost imperceptible to anyone who wasn't willing it with every ounce of her being.

I felt the thump, heard the beep, and watched Key's face for some sign that he really was in there. This was how I spent my days now. I had nowhere I needed to be, no training that couldn't wait. I'd become the first-ever recipient of the Avery Ray Scholarship, funded by Frank's Books. Anything, he'd said, to keep me off of the trails for a while. He'd refused to take no for an answer. Accepting allowed him to atone, and I was glad for the help—and for the break. Yeah, I'd still run. I always would.

But not now.

Like everyone else in town, my mom had been shocked at what might have happened—if Stella hadn't found Key and me by the edge of the pond. Actually, Mom had been knocked speechless for once, wrapping Stella in a very uncharacteristic bear hug at the first available opportunity. The only thing I'd asked was that Mom never tell Lily, which was an easy agreement between us, although when I'd gone to visit her, the way Lily had looked, I couldn't shake the feeling that maybe she already knew.

What had happened in the meadow—I couldn't explain that. The last thing I remembered was the water bubbling and then Stella, drenched and shrieking, looming over me in the pines with my phone in her hand. All I knew was the black water would have kept at least one of us if it could have, but while the black water may have anticipated me coming for it, I guess it didn't expect all my ancestors to have my back. They'd been watching me all this time, maybe through Lily's eyes, watching and loving me, and I'd never given them a thought.

I'd been drowning, and Turtle had lifted me up. I'd crawled out of the black water and brought Key with me.

And what else?

A flash of movement behind me, of splashing not my own. I pushed that thought away. I had Key, and the Ragged Man was gone—that was all that mattered.

"Are you coming?" Stella asked from the doorway, low-key worried about me still, always trying to coax me out of the room with offers of ice cream or "keeping an eye on your boy" while I took a break. Sometimes I accepted. Stella had had to answer questions, too, about that day—what we'd been doing in the forest off the trail.

Everyone had questions, including me—a lot, actually—things I'd never cared about before, or felt entitled to know, but not about the black water. I wanted to learn the words for the things I didn't know how to say, to be brave enough to hope for the things I really wanted and to try to make them happen. I wanted to learn how to dance. My culture, like the black water, had been waiting for me for a long time. The Kanyen'kehá:ka weren't going anywhere; hopefully the black water was gone for good.

The pond was still out there, but now anyone could find it. "The big pond"—that's what they were calling it, because that's what it was. A large, almost-perfect circle of water that reflected the blue of the sky, clear enough to see the long grass undulating underneath if you got close enough. Stella had been out there and taken a video from the fence line that now surrounded the area. It looked normal. Pretty, even. There was no trail leading to it, and there never would be, but for now, the tracks of the paramedics who'd brought Key and me out were still visible for the curious to follow. The forest would take care of that as it had many times before, I knew, erasing any trace of people and reabsorbing its secret. Not soon enough, in my opinion.

There wasn't anything unusual about the water now, but the local paper reported that when recovery divers approached the center of the pond where the depth plunged, they became disoriented and were forced to surface, unsure of whether they had been swimming up or down. They'd found no bodies and the whole thing had been fenced off after that. It was deemed too risky to continue, although the mayor insisted that the search for the others would go on, and he would get the town council to pay for drones to send through the forest.

When I'd read that, an unpleasantly familiar chill had danced down my spine. If the black water was gone, shouldn't people have woken up? Everyone should be clamoring for investigation and the truth—unless it hadn't just been the black water's influence; people preferred to believe what was most convenient for them. But I was hopeful that change would come. Rumors had started that the water was contaminated somehow, that it gave off disorienting fumes; naturally, whispers of government or industrial conspiracy had started to circulate. People would forget, like Maxine said, but maybe this time would be different. Maybe I had forced us off the loop. The rumors going around were better than nothing; I certainly wasn't going to do anything to stop them. But still.

CHERYL ISAACS

Warning signs and a fence. I had shaken my head in disgust and tossed the paper aside.

I worried that it would only be a matter of time now that anyone could find it. The water had changed, but the fact that it was still there at all disturbed me.

Every last bit of bone had burned, Stella swore, and Frank backed her up. I believed them; besides, the Ragged Man's dissolution was proof of it.

It sleeps. . . .

"We could go for coffee?" Stella tried now.

But I didn't bite.

"I'm going to stay," I said quietly. The chair squeaked as I changed position, my back sending out its own twinge of protest. Suck it up, back. We're not going anywhere.

"She's still stubborn." My mom appeared behind Stella, in her scrubs, up from Radiology. "You should know that. I'll make her leave at the end of my shift." She patted Stella's arm.

"Okay." Stella knew there was no use reasoning or trying to negotiate. A lot of things about me had changed, but like my mom said, I was as stubborn as ever.

"I'll text later." Stella crept up and kissed the top of my head, a move that I would never have tolerated before, but Stella needed support now, too. When she wasn't with Luci's older sister, she was filling in for Key—his photography club had reconvened for a special summer meeting to make a memorial exhibit for Jackie and the others who'd disappeared in the forest. She was clearly trying to atone for whatever guilt she carried, and I hoped she could; Stella was the last person who needed to feel bad about anything that had happened. When Key found out how easily and ably Stella had replaced him, though, he'd be spitting mad. I couldn't wait to hear them bicker about it.

Stella patted Key's hand and padded out.

Another kiss on my head, and my mom whispered in my ear, "I'll be back for you."

I nodded, dying to rest my eyes, just for a few minutes.

The light outside had faded, the window now showing me only myself, sitting in my chair. I tilted my head to one side, watching the other girl copy. I yawned, and the other girl joined in. We both stroked the silver turtle around my neck. My body felt heavy and warm, ready to be pulled down by sleep if I'd only let it happen. But sleep was still complicated.

I didn't have nightmares anymore, not like before. Nothing comparable to that crushing panic I'd felt being dragged across the meadow night after night. This was different. Now, most often, when I slipped off in the dark, I was falling.

I was falling through the sky, the wind whistling in my ears, cold air biting at my face.

Falling toward a bright blue ocean, diamonds of light dancing on the waves.

Down, down I fell,

but I wasn't afraid.

He was there already, treading water patiently.

And when I finally landed, splashed down beside him,

I knew.

I would surface.

We would swim together.

We would find land.

I'd once feared speaking things into existence. Now I was counting on it. When he woke up, things would be different. All the things I never said, all the words that had caught in my throat when I tried, I'd say them now.

I shifted forward in the chair and lowered my face right next to Key's. The soft sound of his breath was all it took to keep the world turning. His eyelashes were dense and dark, curled against his cheek. Number three on my Top Ten Things I Love but Will Never Tell. I slipped one hand under his, the other on top, curling my fingers gently, remembering the last time.

"Wake up," I whispered.

Drawing a breath in with him, breathing out together.

"Key."

Breathing in.

I squeezed his hand twice.

You there?

I needed him to answer.

One breath.

Another.

His eyes fluttered open and settled on my face.

"Shé:kon," I whispered.

A week later, I had my face turned to the window, eyes closed and enjoying the sweet-scented breeze that washed over my skin.

"Here?" My mom squinted at the mailbox, leaning forward over the steering wheel as she turned up the skinny driveway.

"This is it." I nodded. "Careful of the potholes."

At the end of the drive, Foster stood waiting in the open door.

The little blue house looked the same, but I knew that some of the windows were new and the back door was no longer wood but steel-framed.

I unbuckled my seat belt and turned to my mom, wanting to check one last time. "Sure you don't want to come in?"

She gave a tight smile and a shake of the head. "This is your thing, Ave."

I shrugged and got out, because it really wasn't "my thing," but whatever. I thought of all the powwow invitations she'd turned down and climbed the porch with a sigh.

"Shé:kon, Uncle."

"Niece." He called me that now. I hadn't noticed that he had never called me anything—never used my name or called me anything else. Maybe knowing what he did, he hadn't wanted to get attached. But things between us were different now; they'd changed quickly, and for the better.

I surveyed the living room, still familiar, but like everything else in my life—changed. "You've done some shopping."

Foster shrugged. "It was time."

In front of me on the table, a teacup already sat, steaming far too much for me to want to lose my fingerprints picking it up. Tea wasn't that bad. It would never replace coffee in my heart, but with a little sugar and milk, I had to admit that I'd actually developed a taste for it.

Seated in the new green easy chair that had replaced the old blue one, Foster blew on his tea and waited, looking at me from under his bushy brows, living proof that the black water really didn't take the first. "So."

"I'd . . . like to hear some stories," I said with a shrug. Foster's eyebrows shot up, but I quickly shook my head.

"Not—" Raising my hands. "Not about that." If I never heard about the black water again, that would be awesome. I wanted the stories that I'd been missing and not even known it. The stories Lily had told me when she was still Lily.

Foster nodded, apparently approving. "Hmm. Well." He rubbed his chin, contemplating. I was sure he had a million to choose from.

While Foster pondered his internal menu of stories, I contemplated the changes he'd made. The house was still full, "clutter" being Foster's default setting, but the photos had been rearranged, the curtains were new—pale blue that almost matched the outside of the house—and they were pulled back, letting light stream in the big front window. It felt like the house had finally let its shoulders drop, had let out the breath it had been holding for years.

A knock at the door, so soft that at first I wasn't sure I'd heard it, then again, barely louder. I turned to find Foster looking at me, then tilting his head as if to say he wasn't getting up to answer it.

Three seconds later and I was glad he hadn't.

"I . . . changed my mind." Mom nodded at Foster. "Uncle. Is that okay?"

I shot Foster a look, trying to communicate telepathically. *Act casual; don't scare her off.*

"Shé:kon." Foster swallowed the surprise that had been about to bloom on his face and waved my mom in.

Mom looked unsure, even nervous, so I took her hand and led her to the little floral sofa, one of the pieces of furniture Foster hadn't replaced, and poured her a cup of tea.

"You remember me?" Foster smiled and my mom nodded with a shy smile I'd never seen on her face in my life. "I had a lot more up top back then." He rubbed his wispy baby chicken hair and chuckled.

Beside me, mom was twisting her fingers together and trying to discreetly check things out while I let warm contentment bubble up in my chest and a smile bloom. Why not?

"We were going to tell a story," Foster informed my mom. "Where should I start?" Foster mused, rubbing his papery palms together.

On the far wall, the painting—Sky Woman's fall—still hung in the same spot. I'd always thought she must have been terrified, but maybe she'd had faith that there would be someone below to catch her. I imagined it now, the wind rushing by, the vantage point from which she could see everything in existence; it must have felt like flying. Maybe her fall had felt like freedom. I'd found the painting disturbing the first time I saw it, but now I found it . . . hopeful, the story of a new beginning.

Foster followed my eyes. "The beginning it is." He patted his knees, decided. I folded my feet underneath me and leaned against my mom the way I had as a child, when she read me stories at night, prompting her to look at me like she was seeing someone mysterious who'd replaced the daughter she knew. I crunched my cookie and felt her fingers stroke my hair.

"But don't get bored on me." Foster pointed one finger in my direction. "You've heard this story already."

"I won't," I promised. I had heard it before, more than once, but this telling would be like the first.

Beside me, I felt my mom's body relax, like she'd needed to rest for a very long time. The cup was now comfortably warm in my hands, and the clock in the kitchen ticked softly. Foster looked toward the ceiling and took a deep breath, cleared his throat, and opened his hands. "In the beginning, there was only water here and the Sky World up above."

It might be the same story, but it was a different me.

I was finally ready to listen.

A NOTE FROM THE AUTHOR

This book started where it is set—out on the trails.

I generally run the trails because they're quiet and peaceful and my mind is free to drift. Sometimes I explore new trails for variety, but they also occasionally offer surprises—a bird I've heard but never seen, a challenging hill, or just the same forest from a different perspective. Sometimes I see things out on the trails—shadows created by dappled sunlight and moss-covered chunks of limestone that aren't really there.

But what if they were? What if I saw something that changed my reality?

This story is about transparency and change, about ending the habit of hiding in murky words, relationships, and thoughts. If you're afraid of the truth, a lack of clarity can be comforting, can keep you in a kind of limbo where choices aren't necessary and uncomfortable truths don't need to be spoken. As Avery learns, the price of this comfort is that not naming what you want means that you'll never get it.

Although the legend of the black water is my own invention, Sky Woman's fall is drawn from Haudenosaunee culture. I thought of Sky Woman and what she must have felt as she fell, not knowing what was waiting for her in the limitless water far below. But her misadventure led to the creation of Turtle Island for us. So as Avery finds out, not all change has to be bad. Sometimes different is good.

All of Avery's hiding and fence-sitting is misguided, because once she accepts her shaky connection to her culture, she finds that she isn't alone, and never has been. Becoming lost isn't forever; being vulnerable isn't death. Once Avery can be truthful about what she wants and who she is—to herself and others—she's able to take steps to make positive things happen.

Avery learns that if she is strong enough to face the past and present, if she stops running away, she has the power to change the narrative and the outcome. She can break the cycle that the black water began. Stolen children, women who left home and never returned—these are all true things that have made Avery who she is, not through her personal experience but through the pain of her family that will echo until someone stops it. In a way, the black water gives her that chance. One day and one new trail can't change all of it, but it does set Avery and her family, at least, on a new course. The story doesn't always have to end the same.

There are enough new trails for all of us. I hope we find them.

ACKNOWLEDGMENTS

Many, many thanks to the people who made this story into a book:

Cynthia Leitich Smith.
Rosemary Brosnan.
Courtney Stevenson, Mikayla Lawrence, and Britt Newton.
The professional and moral support team:
Natalie Lakosil, an amazing guide and advocate.
Jen Ferguson, for her big auntie energy.
Maria Tureaud, the first believer.
The early readers and my Emotional Support Nancy.
My family:
Pete, Brad, and Amanda.
Gaius, Olivia, and Wilton, the best humans I know.
My mum, who is her own map.
My dad, who always blazed his own trail.
And you, reader. You.

KANYEN'KÉHA GLOSSARY

akhsótha (uck-so-ta): my grandmother / my granny

ihstá (eeh-sta): auntie

karhá:kon (gar-ha-goo): in the woods/forest

nyá:wen (nya-wa): thank you

ó:nen ki' wáhi (o-na-gee-wa-hee): goodbye (until we meet again)

Sakatathré:wa't (sa-ga-dut-lay-wat): I'm sorry (apology)

shé:kon (say-goo): hello/hi

Wakata'karí:te (wa-ga-dut-ga-lee-day): I am healthy

To learn more about the language or to take an online course, visit onkwawenna.info.

A NOTE FROM CYNTHIA LEITICH SMITH, AUTHOR-CURATOR OF HEARTDRUM

Dear Reader,

Why do eerie novels like *The Unfinished* captivate us? Is it the thrill of a "safe scare" through the power of fiction? That's part of it, I think, but there's also a deeper, more vital dynamic at work.

For all its blessings, our world can be an uncertain, unsettling place—with haunting mysteries and deadly dangers. Sometimes, in real life, people do seem to disappear. Eventually, we all experience tragedy and trauma.

Through Avery's story, author Cheryl Isaacs offers us a path to understanding and empathy, to healing from fear and insecurity. She prompts us to reflect on how embracing our own full humanity can provide us with community and support, with wisdom and strength.

The Unfinished is published by Heartdrum, a Native-focused imprint of HarperCollins, which offers books about young Native heroes by Indigenous authors and illustrators. I'm so pleased that this novel is on our list. It's suspenseful, with a compelling protagonist in an engrossing setting, or, put another way, it's exactly the kind of story that made me an avid reader.

Have you read many books by and about Mohawk characters or other Native people? Hopefully *The Unfinished* will inspire you to read more.

Mvto,

Cynthia Leitich Smith

Cheryl Isaacs is a Kanyenke'há:ka/white writer from southern Ontario, Canada. She loves everything furry, anything that occurs outdoors, and running the local trails, where she's never encountered anything eerie. Not once.

Cynthia Leitich Smith is the *New York Times* bestselling, acclaimed author of books for all ages, including *Sisters of the Neversea, Rain Is Not My Indian Name, Indian Shoes, Jingle Dancer, Harvest House,* and *Hearts Unbroken,* which won the American Indian Youth Literature Award; she is also the anthologist of *Ancestor Approved: Intertribal Stories for Kids.* Cynthia is the author-curator of Heartdrum, a Native-focused imprint at HarperCollins Children's Books, and serves on the core faculty of the MFA program in writing for children and young adults at Vermont College of Fine Arts. She is an enrolled citizen of the Muscogee Nation and lives in Austin, Texas.

In 2014, We Need Diverse Books (WNDB) began as a simple hashtag on Twitter. The social media campaign soon grew into a 501(c)(3) nonprofit with a team that spans the globe. WNDB is supported by a network of writers, illustrators, agents, editors, teachers, librarians, and book lovers, all united under the same goal—to create a world where every child can see themselves in the pages of a book. You can learn more about WNDB programs at www.diversebooks.org.